To Barbara Allean
from Auntie Olga
Xmas 1942.

THE WORKS OF
ROBERT LOUIS STEVENSON
TUSITALA EDITION
VOL. XIII

ISLAND NIGHTS' ENTERTAINMENTS
THE MISADVENTURES OF JOHN NICHOLSON

BY

ROBERT LOUIS STEVENSON

LONDON: WILLIAM HEINEMANN, Ltd:
IN ASSOCIATION WITH CHATTO & WINDUS:
CASSELL & COMPANY, LTD: AND LONGMANS,
GREEN & COMPANY, LTD.

First published, TUSITALA EDITION, March   1924.
Second Impression . . . . November 1924.
Third Impression . . . . April   1926.
Fourth Impression . . . . December 1930.

PRINTED IN GREAT BRITAIN.

TO

THREE OLD SHIPMATES
AMONG THE ISLANDS

Harry Henderson

Ben Hird

Jack Buckland

Their Friend

R. L. S.

CONTENTS

PREFATORY NOTE

By Mrs. R. L. Stevenson

AMONG our English friends whom we first met in Bournemouth were Sir Percy Shelley, the son of the poet, and his charming wife. They lived at Boscombe Manor, in a rambling, comfortable house set in the midst of trees and lawn and shrubbery, where Sir Percy was always seriously busied in play of a more or less practical nature. He even worked with carpenter's tools—much to the disgust of his butler, who once gave warning for that reason, his dignity being unable to stand the strain of his master's low occupation. Sir Percy also took photographs in a studio he helped to build with his own hands. For backgrounds for his pictures he painted out-of-door scenes in the most realistic manner, his sitters being posed on a piece of canvas made to represent a greensward.

One wing of the house had been turned into a private theatre holding about three hundred guests. All the stage accessories were planned and many of them by Sir Percy. Both he and Lady Shelley took part in the plays—usually old-fashioned melodramas—that they produced for the pleasure and amusement of their friends. Of these melodramas Sir Percy had a large assortment, principally by an author, even then almost forgotten, named Fitzball. After Sir Percy's death (my husband's dedication to *The Master of Ballantrae* reached him just before the end) the little theatre being closed for ever, Lady Shelley gave the stock of Fitzball melodramas to my husband.

Fitzball, following the example of greater dramatists, took ideas for his plays where he could find them, and after changing or elaborating them as the occasion required, reproduced them as melodramas. One of these, adapted from an old German legend, caught my husband's fancy ; he spoke of it several times when we were living in Hono- lulu, as being, in its ingenuity and imaginative qualities, singularly like the Hawaiian tales. No doubt Fitzball's melodrama differed widely from the original *German Bottle Imp ;* certainly there was very little resemblance between his version and my husband's story that was meant to appeal more particularly to the native mind. The tale was first published in England in *Black and White*, and then translated by one of the missionaries into the Samoan tongue for the Sulu (the torch of Samoa) under the title of *O Le Fangu Aitu*, running in weekly numbers as a serial.

The Bottle Imp was the first piece of fiction ever offered to the Samoan people, its publication raising the circulation of the paper to an unprecedented extent. Samoans are in the habit of speaking in parables ; they found many different morals in *The Bottle Imp*, some very ingeniously extracted. Yet the story was so circumstantial in its details, and its incidents seemed so like reality, that doubts would occasionally assail some inquiring mind ; perhaps, after all, it might be true, and the magic bottle still be in existence. We wondered why so many of our native visitors demanded a view of the large safe in Vailima, and were puzzled by the expression of disappointment that crossed their faces when they were shown its interior and saw that it contained nothing more than papers and a little money. We afterwards discovered there was a popular belief that Tusitala still possessed the magic bottle, and the great iron safe had been placed in Vailima solely for its protection.

The magic bottle was the natural explanation of the source of Tusitala's immense wealth, which enabled him not only to purchase many tins of ship's biscuits and barrels of salt beef, but to regale his Samoan friends in the most princely fashion on cans of salmon and other expensive foreign luxuries. I do not understand what civilising effect the story of *The Bottle Imp* was supposed to have on the natives, but I cannot think it quite fulfilled the expectations of the missionary who translated it. At all events, *The Isle of Voices* was allowed to remain in the obscurity of the *'Palangi* (English) language, and was not translated, as had been intended, into Samoan.

On our first South Sea cruise we stopped, among other places, at Fakarava, in the Dangerous Archipelago. Leaving the yacht *Casco* in the lagoon, my husband hired a little cottage on the beach, where we lived for several weeks. Fakarava is an atoll of the usual horseshoe shape, so narrow that one can walk across it in ten minutes, but of great circumference ; it lay so little above the sea-level that one had a sense of insecurity ; justified by the terrible disasters following the last hurricane in the group. Not far from where we lived the waves had recently swept over the narrow strip of coral during a storm.

Though we had before us the evidences of what had happened, and might happen again, our life on the island passed in a gentle monotony of peace. At sunrise we walked from our front door into the warm, shallow waters of the lagoon for our bath ; we cooked our breakfast on the remains of an old American cooking-stove I discovered on the beach, and spent the rest of the morning sorting over the shells we had found the previous day. After lunch and a siesta, we crossed the island to the windward side and gathered more shells. Sometimes we would find the strangest fish stranded in pools between the rocks by the outgoing tide, many of them curiously shaped and brilliantly coloured ; some of the most gorgeous were poisonous to eat, and capable of inflicting very unpleasant wounds with their fins. I remember our captain suffered during all the remainder of our voyage from a numbness resembling paralysis, in one of his fingers that he had scratched while handling a strange fish with a beak like a parrot.

The close of the placid day marked the beginning of the most agreeable part of the twenty-four hours ; it was the time of the moon, and the shadows that fell from the cocoa-nut leaves were so sharply defined that one involuntarily stepped over them. After a simple dinner, and a dip in the soft sea, we sat expectant of our invariable

visitor, the governor of the island, M. Donat Rimareau.
There were no white men on the island that I remember,
it not being the season for pearl fishing, though now and
again a schooner with its French captain would appear and
disappear like a phantom ship.

While the days were almost intolerably hot, with the
setting of the sun a gentle breeze sprang up, cooling the
air to a comfortable temperature. We spent the evenings
in the moonlight, sitting on our mattresses that were spread
out on the verandah, the only chair being reserved for our
guest. Our conversation with M. Rimareau, who was half
Tahitian, and altogether delightful, was at first rather of the
Shakespeare and musical glasses order, but after the recital
of several Scottish legends—I remember particularly my
husband's telling the story of Ticonderoga—the governor
felt more at his ease, and gradually he became the narrator
and we the spell-bound listeners. Night after night we
literally sat at his feet entranced and thrilled by stories of
Tahiti and the Paumotus, always of a supernatural character.

There is a strange sect in Fakarava called The Whistlers,
resembling the spiritualists of our country, but greater
adepts. When M. Rimareau spoke of these people and
their superstitions his voice sank almost to a whisper,
and he cast fearful glances over his shoulder at the black
shadows of the palms. "Who knows," said he, "how much
truth there may be in it all? It is a strange country, and
I, myself, have seen and heard things that are not to be
explained away." I remember one of the stories was of
the return of the soul of a dead child, the soul being
wrapped in a leaf and dropped in at the door of the
sorrowing parents.

I am sure that when my husband came to write *The
Isle of Voices* he had our evenings in Fakarava and the
stories of M. Rimareau in his mind. I know that I never
read *The Isle of Voices* without a mental picture rising
before me of the lagoon, and the cocoa palms, and the
wonderful moonlight of Fakarava.

F. V. DE G. S.

ISLAND NIGHTS' ENTERTAINMENTS

ISLAND NIGHTS' ENTERTAINMENTS

THE BEACH OF FALESÁ

BEING THE NARRATIVE OF A SOUTH SEA TRADER

CHAPTER I

A SOUTH SEA BRIDAL

I SAW that island first when it was neither night nor morning. The moon was to the west, setting, but still broad and bright. To the east, and right amidships of the dawn, which was all pink, the daystar sparkled like a diamond. The land breeze blew in our faces, and smelt strong of wild lime and vanilla ; other things besides, but these were the most plain ; and the chill of it set me sneezing. I should say I had been for years on a low island near the line, living for the most part solitary among natives. Here was a fresh experience ; even the tongue would be quite strange to me ; and the look of these woods and mountains, and the rare smell of them, renewed my blood.

The captain blew out the binnacle lamp.

" There ! " said he, " there goes a bit of smoke, Mr. Wiltshire, behind the break of the reef. That's Falesá, where your station is, the last village to the east ; nobody lives to windward—I don't know why. Take my glass, and you can make the houses out."

I took the glass ; and the shores leaped nearer, and I saw the tangle of the woods and the breach of the surf, and the brown roofs and the black insides of houses peeped among the trees.

"Do you catch a bit of white there to the east'ard?" the captain continued. "That's your house. Coral built, stands high, verandah you could walk on three abreast; best station in the South Pacific. When old Adams saw it, he took and shook me by the hand. 'I've dropped into a soft thing here,' says he. 'So you have,' says I, 'and time too!' Poor Johnny! I never saw him again but the once, and then he had changed his tune—couldn't get on with the natives, or the whites, or something; and the next time we came round there, he was dead and buried. I took and put up a bit of a stick to him: 'John Adams, *obit* eighteen and sixty-eight. Go thou and do likewise.' I missed that man. I never could see much harm in Johnny."

"What did he die of?" I inquired.

"Some kind of sickness," says the captain. "It appears it took him sudden. Seems he got up in the night, and filled up on Pain Killer and Kennedy's Discovery. No go—he was booked beyond Kennedy. Then he had tried to open a case of gin. No go again—not strong enough. Then he must have turned to and run out on the verandah, and capsized over the rail. When they found him, the next day, he was clean crazy—carried on all the time about somebody watering his copra. Poor John!"

"Was it thought to be the island?" I asked.

"Well, it was thought to be the island, or the trouble, or something," he replied. "I never could hear but what it was a healthy place. Our last man, Vigours, never turned a hair. He left because of the beach—said he was afraid of Black Jack and Case and Whistling Jimmie, who was still alive at the time, but got drowned soon afterward when drunk. As for old Captain Randall, he's been here any time since eighteen-forty, forty-five. I never could see much harm in Billy, nor much change. Seems as if he might live to be Old Kafoozleum. No, I guess it's healthy."

"There's a boat coming now," said I. "She's right

in the pass ; looks to be a sixteen-foot whale ; two white men in the stern-sheets."

"That's the boat that drowned Whistling Jimmie!" cried the captain ; " let's see the glass. Yes, that's Case, sure enough, and the darkie. They've got a gallows bad reputation, but you know what a place the beach is for talking. My belief, that Whistling Jimmie was the worst of the trouble ; and he's gone to glory, you see. What'll you bet they ain't after gin? Lay you five to two they take six cases."

When these two traders came aboard I was pleased with the looks of them at once, or, rather, with the looks of both, and the speech of one. I was sick for white neighbours after my four years at the line, which I always counted years of prison ; getting tabooed, and going down to the Speak House to see and get it taken off ; buying gin and going on a break, and then repenting ; sitting in the house at night with the lamp for company ; or walking on the beach and wondering what kind of a fool to call myself for being where I was. There were no other whites upon my island, and when I sailed to the next, rough customers made the most of the society. Now to see these two when they came aboard was a pleasure. One was a negro, to be sure ; but they were both rigged out smart in striped pyjamas and straw hats, and Case would have passed muster in a city. He was yellow and smallish, had a hawk's nose to his face, pale eyes, and his beard trimmed with scissors. No man knew his country, beyond he was of English speech ; and it was clear he came of a good family and was splendidly educated. He was accomplished too ; played the accordion first rate ; and give him a piece of a string or a cork or a pack of cards, and he could show you tricks equal to any professional. He could speak, when he chose, fit for a drawing-room ; and when he chose he could blaspheme worse than a Yankee boatswain, and talk smart to sicken a Kanaka. The way he thought would pay best at the moment, that was Case's way, and it always seemed to come natural, and like as if he was born to it. He had the courage of a

lion and the cunning of a rat ; and if he's not in hell to-day,
there's no such place. I know but one good point to the
man—that he was fond of his wife, and kind to her. She
was a Samoa woman, and dyed her hair red—Samoa
style ; and when he came to die (as I have to tell of) they
found one strange thing—that he had made a will, like a
Christian, and the widow got the lot ; all his, they said,
and all Black Jack's, and the most of Billy Randall's in
the bargain, for it was Case that kept the books. So she
went off home in the schooner *Manu'a*, and does the lady
to this day in her own place.

But of all this on the first morning I knew no more than
a fly. Case used me like a gentleman and like a friend,
made me welcome to Falesá, and put his services at
my disposal, which was the more helpful from my ignorance of the natives. All the better part of the day
we sat drinking better acquaintance in the cabin, and I
never heard a man talk more to the point. There was no
smarter trader, and none dodgier, in the islands. I thought
Falesá seemed to be the right kind of a place ; and the more
I drank the lighter my heart. Our last trader had fled
the place at half an hour's notice, taking a chance passage
in a labour ship from up west. The captain, when he
came, had found the station closed, the keys left with the
native pastor, and a letter from the runaway, confessing
he was fairly frightened of his life. Since then the firm
had not been represented, and of course there was no
cargo. The wind, besides, was fair, the captain hoped he
could make his next island by dawn, with a good tide,
and the business of landing my trade was gone about
lively. There was no call for me to fool with it, Case
said ; nobody would touch my things, every one was
honest in Falesá, only about chickens or an odd knife or
an odd stick of tobacco ; and the best I could do was to
sit quiet till the vessel left, then come straight to his house,
see old Captain Randall, the father of the beach, take pot-
luck, and go home to sleep when it got dark. So it was
high noon, and the schooner was under way before I
set my foot on shore at Falesá.

I had a glass or two on board ; I was just off a long cruise, and the ground heaved under me like a ship's deck. The world was like all new painted ; my foot went along to music ; Falesá might have been Fiddler's Green, if there is such a place, and more's the pity if there isn't ! It was good to foot the grass, to look aloft at the green mountains, to see the men with their green wreaths and the women in their bright dresses, red and blue. On we went, in the strong sun and the cool shadow, liking both ; and all the children in the town came trotting after with their shaven heads and their brown bodies, and raising a thin kind of a cheer in our wake, like crowing poultry.

" By the by," says Case, " we must get you a wife."

" That's so," said I ; " I had forgotten."

There was a crowd of girls about us, and I pulled myself up and looked among them like a bashaw. They were all dressed out for the sake of the ship being in ; and the women of Falesá are a handsome lot to see. If they have a fault, they are a trifle broad in the beam ; and I was just thinking so when Case touched me.

" That's pretty," says he.

I saw one coming on the other side alone. She had been fishing ; all she wore was a chemise, and it was wetted through. She was young and very slender for an island maid, with a long face, a high forehead, and a shy, strange, blindish look, between a cat's and a baby's.

" Who's she ? " said I. " She'll do."

" That's Uma," said Case, and he called her up and spoke to her in the native. I didn't know what he said ; but when he was in the midst she looked up at me quick and timid, like a child dodging a blow, then down again, and presently smiled. She had a wide mouth, the lips and the chin cut like any statue's ; and the smile came out for a moment and was gone. Then she stood with her head bent, and heard Case to an end, spoke back in the pretty Polynesian voice, looking him full in the face, heard him again in answer, and then with an obeisance started off.

I had just a share of the bow, but never another shot of her eye, and there was no more word of smiling.

" I guess it's all right," said Case. " I guess you can have her. I'll make it square with the old lady. You can have your pick of the lot for a plug of tobacco," he added, sneering.

I suppose it was the smile that stuck in my memory, for I spoke back sharp. " She doesn't look that sort," I cried.

" I don't know that she is," said Case. " I believe she's as right as the mail. Keeps to herself, don't go round with the gang, and that. Oh, no, don't you misunderstand me—Uma's on the square." He spoke eager, I thought, and that surprised and pleased me. " Indeed," he went on, " I shouldn't make so sure of getting her, only she cottoned to the cut of your jib. All you have to do is to keep dark and let me work the mother my own way ; and I'll bring the girl round to the captain's for the marriage."

I didn't care for the word marriage, and I said so.

" Oh, there's nothing to hurt in the marriage," says he. " Black Jack's the chaplain."

By this time we had come in view of the house of these three white men ; for a negro is counted a white man, and so is a Chinese ! A strange idea, but common in the islands. It was a board house with a strip of rickety verandah. The store was to the front, with a counter, scales, and the finest possible display of trade : a case or two of tinned meats ; a barrel of hard bread, a few bolts of cotton stuff, not to be compared with mine ; the only thing well represented being the contraband firearms and liquor. " If these are my only rivals," thinks I, " I should do well in Falesá." Indeed, there was only the one way they could touch me, and that was with the guns and drink.

In the back room was old Captain Randall, squatting on the floor native fashion, fat and pale, naked to the waist, grey as a badger, and his eyes set with drink. His body was covered with grey hair and crawled over by flies ; one was in the corner of his eye—he never heeded ; and the mosquitoes hummed about the man like bees. Any clean-minded man would have had the creature out at once and buried him ; and to see him, and think he was seventy, and remember he had once commanded a ship, and come ashore in his smart togs, and talked big in bars and consulates, and sat in club verandahs, turned me sick and sober.

He tried to get up when I came in, but that was hopeless ; so he reached me a hand instead, and stumbled out some salutation.

" Papa's * pretty full this morning," observed Case. " We've had an epidemic here ; and Captain Randall takes gin for a prophylactic—don't you, Papa ? "

" Never took such a thing in my life ! " cried the captain, indignantly. " Take gin for my health's sake, Mr. Wha's-ever-your-name—'s a precautionary measure."

" That's all right, Papa," said Case. " But you'll have to brace up. There's going to be a marriage—Mr. Wiltshire here is going to get spliced."

The old man asked to whom.

" To Uma," said Case.

" Uma ! " cried the captain. " Wha's he want Uma for ? 's he come here for his health, anyway ? Wha' 'n hell's he want Uma for ? "

" Dry up, Papa," said Case. " 'Tain't you that's to marry her. I guess you're not her godfather and godmother. I guess Mr. Wiltshire's going to please himself."

With that he made an excuse to me that he must move about the marriage, and left me alone with the poor wretch that was his partner and (to speak truth) his gull. Trade and station belonged both to Randall ; Case and the negro were parasites ; they crawled and fed upon him like the flies, he none the wiser. Indeed, I have no harm to say of Billy Randall beyond the fact that my gorge rose at him, and the time I now passed in his company was like a nightmare.

The room was stifling hot and full of flies ; for the house

* Please pronounce *pappa* throughout.

was dirty and low and small, and stood in a bad place, behind the village, in the borders of the bush, and sheltered from the trade. The three men's beds were on the floor, and a litter of pans and dishes. There was no standing furniture ; Randall, when he was violent, tearing it to laths. There I sat and had a meal which was served us by Case's wife ; and there I was entertained all day by that remains of man, his tongue stumbling among low old jokes and long old stories, and his own wheezy laughter always ready, so that he had no sense of my depression. He was nipping gin all the while. Sometimes he fell asleep, and awoke again, whimpering and shivering, and every now and again he would ask me why I wanted to marry Uma. "My friend," I was telling myself all day, "you must not come to be an old gentleman like this."

It might be four in the afternoon, perhaps, when the back door was thrust slowly open, and a strange old native woman crawled into the house almost on her belly. She was swathed in black stuff to her heels ; her hair was grey in swatches ; her face was tattooed, which was not the practice in that island ; her eyes big and bright and crazy. These she fixed upon me with a rapt expression that I saw to be part acting. She said no plain word, but smacked and mumbled with her lips, and hummed aloud, like a child over its Christmas pudding. She came straight across the house, heading for me, and, as soon as she was alongside, caught up my hand and purred and crooned over it like a great cat. From this she slipped into a kind of song.

"Who the devil's this ? " cried I, for the thing startled me.

"It's Fa'avao," says Randall ; and I saw he had hitched along the floor into the farthest corner.

"You ain't afraid of her ? " I cried.

"Me 'fraid ! " cried the captain. "My dear friend, I defy her ! I don't let her put her foot in here, only I suppose's different to-day for the marriage. 's Uma's mother."

"Well, suppose it is ; what's she carrying on about ? "

I asked, more irritated, perhaps more frightened, than I cared to show ; and the captain told me she was making up a quantity of poetry in my praise because I was to marry Uma. " All right, old lady," says I, with rather a failure of a laugh, " anything to oblige. But when you're done with my hand, you might let me know."

She did as though she understood ; the song rose into a cry, and stopped ; the woman crouched out of the house the same way that she came in, and must have plunged straight into the bush, for when I followed her to the door she had already vanished.

" These are rum manners," said I.

" 's a rum crowd," said the captain, and, to my surprise, he made the sign of the cross on his bare bosom.

" Hillo ! " says I, " are you a Papist ? "

He repudiated the idea with contempt. " Hard-shell Baptis'," said he. " But, my dear friend, the Papists got some good ideas too ; and tha' 's one of 'em. You take my advice, and whenever you come across Uma or Fa'avao or Vigours, or any of that crowd, you take a leaf out o' the priests, and do what I do. Savvy ? " says he, repeated the sign, and winked his dim eye at me. " No, *sir* ! " he broke out again, " no Papists here ! " and for a long time entertained me with his religious opinions.

I must have been taken with Uma from the first, or I should certainly have fled from that house, and got into the clean air, and the clean sea, or some convenient river— though, it's true, I was committed to Case ; and, besides, I could never have held my head up in that island if I had run from a girl upon my wedding-night.

The sun was down, the sky all on fire, and the lamp had been some time lighted, when Case came back with Uma and the negro. She was dressed and scented ; her kilt was of fine tapa, looking richer in the fold than any silk ; her bust, which was of the colour of dark honey, she wore bare, only for some half a dozen necklaces of seeds and flowers ; and behind her ears and in her hair she had the scarlet flowers of the hibiscus. She showed the best bearing for a bride conceivable, serious and still ; and I thought shame to stand up with her in that mean house and before that grinning negro. I thought shame, I say; for the mountebank was dressed with a big paper collar, the book he made believe to read from was an old volume of a novel, and the words of his service not fit to be set down. My conscience smote me when we joined hands; and when she got her certificate I was tempted to throw up the bargain and confess. Here is the document. It was Case that wrote it, signatures and all, in a leaf out of the ledger:

This is to certify that Uma, daughter of Fa'avao of Falesá, Island of ——, is illegally married to Mr. John Wiltshire for one week, and Mr. John Wiltshire is at liberty to send her to hell when he pleases.

JOHN BLACKAMOAR,
Chaplain to the Hulks.

Extracted from the Register
by William T. Randall,
Master Mariner.

A nice paper to put in a girl's hand and see her hide away like gold. A man might easily feel cheap for less. But it was the practice in these parts, and (as I told myself) not the least the fault of us white men, but of the missionaries. If they had let the natives be, I had never needed this deception, but taken all the wives I wished and left them when I pleased, with a clear conscience.

The more ashamed I was, the more hurry I was in to be gone; and our desires thus jumping together, I made the less remark of a change in the traders. Case had been all eagerness to keep me; now, as though he had attained a purpose, he seemed all eagerness to have me go. Uma, he said, could show me to my house, and the three bade us farewell indoors.

The night was nearly come; the village smelt of trees and flowers and the sea and bread-fruit-cooking; there came a fine roll of sea from the reef, and from a distance, among the woods and houses, many pretty sounds of men and children. It did me good to breathe free air; it did me good to be done with the captain, and see, instead, the creature at my side. I felt for all the world as though

she were some girl at home in the Old Country, and for-
getting myself for the minute, took her hand to walk with.
Her fingers nestled into mine, I heard her breathe deep
and quick, and all at once she caught my hand to her face
and pressed it there. " You good ! " she cried, and ran
ahead of me, and stopped and looked back and smiled,
and ran ahead of me again, thus guiding me through the
edge of the bush, and by a quiet way to my own house.

The truth is, Case had done the courting for me in style—
told her I was mad to have her, and cared nothing for the
consequences ; and the poor soul, knowing that which I
was still ignorant of, believed it, every word, and had her
head nigh turned with vanity and gratitude. Now, of all
this I had no guess ; I was one of those most opposed to
any nonsense about native women, having seen so many
whites eaten up by their wives' relatives, and made fools of
into the bargain ; and I told myself I must make a stand at
once, and bring her to her bearings. But she looked so
quaint and pretty as she ran away and then awaited me,
and the thing was done so like a child or a kind dog, that
the best I could do was just to follow her whenever she
went on, to listen for the fall of her bare feet, and to watch
in the dusk for the shining of her body. And there was
another thought came in my head. She played kitten with
me now when we were alone ; but in the house she had
carried it the way a countess might, so proud and humble.
And what with her dress—for all there was so little of it,
and that native enough—what with her fine tapa and fine
scents, and her red flowers and seeds, that were quite as
bright as jewels, only larger—it came over me she was a
kind of countess really, dressed to hear great singers at a
concert, and no even mate for a poor trader like myself.

She was the first in the house ; and while I was still
without I saw a match flash and the lamplight kindle in
the windows. The station was a wonderful fine place,
coral built, with quite a wide verandah, and the main room
high and wide. My chests and cases had been piled in,
and made rather of a mess ; and there, in the thick of the
confusion, stood Uma by the table, awaiting me. Her

shadow went all the way up behind her into the hollow of the iron roof ; she stood against it bright, the lamplight shining on her skin. I stopped in the door, and she looked at me, not speaking, with eyes that were eager and yet daunted ; then she touched herself on the bosom.

" Me—your wifie," she said. It had never taken me like that before ; but the want of her took and shook all through me, like the wind in the luff of a sail.

I could not speak if I had wanted ; and if I could, I would not. I was ashamed to be so much moved about a native, ashamed of the marriage too, and the certificate she had treasured in her kilt ; and I turned aside and made believe to rummage among my cases. The first thing I lighted on was a case of gin, the only one that I had brought ; and partly for the girl's sake and partly for horror of the recollections of old Randall, took a sudden resolve. I pried the lid off. One by one I drew the bottles with a pocket corkscrew, and sent Uma out to pour the stuff from the verandah.

She came back after the last, and looked at me puzzled like.

" No good," said I, for I was now a little better master of my tongue. " Man he drink, he no good."

She agreed with this, but kept considering. " Why you bring him ? " she asked presently. " Suppose you no want drink, you no bring him, I think."

" That's all right," said I. " One time I want drink too much ; now no want. You see, I no savvy I get one little wifie. Suppose I drink gin, my little wifie be 'fraid."

To speak to her kindly was about more than I was fit for ; I had made my vow I would never let on to weakness with a native, and I had nothing for it but to stop.

She stood looking gravely down at me where I sat by the open case. " I think you good man," she said. And suddenly she had fallen before me on the floor. " I belong you all-e-same pig ! " she cried.

CHAPTER II

THE BAN

I CAME on the verandah just before the sun rose on the morrow. My house was the last on the east; there was a cape of woods and cliffs behind that hid the sunrise. To the west, a swift, cold river ran down, and beyond was the green of the village, dotted with cocoa-palms and bread-fruits and houses. The shutters were some of them down and some open; I saw the mosquito bars still stretched with shadows of people new-awakened sitting up inside; and all over the green others were stalking silent, wrapped in their many-coloured sleeping clothes, like Bedouins in Bible pictures. It was mortal still and solemn and chilly, and the light of the dawn on the lagoon was like the shining of a fire.

But the thing that troubled me was nearer hand. Some dozen young men and children made a piece of a half-circle, flanking my house: the river divided them, some were on the near side, some on the far, and one on a boulder in the midst; and they all sat silent, wrapped in their sheets, and stared at me and my house as straight as pointer dogs. I thought it strange as I went out. When I had bathed and come back again, and found them all there, and two or three more along with them, I thought it stranger still. What could they see to gaze at in my house, I wondered, and went in.

But the thought of these starers stuck in my mind, and presently I came out again. The sun was now up, but it was still behind the cape of woods. Say a quarter of an hour had come and gone. The crowd was greatly increased, the far bank of the river was lined for quite a

way—perhaps thirty grown folk, and of children twice as
many, some standing, some squatted on the ground, and
all staring at my house. I have seen a house in a South
Sea village thus surrounded, but then a trader was thrashing
his wife inside, and she singing out. Here was nothing—
the stove was alight, the smoke going up in a Christian
manner; all was shipshape and Bristol fashion. To be
sure, there was a stranger come, but they had a chance to
see that stranger yesterday, and took it quiet enough.
What ailed them now? I leaned my arms on the rail
and stared back. Devil a wink they had in them! Now
and then I could see the children chatter, but they spoke so
low not even the hum of their speaking came my length.
The rest were like graven images: they stared at me,
dumb and sorrowful, with their bright eyes; and it came
upon me things would look not much different if I were on
the platform of the gallows and these good folk had come
to see me hanged.

I felt I was getting daunted, and began to be afraid I
looked it, which would never do. Up I stood, made
believe to stretch myself, came down the verandah stair,
and strolled towards the river. There went a short buzz
from one to the other, like what you hear in theatres when
the curtain goes up; and some of the nearest gave back
the matter of a pace. I saw a girl lay one hand on a
young man and make a gesture upward with the other;
at the same time she said something in the native with a
gasping voice. Three little boys sat beside my path,
where I must pass within three feet of them. Wrapped
in their sheets with their shaved heads and bits of top-
knots, and queer faces, they looked like figures on a
chimney-piece. A while they sat their ground, solemn
as judges. I came up hand over fist, doing my five knots,
like a man that meant business; and I thought I saw a sort
of a wink and gulp in the three faces. Then one jumped
up (he was the farthest off) and ran for his mammy. The
other two, trying to follow suit, got foul, came to the
ground together bawling, wriggled right out of their sheets,
and in a moment there were all three of them scampering

for their lives, and singing out like pigs. The natives, who would never let a joke slip, even at a burial, laughed and let up, as short as a dog's bark.

They say it scares a man to be alone. No such thing. What scares him in the dark or the high bush is that he can't make sure, and there might be an army at his elbow. What scares him worst is to be right in the midst of a crowd, and have no guess of what they're driving at. When that laugh stopped, I stopped too. The boys had not yet made their offing; they were still on the full stretch going the one way, when I had already gone about ship and was sheering off the other. Like a fool I had come out, doing my five knots; like a fool I went back again. It must have been the funniest thing to see, and what knocked me silly, this time no one laughed; only one old woman gave a kind of pious moan, the way you have heard Dissenters in their chapels at the sermon.

" I never saw such fools of Kanakas as your people here," I said once to Uma, glancing out of the window at the starers.

" Savvy nothing," says Uma, with a kind of disgusted air that she was good at.

And that was all the talk we had upon the matter, for I was put out, and Uma took the thing so much as a matter of course that I was fairly ashamed.

All day, off and on, now fewer and now more, the fools sat about the west end of my house and across the river, waiting for the show, whatever that was—fire to come down from heaven, I suppose, and consume me, bones and baggage. But by evening, like real islanders, they had wearied of the business, and got away, and had a dance instead in the big house of the village, where I heard them singing and clapping hands till, maybe, ten at night, and the next day it seemed they had forgotten I existed. If fire had come down from heaven or the earth opened and swallowed me, there would have been nobody to see the sport or take the lesson, or whatever you like to call it. But I was to find they hadn't forgot either, and kept an eye lifting for phenomena over my way.

I was hard at it these days both getting my trade in order and taking stock of what Vigours had left. This was a job that made me pretty sick, and kept me from thinking on much else. Ben had taken stock the trip before—I knew I could trust Ben—but it was plain somebody had been making free in the meantime. I found I was out by what might easily cover six-months' salary and profit, and I could have kicked myself all round the village to have been such a blamed ass, sitting boozing with that Case instead of attending to my own affairs and taking stock.

However, there's no use crying over spilt milk. It was done now, and couldn't be undone. All I could do was to get what was left of it, and my new stuff (my own choice) in order, to go round and get after the rats and cockroaches, and to fix up that store regular Sydney style. A fine show I made of it ; and the third morning, when I had lit my pipe and stood in the doorway and looked in, and turned and looked far up the mountain and saw the cocoanuts waving and posted up the tons of copra, and over the village green and saw the island dandies and reckoned up the yards of print they wanted for their kilts and dresses, I felt as if I was in the right place to make a fortune, and go home again and start a public-house. There was I, sitting in that verandah, in as handsome a piece of scenery as you could find, a splendid sun, and a fine, fresh, healthy trade that stirred up a man's blood like sea-bathing ; and the whole thing was clean gone from me, and I was dreaming England, which is, after all, a nasty, cold, muddy hole, with not enough light to see to read by ; and dreaming the looks of my public, by a cant of a broad high-road like an avenue and with the sign on a green tree.

So much for the morning, but the day passed and the devil any one looked near me, and from all I knew of natives in other islands I thought this strange. People laughed a little at our firm and their fine stations, and at this station of Falesá in particular ; all the copra in the district wouldn't pay for it (I heard them say) in fifty years, which I suppose was an exaggeration. But when the day went, and no business came at all, I began to get downhearted ; and, about three in the afternoon, I went out for a stroll to cheer me up. On the green I saw a white man coming with a cassock on, by which and by the face of him I knew he was a priest. He was a good-natured old soul to look at, gone a little grizzled, and so dirty you could have written with him on a piece of paper.

" Good-day, sir," said I.

He answered me eagerly in native.

" Don't you speak any English ? " said I.

" French," says he.

" Well," said I, " I'm sorry, but I can't do anything there."

He tried me a while in the French, and then again in native, which he seemed to think was the best chance. I made out he was after more than passing the time of day with me, but had something to communicate, and I listened the harder. I heard the names of Adams and Case and of Randall — Randall the oftenest — and the word " poison," or something like it, and a native word that he said very often. I went home, repeating it to myself.

" What does fussy-ocky mean ? " I asked of Uma, for that was as near as I could come to it.

" Make dead," said she.

" The devil it does ! " says I. " Did ever you hear that Case had poisoned Johnny Adams ? "

" Every man he savvy that," says Uma, scornful-like. " Give him white sand—bad sand. He got the bottle still. Suppose he give you gin, you no take him."

Now I had heard much of the same sort of story in other islands, and the same white powder always to the front, which made me think the less of it. For all that, I went over to Randall's place to see what I could pick up, and found Case on the doorstep, cleaning a gun.

" Good shooting here ? " says I.

" A 1," says he. " The bush is full of all kinds of birds I wish copra was as plenty," says he—I thought, slyly—" but there don't seem anything doing."

c

I could see Black Jack in the store, serving a customer.

" That looks like business, though," said I.

" That's the first sale we've made in three weeks," said he.

" You don't tell me ? " says I. " Three weeks ? Well, well."

" If you don't believe me," he cries, a little hot, " you can go and look at the copra-house. It's half empty to this blessed hour."

" I shouldn't be much the better for that, you see," says I. " For all I can tell, it might have been whole empty yesterday."

" That's so," says he, with a bit of a laugh.

" By the by," I said, " what sort of a party is that priest ? Seems rather a friendly sort."

At this Case laughed right out loud. " Ah ! " says he, " I see what ails you now. Galuchet's been at you." *Father Galoshes* was the name he went by most, but Case always gave it the French quirk, which was another reason we had for thinking him above the common.

" Yes, I have seen him," I says. " I made out he didn't think much of your Captain Randall."

" That he don't ! " says Case. " It was the trouble about poor Adams. The last day, when he lay dying, there was young Buncombe round. Ever met Buncombe ? "

I told him no.

" He's a cure, is Buncombe ! " laughs Case. " Well, Buncombe took it in his head that, as there was no other clergyman about, bar Kanaka pastors, we ought to call in Father Galuchet, and have the old man administered and take the sacrament. It was all the same to me, you may suppose ; but I said I thought Adams was the fellow to consult. He was jawing away about watered copra and a sight of foolery. ' Look here,' I said, ' you're pretty sick. Would you like to see Galoshes ? ' He sat right up on his elbow. ' Get the priest,' says he, ' get the priest ; don't let me die here like a dog ! ' He spoke kind of fierce and eager, but sensible enough. There was nothing to say against that, so we sent and asked Galuchet if he would come. You bet he would. He jumped in his dirty linen at the thought of it. But we had reckoned without Papa. He's a hard-shelled Baptist, is Papa ; no Papists need apply. And he took and locked the door. Buncombe told him he was bigoted, and I thought he would have had a fit. ' Bigoted ! ' he says. ' Me bigoted ? Have I lived to hear it from a jackanapes like you ? ' And he made for Buncombe, and I had to hold them apart ; and there was Adams in the middle, gone luny again, and carrying on about copra like a born fool. It was good as the play, and I was about knocked out of time with laughing, when all of a sudden Adams sat up, clapped his hands to his chest, and went into the horrors. He died hard, did John Adams," says Case, with a kind of a sudden sternness.

" And what became of the priest ? " I asked.

" The priest ? " says Case. " Oh ! he was hammering on the door outside, and crying on the natives to come and beat it in, and singing out it was a soul he wished to save, and that. He was in a rare taking, was the priest. But what would you have ? Johnny had slipped his cable ; no more Johnny in the market ; and the administration racket clean played out. Next thing, word came to Randall that the priest was praying upon Johnny's grave. Papa was pretty full, and got a club, and lit out straight for the place, and there was Galoshes on his knees, and a lot of natives looking on. You wouldn't think Papa cared that much about anything, unless it was liquor ; but he and the priest stuck to it two hours, slanging each other in native, and every time Galoshes tried to kneel down Papa went for him with a club. There never were such larks in Falesá. The end of it was that Captain Randall knocked over with some kind of a fit or stroke, and the priest got in his goods after all. But he was the angriest priest you ever heard of, and complained to the chiefs about the outrage, as he called it. That was no account, for our chiefs are Protestant here ; and, anyway, he had been making trouble about the drum for morning school, and they were glad to give him a wipe. Now he swears old Randall gave Adams poison or something, and when the two meet they grin at each other like baboons."

He told this story as natural as could be, and like a man that enjoyed the fun ; though now I come to think of it after so long, it seems rather a sickening yarn. However, Case never set up to be soft, only to be square and hearty, and a man all round ; and, to tell the truth, he puzzled me entirely.

I went home and asked Uma if she were a Popey, which I made out to be the native word for Catholics.

" *E le ai !* " says she. She always used the native when she meant " no " more than usually strong, and, indeed, there's more of it. " No good Popey," she added.

Then I asked her about Adams and the priest, and she told me much the same yarn in her own way. So that I was left not much further on, but inclined, upon the whole, to think the bottom of the matter was the row about sacrament, and the poisoning only talk.

The next day was a Sunday, when there was no business to be looked for. Uma asked me in the morning if I was going to " pray " ; I told her she bet not, and she stopped home herself, with no more words. I thought this seemed unlike a native, and a native woman, and a woman that had new clothes to show off ; however, it suited me to the ground, and I made the less of it. The queer thing was that I came next door to going to church after all, a thing I'm little likely to forget. I had turned out for a stroll, and heard the hymn tune up. You know how it is. If you hear folk singing, it seems to draw you ; and pretty soon I found myself alongside the church. It was a little, long, low place, coral built, rounded off at both ends like a whale-boat, a big native roof on the top of it, windows without sashes and doorways without doors. I stuck my head into one of the windows, and the sight was so new to me—for things went quite different in the islands I was acquainted with—that I stayed and looked on. The congregation sat on the floor on mats, the women on one side, the men on the other, all rigged out to kill—the women with dresses and trade hats, the men in white jackets and shirts. The hymn was over; the pastor, a big buck Kanaka, was in the pulpit, preaching for his life; and by the way he wagged his hand, and worked his voice, and made his points, and seemed to argue with the folk, I made out he was a gun at the business. Well, he looked up suddenly and caught my eye, and I give you my word he staggered in the pulpit; his eyes bulged out of his head, his hand rose and pointed at me like as if against his will, and the sermon stopped right there.

It isn't a fine thing to say for yourself, but I ran away; and if the same kind of a shock was given me, I should run away again to-morrow. To see that palavering Kanaka struck all of a heap at the mere sight of me gave me a feeling as if the bottom had dropped out of the world. I went right home, and stayed there, and said nothing. You might think I would tell Uma, but that was against my system. You might have thought I would have gone over and consulted Case; but the truth was I was ashamed to speak of such a thing, I thought every one would blurt out laughing in my face. So I held my tongue, and thought all the more; and the more I thought, the less I liked the business.

By Monday night I got it clearly in my head I must be tabooed. A new store to stand open two days in a village and not a man or woman come to see the trade, was past believing.

" Uma," said I, " I think I'm tabooed."

" I think so," said she.

I thought a while whether I should ask her more, but it's a bad idea to set natives up with any notion of consulting them, so I went to Case. It was dark, and he was sitting alone, as he did mostly, smoking on the stairs.

" Case," said I, " here's a queer thing. I'm tabooed."

" Oh, fudge ! " says he ; " tain't the practice in these islands."

" That may be, or it mayn't," said I. " It's the practice where I was before. You can bet I know what it's like ; and I tell it you for a fact, I'm tabooed."

" Well," said he, " what have you been doing ? "

" That's what I want to find out," said I.

" Oh, you can't be," said he ; " it ain't possible. However, I'll tell you what I'll do. Just to put your mind at rest, I'll go round and find out for sure. Just you waltz in and talk to Papa."

" Thank you," I said, " I'd rather stay right out here on the verandah. Your house is so close."

" I'll call Papa out here, then," says he.

" My dear fellow," I says, " I wish you wouldn't. The fact is, I don't take to Mr. Randall."

Case laughed, took a lantern from the store, and set out into the village. He was gone perhaps a quarter of an hour, and he looked mighty serious when he came back.

" Well," said he, clapping down the lantern on the verandah steps, " I would never have believed it. I don't know where the impudence of these Kanakas'll go next ; they seem to have lost all idea of respect for whites. What we want is a man-of-war—a German, if we could—they know how to manage Kanakas."

" I *am* tabooed then ? " I cried.

" Something of the sort," said he. " It's the worst thing of the kind I've heard of yet. But I'll stand by you, Wiltshire, man to man. You come round here to-morrow about nine, and we'll have it out with the chiefs. They're afraid of me, or they used to be ; but their heads are so big by now, I don't know what to think. Understand me, Wiltshire ; I don't count this your quarrel," he went on, with a great deal of resolution, " I count it all of our quarrel, I count it the White Man's Quarrel, and I'll stand to it through thick and thin, and there's my hand on it."

" Have you found out what's the reason ? " I asked.

" Not yet," said Case. " But we'll fire them down to-morrow."

Altogether I was pretty well pleased with his attitude, and almost more the next day, when we met to go before the chiefs, to see him so stern and resolved. The chiefs awaited us in one of their big oval houses, which was marked out to us from a long way off by the crowd about the eaves, a hundred strong if there was one—men, women, and children. Many of the men were on their way to work and wore green wreaths, and it put me in thoughts of the first of May at home. This crowd opened and buzzed about the pair of us as we went in, with a sudden angry animation. Five chiefs were there ; four mighty, stately men, the fifth old and puckered. They sat on mats in their white kilts and jackets ; they had fans in their hands, like fine ladies ; and two of the younger ones wore Catholic medals, which gave me matter of reflection. Our place was set, and the mats laid for us over against these grandees, on the near side of the house ; the midst was empty ; the crowd, close at our backs, murmured and craned and jostled to look on, and the shadows of them tossed in front of us on the clean pebbles on the floor. I was just a hair put out by the excitement of the commons, but the quiet, civil appearance of the chiefs reassured me, all the more when their spokesman began and made a long speech in a low tone of voice, sometimes waving his hand towards Case, sometimes towards me, and sometimes knocking with his knuckles on the mat. One thing was clear : there was no sign of anger in the chiefs.

" What's he been saying ? " I asked, when he had done.

" Oh, just that they're glad to see you, and they understand by me you wish to make some kind of complaint, and you're to fire away, and they'll do the square thing."

" It took a precious long time to say that," said I.

" Oh, the rest was sawder and *bonjour* and that," said Case. " You know what Kanakas are."

" Well, they don't get much *bonjour* out of me," said I. " You tell them who I am. I'm a white man, and a British subject, and no end of a big chief at home ; and I've come here to do them good, and bring them civilisation ; and no sooner have I got my trade sorted out than they go and taboo me, and no one dare come near my place ! Tell them I don't mean to fly in the face of anything legal ; and if what they want's a present, I'll do what's fair. I don't blame any man looking out for himself, tell them for that's human nature ; but if they think they're going to come any of their native ideas over me, they'll find themselves mistaken. And tell them plain that I demand the reason of this treatment as a white man and a British subject."

That was my speech. I knew how to deal with Kanakas : give them plain sense and fair dealing, and—I'll do them that much justice—they knuckle under every time. They haven't any real government or any real law, that's what you've got to knock into their heads ; and even if they had, it would be a good joke if it was to apply to a white man. It would be a strange thing if we came all this way and couldn't do what we pleased. The mere idea has always put my monkey up, and I rapped my speech out pretty big. Then Case translated it—or made believe to, rather—and the first chief replied, and then a second, and a third, all in the same style—easy and genteel, but solemn underneath. Once a question was put to Case, and he answered it, and all hands (both chiefs and commons) laughed out aloud, and looked at me. Last of all, the puckered old fellow and the big young chief that spoke first started in to put Case through a kind of catechism. Sometimes I made out that Case was trying to fence, and they stuck to him like hounds, and the sweat ran down his face, which was no very pleasant sight to me, and at some of his answers the crowd moaned and murmured, which was a worse hearing. It's a cruel shame I knew no native, for (as I now believe) they were asking Case about my marriage, and he must have had a tough job of it to clear his feet. But leave Case alone ; he had the brains to run a parliament.

" Well, is that all ? " I asked, when a pause came.

" Come along," says he, mopping his face ; " I'll tell you outside."

" Do you mean they won't take the taboo off ? " I cried.

" It's something queer," said he. " I'll tell you outside. Better come away."

" I won't take it at their hands," cried I. " I ain't that kind of a man. You don't find me turn my back on a parcel of Kanakas."

" You'd better," said Case.

He looked at me with a signal in his eye ; and the five chiefs looked at me civilly enough, but kind of pointed ; and the people looked at me and craned and jostled. I remembered the folks that watched my house, and how the pastor had jumped in his pulpit at the bare sight of me ; and the whole business seemed so out of the way that I rose and followed Case. The crowd opened again to let us through, but wider than before, the children on the skirts running and singing out, and as we two white men walked away they all stood and watched us.

" And now," said I, " what is all this about ? "

" The truth is I can't rightly make it out myself. They have a down on you," says Case.

" Taboo a man because they have a down on him ! " I cried. " I never heard the like."

" It's worse than that, you see," said Case. " You ain't tabooed—I told you that couldn't be. The people won't go near you, Wiltshire, and there's where it is."

" They won't go near me ? What do you mean by that ? Why won't they go near me ? " I cried.

Case hesitated. " Seems they're frightened," says he, in a low voice.

I stopped dead short. " Frightened ? " I repeated. " Are you gone crazy, Case ? What are they frightened of ? "

" I wish I could make out," Case answered, shaking his head. " Appears like one of their tomfool superstitions. That's what I don't cotton to," he said. " It's like the business about Vigours."

" I'd like to know what you mean by that, and I'll trouble you to tell me," says I.

" Well, you know, Vigours lit out and left all standing," said he. " It was some superstition business—I never got the hang of it ; but it began to look bad before the end."

" I've heard a different story about that," said I, " and I had better tell you so. I heard he ran away because of you."

" Oh ! well, I suppose he was ashamed to tell the truth,"
says Case ; " I guess he thought it silly. And it's a fact
that I packed him off. ' What would you do, old man ? '
says he. ' Get,' says I, ' and not think twice about it.' I
was the gladdest kind of man to see him clear away. It
ain't my notion to turn my back on a mate when he's in a
tight place, but there was that much trouble in the village
that I couldn't see where it might likely end. I was a fool
to be so much about with Vigours. They cast it up to me
to-day. Didn't you hear Maea—that's the young chief,
the big one—ripping out about ' Vika ' ? That was him
they were after. They don't seem to forget it, somehow."

" This is all very well," said I, " but it don't tell me
what's wrong ; it don't tell me what they're afraid of—
what their idea is."

" Well, I wish I knew," said Case. " I can't say fairer
than that."

" You might have asked, I think," says I.

" And so I did," says he. " But you must have seen for
yourself, unless you're blind, that the asking got the other
way. I'll go as far as I dare for another white man ; but
when I find I'm in the scrape myself, I think first of my
own bacon. The loss of me is I'm too good-natured.
And I'll take the freedom of telling you you show a
queer kind of gratitude to a man who's got into all this
mess along of your affairs."

" There's a thing I'm thinking of," said I. " You were
a fool to be so much about with Vigours. One comfort,
you haven't been much about with me. I notice you've
never been inside my house. Own up now ; you had word
of this before ? "

" It's a fact I haven't been," said he. " It was an over-
sight, and I am sorry for it, Wiltshire. But about coming
now, I'll be quite plain."

" You mean you won't ? " I asked.

" Awfully sorry, old man, but that's the size of it," says
Case.

" In short, you're afraid ? " says I.

" In short, I'm afraid," says he.

" And I'm still to be tabooed for nothing ? " I asked.

" I tell you you're not tabooed," said he. " The Kanakas won't go near you, that's all. And who's to make 'em ? We traders have a lot of gall, I must say ; we make these poor Kanakas take back their laws, and take up their taboos, and that, whenever it happens to suit us. But you don't mean to say you expect a law obliging people to deal in your store whether they want to or not ? You don't mean to tell me you've got the gall for that ? And if you had, it would be a queer thing to propose to me. I would just like to point out to you, Wiltshire, that I'm a trader myself."

" I don't think I would talk of gall if I was you," said I. " Here's about what it comes to, as well as I can make out : None of the people are to trade with me, and they're all to trade with you. You're to have the copra, and I'm to go to the devil and shake myself. And I don't know any native, and you're the only man here worth mention that speaks English, and you have the gall to up and hint to me my life's in danger, and all you've got to tell me is you don't know why ! "

" Well, it *is* all I have to tell you," said he. " I don't know—I wish I did."

" And so you turn your back and leave me to myself ! Is that the position ? " says I.

" If you like to put it nasty," says he. " I don't put it so. I say merely, ' I'm going to keep clear of you ; or, if I don't I'll get in danger for myself.' "

" Well," says I, " you're a nice kind of a white man ! "

" Oh, I understand ; you're riled," said he. " I would be myself. I can make excuses."

" All right," I said, " go and make excuses somewhere else. Here's my way, there's yours ! "

With that we parted, and I went straight home in a hot temper and found Uma trying on a lot of trade goods like a baby.

" Here," I said, " you quit that foolery ! Here's pretty mess to have made, as if I wasn't bothered enough anyway ! And I thought I told you to get dinner ! "

And then I believe I gave her a bit of the rough side of my tongue, as she deserved. She stood up at once, like a sentry to his officer ; and I must say she was always well brought up, and had a great respect for whites.

" And now," says I, " you belong round here, you're bound to understand this. What am I tabooed for, any-way ? Or, if I ain't tabooed, what makes the folks afraid of me ? "

She stood and looked at me with eyes like saucers.

" You no savvy ? " she gasps at last.

" No," said I. " How would you expect me to ? We don't have any such craziness where I come from."

" Ese no tell you ? " she asked again.

(*Ese* was the name the natives had for Case ; it may mean foreign, or extraordinary ; or it might mean a mummy apple ; but most like it was only his own name misheard and put in a Kanaka spelling.)

" Not much," said I.

" Damn Ese ! " she cried.

You might think it funny to hear this Kanaka girl come out with a big swear. No such thing. There was no swearing in her—no, nor anger ; she was beyond anger, and meant the word simple and serious. She stood there straight as she said it. I cannot justly say that I ever saw a woman look like that before or after, and it struck me mum. Then she made a kind of an obeisance, but it was the proudest kind, and threw her hands out open.

" I 'shamed," she said. " I think you savvy. Ese he tell me you savvy, he tell me you no mind, tell me you love me too much. Taboo belong me," she said, touching herself on the bosom as she had done upon our wedding-night. " Now I go 'way, taboo he go 'way too. Then you get too much copra. You like more better, I think. *Tofá, alii*," says she in the native—" Farewell, chief ! "

" Hold on ! " I cried. " Don't be in such a hurry."

She looked at me sidelong with a smile. " You see, you get copra," she said, the same as you might offer candies to a child.

" Uma," said I, " hear reason. I didn't know, and that's

a fact ; and Case seems to have played it pretty mean upon the pair of us. But I do know now, and I don't mind ; I love you too much. You no go 'way, you no leave me, I too much sorry."

" You no love me," she cried, " you talk me bad words ! " And she threw herself in a corner of the floor and began to cry.

Well, I'm no scholar, but I wasn't born yesterday, and I thought the worst of that trouble was over. However, there she lay—her back turned, her face to the wall—and shook with sobbing like a little child, so that her feet jumped with it. It's strange how it hits a man when he's in love ; for there's no use mincing things—Kanaka and all, I was in love with her, or just as good. I tried to take her hand, but she would none of that. " Uma," I said, " there's no sense in carrying on like this. I want you stop here, I want my little wifie, I tell you true."

" No tell me true," she sobbed.

" All right," says I, " I'll wait till you're through with this." And I sat right down beside her on the floor, and set to smooth her hair with my hand. At first she wriggled away when I touched her ; then she seemed to notice me no more ; then her sobs grew gradually less, and presently stopped ; and the next thing I knew, she raised her face to mine.

" You tell me true ? You like me stop ? " she asked.

" Uma," I said, " I would rather have you than all the copra in the South Seas," which was a very big expression, and the strangest thing was that I meant it.

She threw her arms about me, sprang close up, and pressed her face to mine, in the island way of kissing, so that I was all wetted with her tears, and my heart went out to her wholly. I never had anything so near me as this little brown bit of a girl. Many things went together, and all helped to turn my head. She was pretty enough to eat ; it seemed she was my only friend in that queer place ; I was ashamed that I had spoken rough to her : and she was a woman, and my wife, and a kind of a baby besides that I was sorry for ; and the salt of her tears was in my mouth.

And I forgot Case and the natives ; and I forgot that I
knew nothing of the story, or only remembered it to banish
the remembrance ; and I forgot that I was to get no copra,
and so could make no livelihood ; and I forgot my employers,
and the strange kind of service I was doing them, when I
preferred my fancy to their business ; and I forgot even
that Uma was no true wife of mine, but just a maid beguiled,
and that in a pretty shabby style. But that is to look too
far on. I will come to that part of it next.

It was late before we thought of getting dinner. The
stove was out, and gone stone cold ; but we fired up after a
while, and cooked each a dish, helping and hindering each
other, and making a play of it like children. I was so
greedy of her nearness that I sat down to dinner with my
lass upon my knee, and made sure of her with one hand,
and ate with the other. Ay, and more than that. She
was the worst cook, I suppose, God made ; the things she
set her hand to it would have sickened an honest horse to
eat of ; yet I made my meal that day on Uma's cookery,
and can never call to mind to have been better pleased.

I didn't pretend to myself, and I didn't pretend to her.
I saw I was clean gone ; and if she was to make a fool of
me, she must. And I suppose it was this that set her
talking, for now she made sure that we were friends. A
lot she told me, sitting in my lap and eating my dish, as I
ate hers from foolery—a lot about herself and her mother
and Case, all which would be very tedious, and fill sheets
if I set it down in Beach de Mar, but which I must give a
hint of in plain English, and one thing about myself, which
had a very big effect on my concerns, as you are soon to
hear.

It seems she was born in one of the Line Islands ;
had been only two or three years in these parts, where she
had come with a white man, who was married to her
mother and then died ; and only the one year in Falesá.
Before that they had been a good deal on the move, trekking
about after the white man, who was one of those rolling
stones that keep going round after a soft job. They talk
about looking for gold at the end of a rainbow ; but if a

man wants an employment that'll last him till he dies, let him start out on the soft-job hunt. There's meat and drink in it too, and beer and skittles, for you never hear of them starving, and rarely see them sober ; and as for steady sport, cock-fighting isn't in the same county with it. Anyway, this beachcomber carried the woman and her daughter all over the shop, but mostly to out-of-the-way islands, where there were no police, and he thought, perhaps, the soft job hung out. I've my own view of this old party ; but I was just as glad he had kept Uma clear of Apia and Papeete and these flash towns. At last he struck Fale-alii on this island, got some trade—the Lord knows how !—muddled it all away in the usual style, and died worth next to nothing, bar a bit of land at Falesá that he had got for a bad debt, which was what put it in the minds of the mother and daughter to come there and live. It seems Case encouraged them all he could, and helped to get their house built. He was very kind those days, and gave Uma trade, and there is no doubt he had his eye on her from the beginning. However, they had scarce settled, when up turned a young man, a native, and wanted to marry her. He was a small chief, and had some fine mats and old songs in his family, and was " very pretty," Uma said ; and, altogether, it was an extraordinary match for a penniless girl and an out-islander.

At the first word of this I got downright sick with jealousy.

" And you mean to say you would have married him ? " I cried.

" *Ioe*, yes," said she. " I like too much ! "

" Well ! " I said. " And suppose I had come round after ? "

" I like you more better now," said she. " But suppose I marry Ioane, I one good wife. I no common Kanaka. Good girl ! " says she.

Well, I had to be pleased with that ; but I promise you I didn't care about the business one little bit. And I liked the end of that yarn no better than the beginning. For it seems this proposal of marriage was a start of all the trouble.

It seems, before that, Uma and her mother had been looked down upon, of course, for kinless folk and out-islanders, but nothing to hurt ; and, even when Ioane came forward, there was less trouble at first than might have been looked for.   And then, all of a sudden, about six months before my coming, Ioane backed out and left that part of the island, and from that day to this Uma and her mother had found themselves alone.   None called at their house—none spoke to them on the roads.   If they went to church, the other women drew their mats away and left them in a clear place by themselves.   It was a regular excommunication, like what you read of in the Middle Ages ; and the cause or sense of it beyond guessing.   It was some *talo pepelo*, Uma said, some lie, some calumny ; and all she knew of it was that the girls who had been jealous of her luck with Ioane used to twit her with his desertion, and cry out, when they met her alone in the woods, that she would never be married.   " They tell me no man he marry me. He too much 'fraid," she said.

The only soul that came about them after this desertion was Master Case.   Even he was chary of showing himself, and turned up mostly by night ; and pretty soon he began to table his cards and make up to Uma.   I was still sore about Ioane, and when Case turned up in the same line of business I cut up downright rough.

" Well," I said, sneering, " and I suppose you thought Case ' very pretty ' and ' liked too much ' ? "

" Now you talk silly," said she.   " White man, he come here, I marry him all-e-same Kanaka ; very well then, he marry me all-e-same white woman.   Suppose he no marry, he go 'way, woman he stop.   All-e-same thief, empty-hand, Tonga-heart—no can love !   Now you come marry me.   You big heart—you no 'shamed island-girl.   That thing I love you far too much.   I proud."

I don't know that ever I felt sicker all the days of my life. I laid down my fork, and I put away the " island-girl " ; I didn't seem somehow to have any use for either, and I went and walked up and down in the house, and Uma followed me with her eyes, for she was troubled, and small wonder ! But troubled was no word for it with me. I so wanted, and so feared, to make a clean breast of the sweep that I had been.

And just then there came a sound of singing out of the sea ; it sprang up suddenly clear and near, as the boat turned the headland, and Uma, running to the window, cried out it was " Misi " come upon his rounds.

I thought it was a strange thing I should be glad to have a missionary ; but if it was strange, it was still true.

" Uma," said I, " you stop here in this room, and don't budge a foot out of it till I come back."

D

CHAPTER III

THE MISSIONARY

A S I came out on the verandah, the mission-boat was shooting for the mouth of the river. She was a long whale-boat painted white; a bit of an awning astern; a native pastor crouched on the wedge of poop, steering; some four-and-twenty paddles flashing and dipping, true to the boat-song; and the missionary under the awning, in his white clothes, reading in a book; and set him up! It was pretty to see and hear; there's no smarter sight in the islands than a missionary boat with a good crew and a good pipe to them; and I considered it for half a minute with a bit of envy perhaps, and then strolled down towards the river.

From the opposite side there was another man aiming for the same place, but he ran and got there first. It was Case; doubtless his idea was to keep me apart from the missionary, who might serve me as interpreter; but my mind was upon other things. I was thinking how he had jockeyed us about the marriage, and tried his hand on Uma before; and at the sight of him rage flew into my nostrils.

" Get out of that, you low, swindling thief ! " I cried.

" What's that you say ? " says he.

I gave him the word again, and rammed it down with a good oath. " And if I ever catch you within six fathoms of my house," I cried, " I'll clap a bullet in your measly carcass."

" You must do as you like about your house," said he, " where I told you I have no thought of going ; but this is a public place."

" It's a place where I have private business," said I. " I

have no idea of a hound like you eavesdropping, and I give you notice to clear out."

" I don't take it, though," says Case.

" I'll show you then," said I.

" We'll have to see about that," said he.

He was quick with his hands, but he had neither the height nor the weight, being a flimsy creature alongside a man like me, and, besides, I was blazing to that height of wrath that I could have bit into a chisel. I gave him first the one and then the other, so that I could hear his head rattle and crack, and he went down straight.

" Have you had enough ? " cried I. But he only looked up white and blank, and the blood spread upon his face like wine upon a napkin. " Have you had enough ? " I cried again. " Speak up and don't lie malingering there, or I'll take my feet to you."

He sat up at that, and held his head—by the look of him you could see it was spinning—and the blood poured on his pyjamas.

" I've had enough for this time," says he, and he got up staggering, and went off by the way that he had come.

The boat was close in ; I saw the missionary had laid his book to one side, and I smiled to myself. " He'll know I'm a man, anyway," thinks I.

This was the first time, in all my years in the Pacific, I had ever exchanged two words with any missionary, let alone asked one for a favour. I didn't like the lot, no trader does ; they look down upon us, and make no concealment ; and, besides, they're partly Kanakaised, and suck up with natives instead of with other white men like themselves. I had on a rig of clean, striped pyjamas—for, of course, I had dressed decent to go before the chiefs ; but when I saw the missionary step out of this boat in the regular uniform, white duck clothes, pith helmet, white shirt and tie, and yellow boots to his feet, I could have bunged stones at him. As he came nearer, queering me pretty curious (because of the fight, I suppose), I saw he looked mortal sick, for the truth was he had a fever on, and had just had a chill in the boat.

" Mr. Tarleton, I believe ? " says I, for I had got his name.

" And you, I suppose, are the new trader ? " says he.

" I want to tell you first that I don't hold with missions," I went on, " and that I think you and the likes of you do a sight of harm, filling up the natives with old wives' tales and bumptiousness."

" You are perfectly entitled to your opinions," says he, looking a bit ugly, " but I have no call to hear them."

" It so happens that you've got to hear them," I said. " I'm no missionary, nor missionary lover ; I'm no Kanaka, nor favourer of Kanakas—I'm just a trader ; I'm just a common low God-damned white man and British subject, the sort you would like to wipe your boots on. I hope that's plain ! "

" Yes, my man," said he. " It's more plain than creditable. When you are sober, you'll be sorry for this."

He tried to pass on, but I stopped him with my hand. The Kanakas were beginning to growl. Guess they didn't like my tone, for I spoke to that man as free as I would to you.

" Now you can't say I've deceived you," said I, " and I can go on. I want a service—I want two services, in fact ; and, if you care to give me them, I'll perhaps take more stock in what you call your Christianity."

He was silent for a moment. Then he smiled. " You are rather a strange sort of man," says he.

" I'm the sort of man God made me," says I. " I don't set up to be a gentleman," I said.

" I am not quite so sure," said he. " And what can I do for you, Mr.—— ? "

" Wiltshire," I says, " though I'm mostly called Welsher ; but Wiltshire is the way it's spelt, if the people on the beach could only get their tongues about it. And what do I want ? Well, I'll tell you the first thing. I'm what you call a sinner—what I call a sweep—and I want you to help me to make it up to a person I've deceived."

He turned and spoke to his crew in the native. " And now I am at your service," said he, " but only for the time my crew are dining. I must be much farther down the coast before night. I was delayed at Papa-Malulu till this morning, and I have an engagement in Fale-alii to-morrow night."

I led the way to my house in silence, and rather pleased with myself for the way I had managed the talk, for I like a man to keep his self-respect.

" I was sorry to see you fighting," says he.

" Oh, that's part of the yarn I want to tell you," I said. " That's service number two. After you've heard it you'll let me know whether you're sorry or not."

We walked right in through the store, and I was surprised to find Uma had cleared away the dinner things. This was so unlike her ways that I saw she had done it out of gratitude, and liked her the better. She and Mr. Tarleton called each other by name, and he was very civil to her seemingly. But I thought little of that ; they can always find civility for a Kanaka, it's us white men they lord it over. Besides, I didn't want much Tarleton just then. I was going to do my pitch.

" Uma," said I, " give us your marriage certificate." She looked put out. " Come," said I, " you can trust me. Hand it up."

She had it about her person, as usual ; I believe she thought it was a pass to heaven, and if she died without having it handy she would go to hell. I couldn't see where she put it the first time, I couldn't see now where she took it from ; it seemed to jump into her hand like that Blavatsky business in the papers. But it's the same way with all island women, and I guess they're taught it when young.

" Now," said I, with the certificate in my hand, " I was married to this girl by Black Jack, the negro. The certificate was wrote by Case, and it's a dandy piece of literature, I promise you. Since then I've found that there's a kind of cry in the place against this wife of mine, and so long as I keep her I cannot trade. Now, what would any man do in my place, if he was a man ? " I said. " The first thing he would do is this, I guess." And I took and tore up the certificate and bunged the pieces on the floor.

" *Aué !* " * cried Uma, and began to clap her hands ; but I caught one of them in mine.

" And the second thing that he would do," said I, " if he was what I would call a man and you would call a man, Mr. Tarleton, is to bring the girl right before you or any other missionary, and to up and say : ' I was wrong married to this wife of mine, but I think a heap of her, and now I want to be married to her right.' Fire away, Mr. Tarleton. And I guess you'd better do it in native ; it'll please the old lady," I said, giving her the proper name of a man's wife upon the spot.

So we had in two of the crew for to witness, and were spliced in our own house ; and the parson prayed a good bit, I must say—but not so long as some—and shook hands with the pair of us.

" Mr. Wiltshire," he says, when he had made out the lines and packed off the witnesses, " I have to thank you for a very lively pleasure. I have rarely performed the marriage ceremony with more grateful emotions."

That was what you would call talking. He was going on, besides, with more of it, and I was ready for as much taffy as he had in stock, for I felt good. But Uma had been taken up with something half through the marriage, and cut straight in.

" How your hand he get hurt ? " she asked.

" You ask Case's head, old lady," says I.

She jumped with joy, and sang out.

" You haven't made much of a Christian of this one," says I to Mr. Tarleton.

" We didn't think her one of our worst," says he, " when she was at Fale-alii ; and if Uma bears malice I shall be tempted to fancy she has good cause."

" Well, there we are at service number two," said I. " I want to tell you our yarn, and see if you can let a little daylight in."

" Is it long ? " he asked.

" Yes," I cried ; " it's a goodish bit of a yarn ! "

" Well, I'll give you all the time I can spare," says he,

* Alas !

looking at his watch. " But I must tell you fairly, I haven't eaten since five this morning, and, unless you can let me have something, I am not likely to eat again before seven or eight to-night."

" By God, we'll give you dinner ! " I cried.

I was a little caught up at my swearing, just when all was going straight ; and so was the missionary, I suppose, but he made believe to look out of the window, and thanked us.

So we ran him up a bit of a meal. I was bound to let the old lady have a hand in it, to show off, so I deputised her to brew the tea. I don't think I ever met such tea as she turned out. But that was not the worst, for she got round with the salt-box, which she considered an extra European touch, and turned my stew into sea-water. Altogether, Mr. Tarleton had a devil of a dinner of it ; but he had plenty entertainment by the way, for all the while that we were cooking, and afterwards, when he was making believe to eat, I kept posting him up on Master Case and the beach of Falesá, and he putting questions that showed he was following close.

" Well," said he at last, " I am afraid you have a dangerous enemy. This man Case is very clever, and seems really wicked. I must tell you I have had my eye on him for nearly a year, and have rather had the worst of our encounters. About the time when the last representative of your firm ran so suddenly away, I had a letter from Namu, the native pastor, begging me to come to Falesá at my earliest convenience, as his flock were all ' adopting Catholic practices.' I had great confidence in Namu ; I fear it only shows how easily we are deceived. No one could hear him preach and not be persuaded he was a man of extraordinary parts. All our islanders easily acquire a kind of eloquence, and can roll out and illustrate, with a great deal of vigour and fancy, second-hand sermons ; but Namu's sermons are his own, and I cannot deny that I have found them means of grace. Moreover, he has a keen curiosity in secular things, does not fear work, is clever at carpentering, and has made himself so much respected among the neighbouring pastors that we call him, in a jest which is half serious, the Bishop of the East. In short, I was proud of the man ; all the more puzzled by his letter, and took an occasion to come this way.   The morning before my arrival, Vigours had been sent on board the *Lion*, and Namu was perfectly at his ease, apparently ashamed of his letter, and quite unwilling to explain it. This, of course, I could not allow, and he ended by confessing that he had been much concerned to find his people using the sign of the cross, but since he had learned the explanation his mind was satisfied.   For Vigours had the Evil Eye, a common thing in a country of Europe called Italy, where men were often struck dead by that kind of devil, and it appeared the sign of the cross was a charm against its power.

" ' And I explain it, Misi,' said Namu, ' in this way : the country in Europe is a Popey country, and the devil of the Evil Eye may be a Catholic devil, or, at least, used to Catholic ways.   So then I reasoned thus : if this sign of the cross were used in a Popey manner it would be sinful, but when it is used only to protect men from a devil, which is a thing harmless in itself, the sign too must be harmless.   For the sign is neither good nor bad.   But if the bottle be full of gin, the gin is bad ; and if the sign made in idolatry be bad, so is the idolatry.'   And, very like a native pastor, he had a text apposite about the casting out of devils.

" ' And who has been telling you about the Evil Eye ? ' I asked.

" He admitted it was Case.   Now, I am afraid you will think me very narrow, Mr. Wiltshire, but I must tell you I was displeased, and cannot think a trader at all a good man to advise or have an influence upon my pastors. And, besides, there had been some flying talk in the country of old Adams and his being poisoned, to which I had paid no great heed ; but it came back to me at the moment.

" ' And is this Case a man of a sanctified life ? ' I asked.

" He admitted he was not ; for, though he did not drink, he was profligate with women, and had no religion.

" ' Then,' said I, ' I think the less you have to do with him the better.'

" But it is not easy to have the last word with a man like Namu. He was ready in a moment with an illustration. ' Misi,' said he, ' you have told me there were wise men, not pastors, not even holy, who knew many things useful to be taught—about trees, for instance, and beasts, and to print books, and about the stones that are burned to make knives of. Such men teach you in your college, and you learn from them, but take care not to learn to be unholy. Misi, Case is my college.'

" I knew not what to say. Mr. Vigours had evidently been driven out of Falesá by the machinations of Case and with something not very unlike the collusion of my pastor. I called to mind it was Namu who had reassured me about Adams and traced the rumour to the ill-will of the priest. And I saw I must inform myself more thoroughly from an impartial source. There is an old rascal of a chief here, Faiaso, whom I daresay you saw to-day at the council; he has been all his life turbulent and sly, a great fomenter of rebellions, and a thorn in the side of the mission and the island. For all that he is very shrewd, and, except in politics or about his own misdemeanours, a teller of the truth. I went to his house, told him what I had heard, and besought him to be frank. I do not think I had ever a more painful interview. Perhaps you will understand me, Mr. Wiltshire, if I tell you that I am perfectly serious in these old wives' tales with which you reproached me, and as anxious to do well for these islands as you can be to please and to protect your pretty wife. And you are to remember that I thought Namu a paragon, and was proud of the man as one of the first ripe fruits of the mission. And now I was informed that he had fallen in a sort of dependence upon Case. The beginning of it was not corrupt; it began, doubtless, in fear and respect, produced by trickery and pretence; but I was shocked to find that another element had been lately added, that Namu helped himself in the store, and was believed to be deep in Case's debt. Whatever the trader said, that Namu believed with trembling. He was not alone in this; many in the village lived in a similar subjection; but Namu's case was the most influential, it was through Namu that Case had wrought most evil; and with a certain following among the chiefs, and the pastor in his pocket, the man was as good as master of the village. You know something of Vigours and Adams, but perhaps you have never heard of old Underhill, Adams's predecessor. He was a quiet, mild old fellow, I remember, and we were told he had died suddenly: white men die very suddenly in Falesá. The truth, as I now heard it, made my blood run cold. It seems he was struck with a general palsy, all of him dead but one eye, which he continually winked. Word was started that the helpless old fellow was now a devil, and this vile fellow Case worked upon the natives' fears, which he professed to share, and pretended he durst not go into the house alone. At last a grave was dug, and the living body buried at the far end of the village. Namu, my pastor, whom I had helped to educate, offered up a prayer at the hateful scene.

" I felt myself in a very difficult position. Perhaps it was my duty to have denounced Namu and had him deposed. Perhaps I think so now, but at the time it seemed less clear. He had a great influence, it might prove greater than mine. The natives are prone to superstition; perhaps by stirring them up I might but ingrain and spread these dangerous fancies. And Namu besides, apart from this novel and accursed influence, was a good pastor, an able man, and spiritually minded. Where should I look for a better? How was I to find as good? At that moment, with Namu's failure fresh in my view, the work of my life appeared a mockery; hope was dead in me. I would rather repair such tools as I had than go abroad in quest of others that must certainly prove worse; and a scandal is, at the best, a thing to be avoided when humanly possible. Right or wrong, then, I determined on a quiet course. All that night I denounced and reasoned with the erring pastor, twitted him with his ignorance and want of faith, twitted him with his wretched attitude, making clean the outside of the cup and platter, callously helping at a murder, childishly flying in excitement about a few childish, unnecessary, and inconvenient gestures ; and long before day I had him on his knees and bathed in the tears of what seemed a genuine repentance. On Sunday I took the pulpit in the morning, and preached from First Kings, nineteenth, on the fire, the earthquake, and the voice, distinguishing the true spiritual power, and referring with such plainness as I dared to recent events in Falesá. The effect produced was great, and it was much increased when Namu rose in his turn and confessed that he had been wanting in faith and conduct, and was convinced of sin. So far, then, all was well ; but there was one unfortunate circumstance. It was nearing the time of our ' May ' in the island, when the native contributions to the missions are received ; it fell in my duty to make a notification on the subject, and this gave my enemy his chance, by which he was not slow to profit.

" News of the whole proceedings must have been carried to Case as soon as church was over, and the same afternoon he made an occasion to meet me in the midst of the village. He came up with so much intentness and animosity that I felt it would be damaging to avoid him.

" ' So,' says he, in native, ' here is the holy man. He has been preaching against me, but that was not in his heart. He has been preaching upon the love of God ; but that was not in his heart, it was between his teeth. Will you know what was in his heart ? ' cries he. ' I will show it to you ! ' And, making a snatch at my head, he made believe to pluck out a dollar, and held it in the air.

" There went that rumour through the crowd with which Polynesians receive a prodigy. As for myself, I stood amazed. The thing was a common conjuring trick which I have seen performed at home a score of times ; but how was I to convince the villagers of that ? I wish I had learned legerdemain instead of Hebrew, that I might have paid the fellow out with his own coin. But there I was ; I could not stand there silent, and the best I could find to say was weak.

" ' I will trouble you not to lay hands on me again,' said I.

" ' I have no such thought,' said he, ' nor will I deprive you of your dollar. Here it is,' he said, and flung it at my feet. I am told it lay where it fell three days.'"

" I must say it was well played," said I.

" Oh ! he is clever," said Mr. Tarleton, " and you can now see for yourself how dangerous. He was a party to the horrid death of the paralytic ; he is accused of poisoning Adams ; he drove Vigours out of the place by lies that might have led to murder ; and there is no question but he has now made up his mind to rid himself of you. How he means to try we have no guess ; only be sure, it's something new. There is no end to his readiness and invention."

" He gives himself a sight of trouble," says I. " And, after all, what for ? "

" Why, how many tons of copra may they make in this district ? " asked the missionary.

" I daresay as much as sixty tons," says I.

" And what is the profit to the local trader ? " he asked.

" You may call it three pounds," said I.

" Then you can reckon for yourself how much he does for it," said Mr. Tarleton. " But the more important thing is to defeat him. It is clear he spread some report against Uma, in order to isolate and have his wicked will of her. Failing of that, and seeing a new rival come upon the scene, he used her in a different way. Now, the first point to find out is about Namu.—Uma, when people began to leave you and your mother alone, what did Namu do ? "

" Stop away all-e-same," says Uma.

" I fear the dog has returned to his vomit," said Mr. Tarleton. " And now what am I to do for you ? I will speak to Namu, I will warn him he is observed ; it will be strange if he allow anything to go amiss when he is put upon his guard. At the same time, this precaution may fail, and then you must turn elsewhere. You have two people at hand to whom you might apply. There is, first of all, the priest, who might protect you by the Catholic

interest ; they are a wretchedly small body, but they count
two chiefs.   And then there is old Faiaso.   Ah ! if it had
been some years ago you would have needed no one else ;
but his influence is much reduced, it has gone into Maea's
hands, and Maea, I fear, is one of Case's jackals.   In fine,
if the worst comes to the worst, you must send up or come
yourself to Fale-alii, and, though I am not due at this end of
the island for a month, I will just see what can be done."

So Mr. Tarleton said farewell ; and half an hour later
the crew were singing and the paddles flashing in the
missionary boat.

CHAPTER IV

DEVIL-WORK

NEAR a month went by without much doing. The same night of our marriage Galoshes called round, and made himself mighty civil, and got into a habit of dropping in about dark and smoking his pipe with the family. He could talk to Uma, of course, and started to teach me native and French at the same time. He was a kind old buffer, though the dirtiest you would wish to see, and he muddled me up with foreign languages worse than the Tower of Babel.

That was one employment we had, and it made me feel less lonesome ; but there was no profit in the thing, for though the priest came and sat and yarned, none of his folks could be enticed into my store, and if it hadn't been for the other occupation I struck out, there wouldn't have been a pound of copra in the house. This was the idea : Fa'avao (Uma's mother) had a score of bearing-trees. Of course we could get no labour, being all as good as tabooed, and the two women and I turned to and made copra with our own hands. It was copra to make your mouth water when it was done—I never understood how much the natives cheated me till I had made that four hundred pounds of my own hand—and it weighed so light I felt inclined to take and water it myself.

When we were at the job a good many Kanakas used to put in the best of the day looking on, and once that nigger turned up. He stood back with the natives and laughed and did the big don and the funny dog, till I began to get riled.

" Here, you nigger ! " says I.

"I don't address myself to you, Sah," says the nigger. "Only speak to gen'le'um."

"I know," says I, "but it happens I was addressing myself to you, Mr. Black Jack. And all I want to know is just this : did you see Case's figure-head about a week ago ? "

"No, Sah," says he.

"That's all right, then," says I ; "for I'll show you the own brother to it, only black, in the outside of about two minutes."

And I began to walk towards him, quite slow, and my hands down ; only there was trouble in my eye, if anybody took the pains to look.

"You're a low, obstropulous fellow, Sah," says he.

"You bet ! " says I.

By that time he thought I was about as near as convenient, and lit out so it would have done your heart good to see him travel. And that was all I saw of that precious gang until what I am about to tell you.

It was one of my chief employments these days to go pot-hunting in the woods, which I found (as Case had told me) very rich in game. I have spoken of the cape which shut up the village and my station from the east. A path went about the end of it, and led into the next bay. A strong wind blew here daily, and as the line of the barrier reef stopped at the end of the cape, a heavy surf ran on the shores of the bay. A little cliffy hill cut the valley in two parts, and stood close on the beach ; and at high water the sea broke right on the face of it, so that all passage was stopped. Woody mountains hemmed the place all round ; the barrier to the east was particularly steep and leafy, the lower parts of it, along the sea, falling in sheer black cliffs streaked with cinnabar ; the upper part lumpy with the tops of the great trees. Some of the trees were bright green, and some red, and the sand of the beach as black as your shoes. Many birds hovered round the bay, some of them snow-white ; and the flying-fox (or vampire) flew there in broad daylight, gnashing its teeth.

For a long while I came as far as this shooting, and went

no farther. There was no sign of any path beyond, and the cocoa-palms in the front of the foot of the valley were the last this way. For the whole "eye" of the island, as natives called the windward end, lay desert. From Falesá round about to Papa-Malulu, there was neither house, nor man, nor planted fruit-tree ; and the reef being mostly absent, and the shores bluff, the sea beat direct among crags, and there was scarce a landing-place.

I should tell you that after I began to go in the woods, although no one appeared to come near my store, I found people willing enough to pass the time of day with me where nobody would see them ; and as I had begun to pick up native, and most of them had a word or two of English, I began to hold little odds and ends of conversation, not to much purpose, to be sure, but they took off the worst of the feeling, for it's a miserable thing to be made a leper of.

It chanced one day towards the end of the month, that I was sitting in this bay in the edge of the bush, looking east, with a Kanaka. I had given him a fill of tobacco, and we were making out to talk as best we could ; indeed, he had more English than most.

I asked him if there was no road going eastward.

" One time one road," said he. " Now he dead."

" Nobody he go there ? " I asked.

" No good," said he. " Too much devil he stop there."

" Oho ! " says I, " got-um plenty devil, that bush ? "

" Man devil, woman devil ; too much devil," said my friend. " Stop there all-e-time. Man he go there, no come back."

I thought if this fellow was so well posted on devils and spoke of them so free, which is not common, I had better fish for a little information about myself and Uma.

" You think me one devil ? " I asked.

" No think devil," said he, soothingly. " Think all-e-same fool."

" Uma, she devil ? " I asked again.

" No, no ; no devil. Devil stop bush," said the young man.

I was looking in front of me across the bay, and I saw the hanging front of the woods pushed suddenly open, and Case, with a gun in his hand, step forth into the sunshine on the black beach. He was got up in light pyjamas, near white, his gun sparkled, he looked mighty conspicuous ; and the land-crabs scuttled from all around him to their holes.

" Hullo, my friend ! " says I, " you no talk all-e-same true. Ese he go, he come back."

" Ese no all-e-same ; Ese *Tiapolo*," says my friend ; and, with a " Good-by," slunk off among the trees.

I watched Case all around the beach, where the tide was low ; and let him pass me on the homeward way to Falesá. He was in deep thought, and the birds seemed to know it, trotting quite near him on the sand, or wheeling and calling in his ears. When he passed me I could see by the working of his lips that he was talking to himself, and what pleased me mightily, he had still my trade-mark on his brow. I tell you the plain truth : I had a mind to give him a gunful in his ugly mug, but I thought better of it.

All this time, and all the time I was following home, I kept repeating that native word, which I remembered by " Polly, put the kettle on and make us all some tea," tea-a-pollo.

" Uma," says I, when I got back, " what does *Tiapolo* mean ? "

" Devil," says she.

" I thought *aitu* was the word for that," I said.

" *Aitu* 'nother kind of devil," said she ; " stop bush, eat Kanaka. Tiapolo big chief devil, stop home ; all-e-same Christian devil."

" Well, then," said I, " I'm no farther forward. How can Case be Tiapolo ? "

" No all-e-same," said she. " Ese belong Tiapolo. Tiapolo too much like ; Ese all-e-same his son. Suppose Ese he wish something, Tiapolo he make him."

" That's mighty convenient for Ese," says I. " And what kind of things does he make for him ? "

Well, out came a rigmarole of all sorts of stories, many of

E

which (like the dollar he took from Mr. Tarleton's head) were plain enough to me, but others I could make nothing of; and the thing that most surprised the Kanakas was what surprised me least—namely, that he would go in the desert among all the *aitus*. Some of the boldest, however, had accompanied him, and had heard him speak with the dead and give them orders, and, safe in his protection, had returned unscathed. Some said he had a church there, where he worshipped Tiapolo, and Tiapolo appeared to him; others swore that there was no sorcery at all, that he performed his miracles by the power of prayer, and the church was no church, but a prison, in which he had confined a dangerous *aitu*. Namu had been in the bush with him once, and returned glorifying God for these wonders. Altogether, I began to have a glimmer of the man's position, and the means by which he had acquired it, and, though I saw he was a tough nut to crack, I was noways cast down.

"Very well," said I, " I'll have a look at Master Case's place of worship myself, and we'll see about the glorifying."

At this Uma fell in a terrible taking; if I went in the high bush I should never return; none could go there but by the protection of Tiapolo.

"I'll chance it on God's," said I. "I'm a good sort of a fellow, Uma, as fellows go, and I guess God'll con me through."

She was silent for a while. " I think," said she, mighty solemn—and then, presently—" Victoreea, he big chief?"

"You bet!" said I.

"He like you too much?" she asked again. I told her, with a grin, I believed the old lady was rather partial to me.

"All right," said she. " Victoreea he big chief, like you too much. No can help you here in Falesá; no can do—too far off. Maea he be small chief—stop here. Suppose he like you—make you all right. All-e-same God and Tiapolo. God he big chief—got too much work. Tiapolo he small chief—he like too much makesee, work very hard."

"I'll have to hand you over to Mr. Tarleton," said I. "Your theology's out of its bearings, Uma."

However, we stuck to this business all the evening, and, with the stories she told me of the desert and its dangers, she came near frightening herself into a fit. I don't remember half a quarter of them, of course, for I paid little heed; but two come back to me kind of clear.

About six miles up the coast there is a sheltered cove they call *Fanga-anaana*—" the haven full of caves." I've seen it from the sea myself, as near as I could get my boys to venture in; and it's a little strip of yellow sand, black cliffs overhang it, full of the black mouths of caves; great trees overhang the cliffs, and dangle-down lianas; and in one place, about the middle, a big brook pours over in a cascade. Well, there was a boat going by here, with six young men of Falesá, " all very pretty," Uma said, which was the loss of them. It blew strong, there was a heavy head sea, and by the time they opened Fanga-anaana, and saw the white cascade and the shady beach, they were all tired and thirsty, and their water had run out. One proposed to land and get a drink, and, being reckless fellows, they were all of the same mind except the youngest. Lotu was his name; he was a very good young gentleman, and very wise; and he held out that they were crazy, telling them the place was given over to spirits and devils and the dead, and there were no living folk nearer than six miles the one way, and maybe twelve the other. But they laughed at his words, and, being five to one, pulled in, beached the boat and landed. It was a wonderful pleasant place, Lotu said, and the water excellent. They walked round the beach, but could see nowhere any way to mount the cliffs, which made them easier in their mind; and at last they sat down to make a meal on the food they had brought with them. They were scarce set, when there came out of the mouth of one of the black caves six of the most beautiful ladies ever seen; they had flowers in their hair, and the most beautiful breasts, and necklaces of scarlet seeds; and began to jest with these young gentlemen, and the young gentlemen to jest back with them, all but Lotu. As for Lotu, he saw there would be no living woman in such a place, and ran, and flung himself in the bottom of the boat, and covered his face, and prayed. All the time the business lasted Lotu made one clean break of prayer, and that was all he knew of it, until his friends came back, and made him sit up, and they put to sea again out of the bay, which was now quite desert, and no word of the six ladies. But, what frightened Lotu most, not one of the five remembered anything of what had passed, but they were all like drunken men, and sang and laughed in the boat, and skylarked. The wind freshened and came squally, and the sea rose extraordinarily high ; it was such weather as any man in the islands would have turned his back to and fled home to Falesá ; but these five were like crazy folk, and cracked on all sail and drove their boat into the seas. Lotu went to the bailing ; none of the others thought to help him, but sang and skylarked and carried on, and spoke singular things beyond a man's comprehension, and laughed out loud when they said them. So the rest of the day Lotu bailed for his life in the bottom of the boat, and was all drenched with sweat and cold sea-water ; and none heeded him. Against all expectation, they came safe in a dreadful tempest to Papa-Malulu, where the palms were singing out, and the cocoanuts flying like cannon-balls about the village green ; and the same night the five young gentlemen sickened, and spoke never a reasonable word until they died.

" And do you mean to tell me you can swallow a yarn like that ? " I asked.

She told me the thing was well known, and with handsome young men alone it was even common ; but this was the only case where five had been slain the same day and in a company by the love of the women-devils ; and it had made a great stir in the island, and she would be crazy if she doubted.

" Well, anyway," says I, " you needn't be frightened about me. I've no use for the women-devils. You're all the women I want, and all the devil too, old lady."

To this she answered there were other sorts, and she had seen one with her own eyes. She had gone one day alone to the next bay, and, perhaps, got too near the margin of

the bad place. The boughs of the high bush overshadowed
her from the cant of the hill, but she herself was outside
on a flat place, very stony and growing full of young
mummy-apples four and five feet high. It was a dark day
in the rainy season, and now there came squalls that tore
off the leaves and sent them flying, and now it was all still
as in a house. It was in one of these still times that a whole
gang of birds and flying-foxes came pegging out of the
bush like creatures frightened. Presently after she heard a
rustle nearer hand, and saw, coming out of the margin of
the trees, among the mummy-apples, the appearance of a
lean grey old boar. It seemed to think as it came, like a
person ; and all of a sudden, as she looked at it coming,
she was aware it was no boar, but a thing that was a man
with a man's thoughts. At that she ran, and the pig after
her, and as the pig ran it holla'd aloud, so that the place
rang with it.

"I wish I had been there with my gun," said I. "I
guess that pig would have holla'd so as to surprise himself."

But she told me a gun was of no use with the like of these,
which were the spirits of the dead.

Well, this kind of talk put in the evening, which was the
best of it ; but of course it didn't change my notion, and
the next day, with my gun and a good knife, I set off upon a
voyage of discovery. I made, as near as I could, for the
place where I had seen Case come out ; for if it was true he
had some kind of establishment in the bush I reckoned I
should find a path. The beginning of the desert was marked
off by a wall, to call it so, for it was more of a long mound of
stones. They say it reaches right across the island, but
how they know it is another question, for I doubt if any
one has made the journey in a hundred years, the natives
sticking chiefly to the sea and their little colonies along the
coast, and that part being mortal high and steep and full of
cliffs. Up to the west side of the wall the ground has been
cleared, and there are cocoa-palms and mummy-apples
and guavas, and lots of sensitive. Just across, the bush
begins outright ; high bush at that, trees going up like the

masts of ships, and ropes of liana hanging down like a
ship's rigging, and nasty orchids growing in the forks like
funguses. The ground where there was no underwood
looked to be a heap of boulders. I saw many green pigeons
which I might have shot, only I was there with a different
idea. A number of butterflies flopped up and down along
the ground like dead leaves ; sometimes I would hear a
bird calling, sometimes the wind overhead, and always
the sea along the coast.

But the queerness of the place it's more difficult to tell
of, unless to one who has been alone in the high bush himself. The brightest kind of a day it is always dim down
there. A man can see to the end of nothing ; whichever
way he looks the wood shuts up, one bough folding with
another like the fingers of your hand ; and whenever he
listens he hears always something new—men talking,
children laughing, the strokes of an axe a far way ahead of
him, and sometimes a sort of a quick, stealthy scurry near
at hand that makes him jump and look to his weapons.
It's all very well for him to tell himself that he's alone,
bar trees and birds ; he can't make out to believe it ; whichever way he turns the whole place seems to be alive and
looking on. Don't think it was Uma's yarns that put me
out ; I don't value native talk a fourpenny-piece ; it's a
thing that's natural in the bush, and that's the end of it.

As I got near the top of the hill, for the ground of the
wood goes up in this place steep as a ladder, the wind began
to sound straight on, and the leaves to toss and switch open
and let in the sun. This suited me better ; it was the same
noise all the time, and nothing to startle. Well, I had got
to a place where there was an underwood of what they
call wild cocoa-nut—mighty pretty with its scarlet fruit—
when there came a sound of singing in the wind that I
thought I had never heard the like of. It was all very fine
to tell myself it was the branches ; I knew better. It was
all very fine to tell myself it was a bird ; I knew never a
bird that sang like that. It rose and swelled, and died away
and swelled again ; and now I thought it was like someone
weeping, only prettier ; and now I thought it was like

harps ; and there was one thing I made sure of, it was a sight too sweet to be wholesome in a place like that. You may laugh if you like ; but I declare I called to mind the six young ladies that came, with their scarlet necklaces, out of the cave at Fanga-anaana, and wondered if they sang like that. We laugh at the natives and their super- stitions ; but see how many traders take them up, splen- didly educated white men, that have been book-keepers (some of them) and clerks in the old country. It's my belief a superstition grows up in a place like the different kinds of weeds ; and as I stood there and listened to that wailing I twittered in my shoes.

You may call me a coward to be frightened ; I thought myself brave enough to go on ahead. But I went mighty carefully, with my gun cocked, spying all about me like a hunter, fully expecting to see a handsome young woman sitting somewhere in the bush, and fully determined (if I did) to try her with a charge of duck-shot. And sure enough, I had not gone far when I met with a queer thing. The wind came on the top of the wood in a strong puff, the leaves in front of me burst open, and I saw for a second something hanging in a tree. It was gone in a wink, the puff blowing by and the leaves closing. I tell you the truth : I had made up my mind to see an *aitu* ; and if the thing had looked like a pig or a woman, it wouldn't have given me the same turn. The trouble was that it seemed kind of square, and the idea of a square thing that was alive and sang knocked me sick and silly. I must have stood quite a while ; and I made pretty certain it was right out of the same tree that the singing came. Then I began to come to myself a bit.

" Well," says I, " if this is really so, if this is a place where there are square things that sing, I'm gone up any- way. Let's have my fun for my money."

But I thought I might as well take the off-chance of a prayer being any good ; so I plumped on my knees and prayed out loud ; and all the time I was praying the strange sounds came out of the tree, and went up and down, and changed, for all the world like music, only you could see it wasn't human—there was nothing there that you could whistle.

As soon as I had made an end in proper style, I laid down my gun, stuck my knife between my teeth, walked right up to that tree and began to climb. I tell you my heart was like ice. But presently, as I went up, I caught another glimpse of the thing, and that relieved me, for I thought it seemed like a box ; and when I had got right up to it I near fell out of the tree with laughing.

A box it was, sure enough, and a candle-box at that, with the brand upon the side of it ; and it had banjo-strings stretched so as to sound when the wind blew. I believe they call the thing a Tyrolean * harp, whatever that may mean.

"Well, Mr. Case," said I, " you frightened me once, but I defy you to frighten me again," I says, and slipped down the tree, and set out again to find my enemy's head office, which I guessed would not be far away.

The undergrowth was thick in this part ; I couldn't see before my nose, and must burst my way through by main force and ply the knife as I went, slicing the cords of the lianas and slashing down whole trees at a blow. I call them trees for the bigness, but in truth they were just big weeds, and sappy to cut through like carrot. From all this crowd and kind of vegetation, I was just thinking to myself, the place might have once been cleared, when I came on my nose over a pile of stones, and saw in a moment it was some kind of a work of man. The Lord knows when it was made or when deserted, for this part of the island has lain undisturbed since long before the whites came. A few steps beyond I hit into the path I had been always looking for. It was narrow, but well beaten, and I saw that Case had plenty of disciples. It seems, indeed it was, a piece of fashionable boldness to venture up here with the trader, and a young man scarce reckoned himself grown till he had got his breech tattooed, for one thing, and seen Case's devils for another. This is mighty like Kanakas :

* Æolian.

but, if you look at it another way, it's mighty like white folks too.

A bit along the path I was brought to a clear stand, and had to rub my eyes. There was a wall in front of me, the path passing it by a gap ; it was tumbledown and plainly very old, but built of big stones very well laid ; and there is no native alive to-day upon that island that could dream of such a piece of building ! Along all the top of it was a line of queer figures, idols or scarecrows, or what not. They had carved and painted faces ugly to view, their eyes and teeth were of shell, their hair and their bright clothes blew in the wind, and some of them worked with the tugging. There are islands up west where they make these kind of figures till to-day ; but if ever they were made in this island, the practice and the very recollection of it are now long forgotten. And the singular thing was that all these bogies were as fresh as toys out of a shop.

Then it came in my mind that Case had let out to me the first day that he was a good forger of island curiosities—a thing by which so many traders turn an honest penny. And with that I saw the whole business, and how this display served the man a double purpose : first of all, to season his curiosities, and then to frighten those that came to visit him.

But I should tell you (what made the thing more curious) that all the time the Tyrolean harps were harping round me in the trees, and even while I looked, a green-and-yellow bird (that, I suppose, was building) began to tear the hair off the head of one of the figures.

A little farther on I found the best curiosity of the museum. The first I saw of it was a longish mound of earth with a twist to it. Digging off the earth with my hands, I found underneath tarpaulin stretched on boards, so that this was plainly the roof of a cellar. It stood right on the top of the hill, and the entrance was on the far side, between two rocks, like the entrance to a cave. I went as far in as the bend, and, looking round the corner, saw a shining face. It was big and ugly, like a pantomime mask, and the brightness of it waxed and dwindled, and at times it smoked.

" Oho ! " says I, " luminous paint ! "

And I must say I rather admired the man's ingenuity. With a box of tools and a few mighty simple contrivances he had made out to have a devil of a temple. Any poor Kanaka brought up here in the dark, with the harps whining all round him, and shown that smoking face in the bottom of a hole, would make no kind of doubt but he had seen and heard enough devils for a lifetime. It's easy to find out what Kanakas think. Just go back to yourself anyway round from ten to fifteen years old, and there's an average Kanaka. There are some pious, just as there are pious boys ; and the most of them, like the boys again, are middling honest and yet think it rather larks to steal, and are easy scared, and rather like to be so. I remember a boy I was at school with at home who played the Case business. He didn't know anything, that boy ; he couldn't do any-thing ; he had no luminous paint and no Tyrolean harps ; he just boldly said he was a sorcerer, and frightened us out of our boots, and we loved it. And then it came in my mind how the master had once flogged that boy, and the surprise we were all in to see the sorcerer catch it and hum like anybody else. Thinks I to myself : " I must find some way of fixing it so for Master Case." And the next moment I had my idea.

I went back by the path, which, when once you had found it, was quite plain and easy walking ; and when I stepped out on the black sands, who should I see but Master Case himself ! I cocked my gun and held it handy, and we marched up and passed without a word, each keeping the tail of his eye on the other ; and no sooner had we passed then we each wheeled round like fellows drilling, and stood face to face. We had each taken the same notion in his head, you see, that the other fellow might give him the load of his gun in the stern.

" You've shot nothing," says Case.

" I'm not on the shoot to-day," said I.

" Well, the devil go with you for me," says he.

" The same to you," says I.

But we stuck just the way we were ; no fear of either of us moving.

Case laughed. " We can't stop here all day, though," said he.

" Don't let me detain you," says I.

He laughed again. " Look here, Wiltshire, do you think me a fool ? " he asked.

" More of a knave, if you want to know," says I.

" Well, do you think it would better me to shoot you here, on this open beach ? " said he. " Because I don't. Folks come fishing every day. There may be a score of them up the valley now, making copra ; there might be half a dozen on the hill behind you, after pigeons ; they might be watching us this minute, and I shouldn't wonder. I give you my word I don't want to shoot you. Why should I ? You don't hinder me any. You haven't got one pound of copra but what you made with your own hands, like a negro slave. You're vegetating—that's what I call it—and I don't care where you vegetate, nor yet how long. Give me your word you don't mean to shoot me, and I'll give you a lead and walk away."

" Well," said I, " you're frank and pleasant, ain't you ? And I'll be the same. I don't mean to shoot you to-day. Why should I ? This business is beginning ; it ain't done yet, Mr. Case. I've given you one turn already. I can see the marks of my knuckles on your head to this blooming hour, and I've more cooking for you. I'm not a paralee, like Underhill. My name ain't Adams, and it ain't Vigours ; and I mean to show you that you've met your match."

" This is a silly way to talk," said he. " This is not the talk to make me move on with."

" All right," said I, " stay where you are. I ain't in any hurry, and you know it. I can put in a day on this beach and never mind. I ain't got any copra to bother with. I ain't got any luminous paint to see to."

I was sorry I said that last, but it whipped out before I knew. I could see it took the wind out of his sails, and he stood and stared at me with his brow drawn up. Then I suppose he made up his mind he must get to the bottom of this.

" I take you at your word," says he, and turned his back, and walked right into the devil's bush.

I let him go, of course, for I had passed my word. But I watched him as long as he was in sight, and after he was gone lit out for cover as lively as you would want to see, and went the rest of the way home under the bush, for I didn't trust him sixpence worth. One thing I saw, I had been ass enough to give him warning, and that which I meant to do I must do at once.

You would think I had had about enough excitement for one morning, but there was another turn waiting me. As soon as I got far enough round the Cape to see my house I made out there were strangers there ; a little farther, and no doubt about it. There was a couple of armed sentinels squatting at my door. I could only suppose the trouble about Uma must have come to a head, and the station been seized. For aught I could think, Uma was taken up already, and these armed men were waiting to do the like with me.

However, as I came nearer, which I did at top speed, I saw there was a third native sitting on the verandah like a guest, and Uma was talking with him like a hostess. Nearer still I made out it was the big young chief, Maea, and that he was smiling away and smoking. And what was he smoking ? None of your European cigarettes fit for a cat, not even the genuine big, knock-me-down native article that a fellow can really put in the time with if his pipe is broke—but a cigar, and one of my Mexicans at that, that I could swear to. At sight of this my heart started beating, and I took a wild hope in my head that the trouble was over, and Maea had come round.

Uma pointed me out to him as I came up, and he met me at the head of my own stairs like a thorough gentleman.

" Vilivili," said he, which was the best they could make of my name, " I pleased."

There is no doubt when an island chief wants to be civil

he can do it. I saw the way things were from the word go. There was no call for Uma to say to me : " He no 'fraid Ese now, come bring copra." I tell you I shook hands with that Kanaka like as if he was the best white man in Europe.

The fact was, Case and he had got after the same girl, or Maea suspected it, and concluded to make hay of the trader on the chance. He had dressed himself up, got a couple of his retainers cleaned and armed to kind of make the thing more public, and, just waiting till Case was clear of the village, came round to put the whole of his business my way. He was rich as well as powerful. I suppose that man was worth fifty thousand nuts per annum. I gave him the price of the beach and a quarter cent better, and as for credit, I would have advanced him the inside of the store and the fittings besides, I was so pleased to see him. I must say he bought like a gentleman : rice and tins and biscuits enough for a week's feast, and stuffs by the bolt. He was agreeable besides ; he had plenty fun to him ; and we cracked jests together, mostly through he interpreter, because he had mighty little English, and my native was still off colour. One thing I made out : he could never really have thought much harm of Uma ; he could never have been really frightened, and must just have made believe from dodginess, and because he thought Case had a strong pull in the village and could help him on.

This set me thinking that both he and I were in a tightish place. What he had done was to fly in the face of the whole village, and the thing might cost him his authority. More than that, after my talk with Case on the beach, I thought it might very well cost me my life. Case had as good as said he would pot me if ever I got any copra ; he would come home to find the best business in the village had changed hands, and the best thing I thought I could do was to get in first with the potting.

" See here, Uma," says I, " tell him I'm sorry I made him wait, but I was up looking at Case's Tiapolo store in the bush."

" He want savvy if you no 'fraid ? " translated Uma.

I laughed out. " Not much ! " says I. " Tell him the place is a blooming toy-shop ! Tell him, in England we give these things to the kid to play with."

" He want savvy if you hear devil sing ? " she asked next.

" Look here," I said, " I can't do it now, because I've got no banjo-strings in stock ; but the next time the ship comes round I'll have one of these same contraptions right here in my verandah, and he can see for himself how much devil there is to it. Tell him, as soon as I can get the strings I'll make one for his pickaninnies. The name of the concern is a Tyrolean harp ; and you can tell him the name means in English that nobody but dam-fools give a cent for it."

This time he was so pleased he had to try his English again. " You talk true ? " says he.

" Rather ! " said I. " Talk all-e-same Bible. Bring out a Bible here, Uma, if you've got such a thing, and I'll kiss it. Or, I'll tell you what's better still," says I, taking a header, " ask him if he's afraid to go up there himself by day."

It appeared he wasn't ; he could venture as far as that by day and in company.

" That's the ticket, then ! " said I. " Tell him the man's a fraud and the place foolishness, and if he'll go up there to-morrow he'll see all that's left of it. But tell him this, Uma, and mind he understands it. If he gets talking it's bound to come to Case, and I'm a dead man ! I'm playing his game, tell him, and if he says one word my blood will be at his door and be the damnation of him here and after."

She told him, and he shook hands with me up to the hilt, and, says he : " No talk. Go up to-mollow. You my friend ? "

" No, sir," says I, " no such foolishness. I've come here to trade, tell him, and not to make friends. But, as to Case, I'll send that man to glory ! "

So off Maea went, pretty well pleased, as I could see.

CHAPTER V

NIGHT IN THE BUSH

WELL, I was committed now ; Tiapolo had to be smashed up before next day, and my hands were pretty full, not only with preparations, but with argument. My house was like a mechanics' debating society. Uma was so made up that I shouldn't go into the bush by night, or that, if I did, I was never to come back again. You know her style of arguing : you've had a specimen about Queen Victoria and the devil ; and I leave you to fancy if I was tired of it before dark.

At last I had a good idea. " What was the use of casting my pearls before her ? " I thought ; some of her own chopped hay would be likelier to do the business.

" I'll tell you what, then," said I. " You fish out your Bible, and I'll take that up along with me. That'll make me right."

She swore a Bible was no use.

" That's just your Kanaka ignorance," said I. " Bring the Bible out."

She brought it, and I turned to the title-page, where I thought there would likely be some English, and so there was. " There ! " said I. " Look at that ! ' *London : Printed for the British and Foreign Bible Society, Blackfriars,*' and the date, which I can't read, owing to its being in three X's. There's no devil in hell can look near the Bible Society, Blackfriars. Why, you silly," I said, " how do you suppose we get along with our own *aitus* at home ! All Bible Society ! "

" I think you no got any," said she. " White man, he tell me you no got."

" Sounds likely, don't it ? " I asked.   " Why would these
islands all be chock full of them and none in Europe ? "

" Well, you no got bread-fruit," said she.

I could have torn my hair.   " Now, look here, old lady,"
said I, " you dry up, for I'm tired of you.   I'll take the
Bible, which'll put me as straight as the mail, and that's
the last word I've got to say."

The night fell extraordinary dark, clouds coming up
with sundown and overspreading all ; not a star showed ;
there was only an end of a moon, and that not due
before the small hours.   Round the village, what with the
lights and the fires in the open houses, and the torches of
many fishers moving on the reef, it kept as gay as an illum-
ination ; but the sea and the mountains and woods were all
clean gone.   I suppose it might be eight o'clock when I
took the road, laden like a donkey.   First there was that
Bible, a book as big as your head, which I had let myself
in for by my own tomfoolery.   Then there was my gun,
and knife, and lantern, and patent matches, all necessary.
And then there was the real plant of the affair in hand,
a mortal weight of gunpowder, a pair of dynamite fishing-
bombs, and two or three pieces of slowmatch that I had
hauled out of the tin cases and spliced together the best
way I could ; for the match was only trade stuff, and a
man would be crazy that trusted it.   Altogether, you see,
I had the materials of a pretty good blow up !   Expense
was nothing to me ; I wanted that thing done right.

As long as I was in the open, and had the lamp in my
house to steer by, I did well.   But when I got to the path,
it fell so dark I could make no headway, walking into
trees and swearing there, like a man looking for the matches
in his bedroom.   I knew it was risky to light up, for my
lantern would be visible all the way to the point of the cape,
and as no one went there after dark, it would be talked
about, and come to Case's ears.   But what was I to do ?
I had either to give the business over and lose caste with
Maea, or light up, take my chance, and get through the
thing the smartest I was able.

As long as I was on the path I walked hard, but when I

came to the black beach I had to run. For the tide was now nearly flowed ; and to get through with my powder dry between the surf and the steep hill, took all the quickness I possessed. As it was, even the wash caught me to the knees, and I came near falling on a stone. All this time the hurry I was in, and the free air and smell of the sea, kept my spirits lively ; but when I was once in the bush and began to climb the path I took it easier. The fearsomeness of the wood had been a good bit rubbed off for me by Master Case's banjo-strings and graven images, yet I thought it was a dreary walk, and guessed, when the disciples were up there, they must be badly scared. The light of the lantern, striking among all these trunks and forked branches and twisted rope-ends of lianas, made the whole place, or all that you could see of it, a kind of a puzzle of turning shadows. They came to meet you, solid and quick like giants, and then spun off and vanished ; they hove up over your head like clubs, and flew away into the night like birds. The floor of the bush glimmered with dead wood, the way the match-box used to shine after you had struck a lucifer. Big, cold drops fell on me from the branches overhead like sweat. There was no wind to mention ; only a little icy breath of a land breeze that stirred nothing ; and the harps were silent.

The first landfall I made was when I got through the bush of wild cocoanuts, and came in view of the bogies on the wall. Mighty queer they looked by the shining of the lantern, with their painted faces and shell eyes, and their clothes, and their hair hanging. One after another I pulled them all up and piled them in a bundle on the cellar roof, so as they might go to glory with the rest. Then I chose a place behind one of the big stones at the entrance, buried my powder and the two shells, and arranged my match along the passage. And then I had a look at the smoking head, just for good-by. It was doing fine.

"Cheer up," says I. "You're booked."

It was my first idea to light up and be getting homeward ; for the darkness and the glimmer of the dead wood and the shadows of the lantern made me lonely. But I

F

knew where one of the harps hung ; it seemed a pity it shouldn't go with the rest ; and at the same time I couldn't help letting on to myself that I was mortal tired of my employment, and would like best to be at home and have the door shut. I stepped out of the cellar and argued it fore and back. There was a sound of the sea far down below me on the coast ; nearer hand not a leaf stirred ; I might have been the only living creature this side of Cape Horn. Well, as I stood there thinking, it seemed the bush woke and became full of little noises. Little noises they were, and nothing to hurt ; a bit of a crackle, a bit of a rush ; but the breath jumped right out of me and my throat went as dry as a biscuit. It wasn't Case I was afraid of, which would have been common sense ; I never thought of Case ; what took me, as sharp as the colic, was the old wives' tales—the devil-women and the man-pigs. It was the toss of a penny whether I should run ; but I got a purchase on myself, and stepped out, and held up the lantern (like a fool) and looked all around.

In the direction of the village and the path there was nothing to be seen ; but when I turned inland it's a wonder to me I didn't drop. There, coming right up out of the desert and the bad bush—there, sure enough, was a devil-woman, just as the way I had figured she would look. I saw the light shine on her bare arms and her bright eyes, and there went out of me a yell so big that I thought it was my death.

"Ah ! No sing out ! " says the devil-woman, in a kind of a high whisper. " Why you talk big voice ? Put out light ! Ese he come."

" My God Almighty, Uma, is that you ? " says I.

" Ioe," * says she. " I come quick. Ese here soon."

" You come alone ? " I asked. " You no 'fraid ? "

" Ah, too much 'fraid ! " she whispered, clutching me. " I think die."

" Well," says I, with a kind of a weak grin, " I'm not the one to laugh at you, Mrs. Wiltshire, for I'm about the worst scared man in the South Pacific myself."

* Yes.

She told me in two words what brought her. I was scarce gone, it seems, when Fa'avao came in, and the old woman had met Black Jack running as hard as he was fit from our house to Case's. Uma neither spoke nor stopped, but lit right out to come and warn me. She was so close at my heels that the lantern was her guide across the beach, and afterward, by the glimmer of it in the trees, she got her line up hill. It was only when I had got to the top or was in the cellar that she wandered—Lord knows where ! —and lost a sight of precious time, afraid to call out lest Case was at the heels of her, and falling in the bush, so that she was all knocked and bruised. That must have been when she got too far to the southward, and how she came to take me in the flank at last and frighten me beyond what I've got the words to tell of.

Well, anything was better than a devil-woman, but I thought her yarn serious enough. Black Jack had no call to be about my house, unless he was set there to watch ; and it looked to me as if my tomfool word about the paint, and perhaps some chatter of Maea's, had got us all in a clove hitch. One thing was clear : Uma and I were here for the night ; we daren't try to go home before day, and even then it would be safer to strike round up the mountain and come in by the back of the village, or we might walk into an ambuscade. It was plain, too, that the mine should be sprung immediately, or Case might be in time to stop it.

I marched into the tunnel, Uma keeping tight hold of me, opened my lantern and lit the match. The first length of it burned like a spill of paper, and I stood stupid, watching it burn, and thinking we were going aloft with Tiapolo, which was none of my views. The second took to a better rate, though faster than I cared about ; and at that I got my wits again, hauled Uma clear of the passage, blew out and dropped the lantern, and the pair of us groped our way into the bush until I thought it might be safe, and lay down together by a tree.

" Old lady," I said, " I won't forget this night. You're a trump, and that's what's wrong with you."

She bumped herself close up to me. She had run out the way she was, with nothing on her but her kilt; and she was all wet with the dews and the sea on the black beach, and shook straight on with cold and the terror of the dark and the devils.

" Too much 'fraid," was all she said.

The far side of Case's hill goes down near as steep as a precipice into the next valley. We were on the very edge of it, and I could see the dead wood shine and hear the sea sound far below. I didn't care about the position, which left me no retreat, but I was afraid to change. Then I saw I had made a worse mistake about the lantern, which I should have left lighted, so that I could have had a crack at Case when he stepped into the shine of it. And since I hadn't had the wit to do that, it seemed a senseless thing to leave the good lantern to blow up with the graven images. The thing belonged to me, after all, and was worth money, and might come in handy. If I could have trusted the match, I might have run in still and rescued it. But who was going to trust to the match? You know what trade is. The stuff was good enough for Kanakas to go fishing with, where they've got to look lively anyway, and the most they risk is only to have their hand blown off. But for any-one that wanted to fool around a blow-up like mine that match was rubbish.

Altogether the best I could do was to lie still, see my shot-gun handy, and wait for the explosion. But it was a solemn kind of a business. The blackness of the night was like solid; the only thing you could see was the nasty bogy glimmer of the dead wood, and that showed you nothing but itself; and as for sounds, I stretched my ears till I thought I could have heard the match burn in the tunnel, and that bush was as silent as a coffin. Now and then there was a bit of a crack; but whether it was near or far, whether it was Case stubbing his toes within a few yards of me, or a tree breaking miles away, I knew no more than the babe unborn.

And then all of a sudden, Vesuvius went off. It was a long time coming; but when it came (though I say it that shouldn't) no man could ask to see a better. At first it was just a son of a gun of a row, and a spout of fire, and the wood lighted up so that you could see to read. And then the trouble began. Uma and I were half buried under a wagonful of earth, and glad it was no worse, for one of the rocks at the entrance of the tunnel was fired clean into the air, fell within a couple of fathoms of where we lay, and bounded over the edge of the hill, and went pounding down into the next valley. I saw I had rather under-calculated our distance, or overdone the dynamite and powder, which you please.

And presently I saw I had made another slip. The noise of the thing began to die off, shaking the island; the dazzle was over; and yet the night didn't come back the way I expected. For the whole wood was scattered with red coals and brands from the explosion; they were all round me on the flat, some had fallen below in the valley, and some stuck and flared in the tree-tops. I had no fear of fire, for these forests are too wet to kindle. But the trouble was that the place was all lit up—not very bright, but good enough to get a shot by; and the way the coals were scattered, it was just as likely Case might have the advantage as myself. I looked all round for his white face, you may be sure; but there was not a sign of him. As for Uma, the life seemed to have been knocked right out of her by the bang and blaze of it.

There was one bad point in my game. One of the blessed graven images had come down all afire, hair and clothes and body, not four yards away from me. I cast a mighty noticing glance all round; there was still no Case, and I made up my mind I must get rid of that burning stick before he came, or I should be shot there like a dog.

It was my first idea to have crawled, and then I thought speed was the main thing, and stood half up to make a rush. The same moment, from somewhere between me and the sea, there came a flash and a report, and a rifle-bullet screeched in my ear. I swung straight round and up with my gun, but the brute had a Winchester, and before I could as much as see him his second shot knocked me over like a ninepin. I seemed to fly in the air, then came down by the run and lay half a minute, silly ; and then I found my hands empty and my gun had flown over my head as I fell. It makes a man mighty wide awake to be in the kind of box that I was in. I scarcely knew where I was hurt, or whether I was hurt or not, but turned right over on my face to crawl after my weapon. Unless you have tried to get about with a smashed leg you don't know what pain is, and I let out a howl like a bullock's.

This was the unluckiest noise that ever I made in my life. Up to then Uma had stuck to her tree like a sensible woman, knowing she would be only in the way ; but as soon as she heard me sing out she ran forward. The Winchester cracked again, and down she went.

I had sat up, leg and all, to stop her ; but when I saw her tumble I clapped down again where I was, lay still, and felt the handle of my knife. I had been scurried and put out before. No more of that for me. He had knocked over my girl, I had got to fix him for it ; and I lay there and gritted my teeth, and footed up the chances. My leg was broke, my gun was gone. Case had still ten shots in his Winchester. It looked a kind of hopeless business. But I never despaired nor thought upon despairing : that man had got to go.

For a goodish bit not one of us let on. Then I heard Case begin to move nearer in the bush, but mighty careful. The image had burned out, there were only a few coals left here and there, and the wood was main dark, but had a kind of a low glow in it like a fire on its last legs. It was by this that I made out Case's head looking at me over a big tuft of ferns, and at the same time the brute saw me and shouldered his Winchester. I lay quite still, and as good as looked into the barrel ; it was my last chance, but I thought my heart would have come right out of its bearings. Then he fired. Lucky for me it was no shot-gun, for the bullet struck within an inch of me and knocked the dirt in my eyes.

Just you try and see if you can lie quiet, and let a man take a sitting shot at you and miss you by a hair. But I did, and lucky, too. A while Case stood with the Winchester at the port-arms; then he gave a little laugh to himself and stepped round the ferns.

"Laugh!" thought I. "If you had the wit of a louse you would be praying!"

I was all as taut as a ship's hawser or the spring of a watch, and as soon as he came within reach of me I had him by the ankle, plucked the feet right out from under him, laid him out, and was upon the top of him, broken leg and all, before he breathed. His Winchester had gone the same road as my shot-gun; it was nothing to me—I defied him now. I'm a pretty strong man anyway, but I never knew what strength was till I got hold of Case. He was knocked out of time by the rattle he came down with, and threw up his hands together, more like a frightened woman, so that I caught both of them with my left. This wakened him up, and he fastened his teeth in my forearm like a weasel. Much I cared. My leg gave me all the pain I had any use for, and I drew my knife and got it in the place.

"Now," said I, "I've got you; and you're gone up, and a good job too! Do you feel the point of that? That's for Underhill! And there's for Adams! And now here's for Uma, and that's going to knock your blooming soul right out of you!"

With that I gave him the cold steel for all I was worth. His body kicked under me like a spring sofa; he gave a dreadful kind of a long moan, and lay still.

"I wonder if you're dead? I hope so!" I thought, for my head was swimming. But I wasn't going to take chances; I had his own example too close before me for that; and I tried to draw the knife out to give it him again. The blood came over my hands, I remember, hot as tea; and with that I fainted clean away, and fell with my head on the man's mouth.

When I came to myself it was pitch dark; the cinders had burned out; there was nothing to be seen but the shine of the dead wood, and I couldn't remember where I was nor why I was in such pain, nor what I was all wetted with,

Then it came back, and the first thing I attended to was to give him the knife again a half a dozen times up to the handle. I believe he was dead already, but it did him no harm and did me good.

" I bet you're dead now," I said, and then I called to Uma.

Nothing answered, and I made a move to go and grope for her, fouled my broken leg, and fainted again.

When I came to myself the second time the clouds had all cleared away, except a few that sailed there, white as cotton. The moon was up—a tropic moon. The moon at home turns a wood black, but even this old butt-end of a one showed up that forest as green as by day. The night birds—or, rather, they're a kind of early morning bird—sang out with their long, falling notes like nightingales. And I could see the dead man, that I was still half resting on, looking right up into the sky with his open eyes, no paler than when he was alive ; and a little way off Uma tumbled on her side. I got over to her the best way I was able, and when I got there she was broad awake and crying, and sobbing to herself with no more noise than an insect. It appears she was afraid to cry out loud, because of the *aitus*. Altogether she was not much hurt, but scared beyond belief ; she had come to her senses a long while ago, cried out to me, heard nothing in reply, made out we were both dead, and had lain there ever since, afraid to budge a finger. The ball had ploughed up her shoulder, and she had lost a main quantity of blood ; but I soon had that tied up the way it ought to be with the tail of my shirt and a scarf I had on, got her head on my sound knee and my back against a trunk, and settled down to wait for morning. Uma was for neither use nor ornament, and could only clutch hold of me and shake and cry. I don't suppose there was ever anybody worse scared, and, to do her justice, she had had a lively night of it. As for me, I was in a good bit of pain and fever, but not so bad when I sat still ; and every time I looked over to Case I could have sung and whistled. Talk about meat and drink ! To see that man lying there dead as a herring filled me full.

The night birds stopped after a while ; and then the light began to change, the east came orange, the whole wood began to whirr with singing like a musical box, and there was the broad day.

I didn't expect Maea for a long while yet ; and, indeed, I thought there was an off-chance he might go back on the whole idea and not come at all. I was the better pleased when, about an hour after daylight, I heard sticks smashing and a lot of Kanakas laughing and singing out to keep their courage up. Uma sat up quite brisk at the first word of it ; and presently we saw a party come stringing out of the path, Maea in front, and behind him a white man in a pith helmet. It was Mr. Tarleton, who had turned up late last night in Falesá, having left his boat and walked the last stage with a lantern.

They buried Case upon the field of glory, right in the hole where he had kept the smoking head. I waited till the thing was done ; and Mr. Tarleton prayed, which I thought tomfoolery, but I'm bound to say he gave a pretty sick view of the dear departed's prospects, and seemed to have his own ideas of hell. I had it out with him afterward, told him he had scamped his duty, and what he had ought to have done was to up like a man and tell the Kanakas plainly Case was damned, and a good riddance ; but I never could get him to see it my way. Then they made me a litter of poles and carried me down to the station. Mr. Tarleton set my leg, and made a regular missionary splice of it, so that I limp to this day. That done, he took down my evidence, and Uma's, and Maea's, wrote it all out fine, and had us sign it ; and then he got the chiefs and marched over to Papa Randall's to seize Case's papers.

All they found was a bit of a diary, kept for a good many years, and all about the price of copra, and chickens being stolen, and that ; and the books of the business and the will I told you of in the beginning, by both of which the whole thing (stock, lock, and barrel) appeared to belong to the Samoa woman. It was I that bought her out at a mighty reasonable figure, for she was in a hurry to get home. As for Randall and the black, they had to tramp ;

got into some kind of a station on the Papa-Malulu side ;
did very bad business, for the truth is neither of the pair
was fit for it, and lived mostly on fish, which was the means
of Randall's death. It seems there was a nice shoal in
one day, and papa went after them with the dynamite ;
either the match burned too fast, or papa was full, or both,
but the shell went off (in the usual way) before he threw it,
and where was papa's hand ? Well, there's nothing to
hurt in that ; the islands up north are all full of one-
handed men like the parties in the *Arabian Nights ;* but
either Randall was too old, or he drank too much, and the
short and the long of it was that he died. Pretty soon
after the nigger was turned out of the island for stealing
from white men, and went off to the west, where he found
men of his own colour, in case he liked that, and the men of
his own colour took and ate him at some kind of a corro-
borree, and I'm sure I hope he was to their fancy !

So there was I, left alone in my glory at Falesá ; and when
the schooner came round I filled her up, and gave her a
deck cargo half as high as the house. I must say Mr.
Tarleton did the right thing by us ; but he took a meanish
kind of a revenge.

"Now, Mr. Wiltshire," said he, "I've put you all
square with everybody here. It wasn't difficult to do,
Case being gone ; but I have done it, and given my pledge
besides that you will deal fairly with the natives. I must
ask you to keep my word."

Well, so I did. I used to be bothered about my balances,
but I reasoned it out this way. We all have queerish
balances, and the natives all know it and water their copra
in a proportion so that it's fair all round ; but the truth is,
it did use to bother me, and, though I did well in Falesá,
I was half glad when the firm moved me on to another
station, where I was under no kind of a pledge and could
look my balances in the face.

As for the old lady, you know her as well as I do. She's
only the one fault. If you don't keep your eye lifting
she would give away the roof off the station. Well, it
seems it's natural in Kanakas. She's turned a powerful

big woman now, and could throw a London bobby over her shoulder. But that's natural in Kanakas too, and there's no manner of doubt that she's an A 1 wife.

Mr. Tarleton's gone home, his trick being over. He was the best missionary I ever struck, and now, it seems, he's parsonising down Somerset way. Well, that's best for him ; he'll have no Kanakas there to get luny over.

My public-house ? Not a bit of it, nor ever likely. I'm stuck here, I fancy. I don't like to leave the kids, you see : and—there's no use talking—they're better here than what they would be in a white man's country, though Ben took the eldest up to Auckland, where he's being schooled with the best. But what bothers me is the girls. They're only half-castes, of course ; I know that as well as you do, and there's nobody thinks less of half-castes than I do ; but they're mine, and about all I've got. I can't reconcile my mind to their taking up with Kanakas, and I'd like to know where I'm to find the whites ?

THE BOTTLE IMP

Note.—Any student of that very un-literary product, the English drama of the early part of the century, will here recognise the name and the root idea of a piece once rendered popular by the redoubtable O. Smith. The root idea is there, and identical, and yet I believe I have made it a new thing. And the fact that the tale has been designed and written for a Polynesian audience may lend it some extraneous interest nearer home.—R. L. S.

THE BOTTLE IMP

THERE was a man of the island of Hawaii, whom I shall call Keawe; for the truth is, he still lives, and his name must be kept secret; but the place of his birth was not far from Honaunau, where the bones of Keawe the Great lie hidden in a cave. This man was poor, brave, and active; he could read and write like a schoolmaster; he was a first-rate mariner besides, sailed for some time in the island steamers, and steered a whale-boat on the Hamakua coast. At length it came in Keawe's mind to have a sight of the great world and foreign cities, and he shipped on a vessel bound to San Francisco.

This is a fine town, with a fine harbour, and rich people uncountable; and, in particular, there is one hill which is covered with palaces. Upon this hill Keawe was one day taking a walk, with his pocket full of money, viewing the great houses upon either hand with pleasure. "What fine houses there are!" he was thinking, "and how happy must these people be who dwell in them, and take no care for the morrow!" The thought was in his mind when he came abreast of a house that was smaller than some others, but all finished and beautified like a toy; the steps of that house shone like silver, and the borders of the garden bloomed like garlands, and the windows were bright like diamonds; and Keawe stopped and wondered at the excellence of all he saw. So stopping, he was aware of a man that looked forth upon him through a window, so clear that Keawe could see him as you see a fish in a pool upon the reef. The man was elderly, with a bald head and a black beard; and his face was heavy with sorrow, and he bitterly sighed. And the truth of it is, that as Keawe looked

79

in upon the man, and the man looked out upon Keawe, each envied the other.

All of a sudden the man smiled and nodded, and beckoned Keawe to enter, and met him at the door of the house.

" This is a fine house of mine," said the man, and bitterly sighed. " Would you not care to view the chambers ? "

So he led Keawe all over it, from the cellar to the roof, and there was nothing there that was not perfect of its kind, and Keawe was astonished.

" Truly," said Keawe, " this is a beautiful house; if I lived in the like of it, I should be laughing all day long. How comes it, then, that you should be sighing ? "

" There is no reason," said the man, " why you should not have a house in all points similar to this, and finer, if you wish. You have some money, I suppose ? "

" I have fifty dollars," said Keawe ; " but a house like this will cost more than fifty dollars."

The man made a computation. " I am sorry you have no more," said he, " for it may raise you trouble in the future ; but it shall be yours at fifty dollars."

" The house ? " asked Keawe.

" No, not the house," replied the man ; " but the bottle. For, I must tell you, although I appear to you so rich and fortunate, all my fortune, and this house itself and its garden, came out of a bottle not much bigger than a pint. This is it."

And he opened a lock-fast place, and took out a round-bellied bottle with a long neck ; the glass of it was white like milk, with changing rainbow colours in the grain. Withinsides something obscurely moved, like a shadow and a fire.

" This is the bottle," said the man ; and, when Keawe laughed, " You do not believe me ? " he added. " Try, then, for yourself. See if you can break it."

So Keawe took the bottle up and dashed it on the floor till he was weary ; but it jumped on the floor like a child's ball, and was not injured.

" This is a strange thing," said Keawe. " For by the

touch of it, as well as by the look, the bottle should be of glass."

" Of glass it is," replied the man, sighing more heavily than ever ; " but the glass of it was tempered in the flames of hell. An imp lives in it, and that is the shadow we behold there moving ; or, so I suppose. If any man buy this bottle the imp is at his command ; all that he desires— love, fame, money, houses like this house, ay, or a city like this city—all are his at the word uttered. Napoleon had this bottle, and by it he grew to be the king of the world ; but he sold it at the last and fell. Captain Cook had this bottle, and by it he found his way to so many islands ; but he, too, sold it, and was slain upon Hawaii. For, once it is sold, the power goes and the protection ; and unless a man remain content with what he has, ill will befall him."

" And yet you talk of selling it yourself ? " Keawe said.

" I have all I wish, and I am growing elderly," replied the man. " There is one thing the imp cannot do—he cannot prolong life ; and, it would not be fair to conceal from you there is a drawback to the bottle ; for if a man die before he sells it, he must burn in hell for ever."

" To be sure, that is a drawback and no mistake," cried Keawe. " I would not meddle with the thing. I can do without a house, thank God ; but there is one thing I could not be doing with one particle, and that is to be damned."

" Dear me, you must not run away with things," returned the man. " All you have to do is to use the power of the imp in moderation, and then sell it to someone else, as I do to you, and finish your life in comfort."

" Well, I observe two things," said Keawe. " All the time you keep sighing like a maid in love, that is one ; and, for the other, you sell this bottle very cheap."

" I have told you already why I sigh," said the man. " It is because I fear my health is breaking up ; and, as you said yourself, to die and go to the devil is a pity for anyone. As for why I sell so cheap, I must explain to you there is a peculiarity about the bottle. Long ago, when the devil brought it first upon earth, it was extremely expensive, and was sold first of all to Prester John for many millions

G

of dollars ; but it cannot be sold at all, unless sold at a loss.
If you sell it for as much as you paid for it, back it comes to
you again like a homing pigeon. It follows that the price
has kept falling in these centuries, and the bottle is now
remarkably cheap. I bought it myself from one of my
great neighbours on this hill, and the price I paid was only
ninety dollars. I could sell it for as high as eighty-nine
dollars and ninety-nine cents, but not a penny dearer, or
back the thing must come to me. Now, about this there
are two bothers. First, when you offer a bottle so singular
for eighty-odd dollars, people suppose you to be jesting.
And second—but there is no hurry about that—and I need
not go into it. Only remember it must be coined money
that you sell it for."

"How am I to know that this is all true ? " asked
Keawe.

"Some of it you can try at once," replied the man.
"Give me your fifty dollars, take the bottle, and wish your
fifty dollars back into your pocket. If that does not happen,
I pledge you my honour I will cry off the bargain and restore
your money."

"You are not deceiving me ? " said Keawe.

The man bound himself with a great oath.

"Well, I will risk that much," said Keawe, "for that
can do no harm," and he paid over his money to the man,
and the man handed him the bottle.

"Imp of the bottle," said Keawe, "I want my fifty
dollars back."   And sure enough, he had scarce said the
word before his pocket was as heavy as ever.

"To be sure this is a wonderful bottle," said Keawe.

"And now good-morning to you, my fine fellow, and
the devil go with you for me," said the man.

"Hold on," said Keawe, " I don't want any more of this
fun.   Here, take your bottle back."

"You have bought it for less than I paid for it," replied
the man, rubbing his hands.   "It is yours now ; and, for
my part, I am only concerned to see the back of you."
And with that he rang for his Chinese servant, and had
Keawe shown out of the house.

Now, when Keawe was in the street, with the bottle under his arm, he began to think. "If all is true about this bottle, I may have made a losing bargain," thinks he. "But, perhaps the man was only fooling me." The first thing he did was to count his money; the sum was exact —forty-nine dollars American money, and one Chili piece. "That looks like the truth," said Keawe. "Now I will try another part."

The streets in that part of the city were as clean as a ship's decks, and though it was noon, there were no passengers. Keawe set the bottle in the gutter and walked away. Twice he looked back, and there was the milky, round-bellied bottle where he left it. A third time he looked back, and turned a corner; but he had scarce done so, when something knocked upon his elbow, and behold! it was the long neck sticking up; and as for the round belly, it was jammed into the pocket of his pilot-coat.

"And that looks like the truth," said Keawe.

The next thing he did was to buy a corkscrew in a shop, and go apart into a secret place in the fields. And there he tried to draw the cork, but as often as he put the screw in, out it came again, and the cork was as whole as ever.

"This is some new sort of cork," said Keawe, and all at once he began to shake and sweat, for he was afraid of that bottle.

On his way back to the port-side he saw a shop where a man sold shells and clubs from the wild islands, old heathen deities, old coined money, pictures from China and Japan, and all manner of things that sailors bring in their sea-chests. And here he had an idea. So he went in and offered the bottle for a hundred dollars. The man of the shop laughed at him at first, and offered him five; but, indeed, it was a curious bottle, such glass was never blown in any human glass-works, so prettily the colours shone under the milky white, and so strangely the shadow hovered in the midst; so, after he had disputed a while after the manner of his kind, the shopman gave Keawe sixty silver dollars for the thing and set it on a shelf in the midst of his window.

" Now," said Keawe, " I have sold that for sixty which I bought for fifty—or, to say truth, a little less, because one of my dollars was from Chili.   Now I shall know the truth upon another point."

So he went back on board his ship, and when he opened his chest, there was the bottle, and had come more quickly than himself.   Now Keawe had a mate on board whose name was Lopaka.

" What ails you ? " said Lopaka, " that you stare in your chest ? "

They were alone in the ship's forecastle, and Keawe bound him to secrecy, and told all.

" This is a very strange affair," said Lopaka ; " and I fear you will be in trouble about this bottle.   But there is one point very clear—that you are sure of the trouble, and you had better have the profit in the bargain.   Make up your mind what you want with it ; give the order, and if it is done as you desire, I will buy the bottle myself ; for I have an idea of my own to get a schooner, and go trading through the islands."

" That is not my idea," said Keawe ; " but to have a beautiful house and garden on the Kona Coast, where I was born, the sun shining in at the door, flowers in the garden, glass in the windows, pictures on the walls, and toys and fine carpets on the tables, for all the world like the house I was in this day—only a story higher, and with balconies all about like the King's palace ; and to live there without care and make merry with my friends and relatives."

" Well," said Lopaka, " let us carry it back with us to Hawaii ; and if all comes true, as you suppose, I will buy the bottle, as I said, and ask a schooner."

Upon that they were agreed, and it was not long before the ship returned to Honolulu, carrying Keawe and Lopaka, and the bottle.   They were scarce come ashore when they met a friend upon the beach, who began at once to condole with Keawe.

" I do not know what I am to be condoled about," said Keawe.

" Is it possible you have not heard," said the friend, " your uncle—that good old man—is dead, and your cousin —that beautiful boy—was drowned at sea ? "

Keawe was filled with sorrow, and, beginning to weep and to lament, he forgot about the bottle. But Lopaka was thinking to himself, and presently, when Keawe's grief was a little abated, " I have been thinking," said Lopaka, " had not your uncle lands in Hawaii, in the district of Kaü ? "

" No," said Leawe, " not in Kaü : they are on the mountain side—a little be-south Hookena."

" These lands will now be yours ? " asked Lopaka.

" And so they will," says Keawe, and began again to lament for his relatives.

" No," said Lopaka, " do not lament at present. I have a thought in my mind. How if this should be the doing of the bottle ? For here is the place ready for your house."

" If this be so," cried Keawe, " it is a very ill way to serve me by killing my relatives. But it may be, indeed ; for it was in just such a station that I saw the house with my mind's eye."

" The house, however, is not yet built," said Lopaka.

" No, nor like to be ! " said Keawe ; " for though my uncle has some coffee and ava and bananas, it will not be more than will keep me in comfort ; and the rest of that land is the black lava."

" Let us go to the lawyer," said Lopaka ; " I have still this idea in my mind."

Now, when they came to the lawyer's, it appeared Keawe's uncle had grown monstrous rich in the last days, and there was a fund of money.

" And here is the money for the house ! " cried Lopaka.

" If you are thinking of a new house," said the lawyer, " here is the card of a new architect of whom they tell me great things."

" Better and better ! " cried Lopaka. " Here is all made plain for us. Let us continue to obey orders."

So they went to the architect, and he had drawings of houses on his table.

" You want something out of the way," said the architect.
" How do you like this ? " and he handed a drawing to
Keawe.

Now, when Keawe set eyes on the drawing, he cried out
aloud, for it was the picture of his thought exactly drawn.

" I am in for this house," thought he. " Little as I
like the way it comes to me, I am in for it now, and I may as
well take the good along with the evil."

So he told the architect all that he wished, and how he
would have that house furnished, and about the pictures on
the wall and the knick-knacks on the tables ; and he asked
the man plainly for how much he would undertake the
whole affair.

The architect put many questions, and took his pen and
made a computation ; and when he had done he named the
very sum that Keawe had inherited.

Lopaka and Keawe looked at one another and nodded.

" It is quite clear," thought Keawe, " that I am to have
this house, whether or no. It comes from the devil, and
I fear I will get little good by that ; and of one thing I am
sure, I will make no more wishes as long as I have this
bottle, But with the house I am saddled, and I may as
well take the good along with the evil."

So he made his terms with the architect, and they signed
a paper ; and Keawe and Lopaka took ship again and sailed
to Australia ; for it was concluded between them they should
not interfere at all, but leave the architect and the bottle
imp to build and to adorn the house at their own pleasure.

The voyage was a good voyage, only all the time Keawe
was holding in his breath, for he had sworn he would utter
no more wishes, and take no more favours, from the
devil. The time was up when they got back. The architect
told them that the house was ready, and Keawe and Lopaka
took a passage in the *Hall*, and went down Kona way to
view the house, and see if all had been done fitly according
to the thought that was in Keawe's mind.

Now, the house stood on the mountain side, visible to
ships. Above, the forest ran up into the clouds of rain ;
below, the black lava fell in cliffs, where the kings of old

lay buried. A garden bloomed about that house with every hue of flowers ; and there was an orchard of papaia on the one hand and an orchard of bread-fruit on the other, and right in front, towards the sea, a ship's mast had been rigged up and bore a flag. As for the house, it was three stories high, with great chambers and broad balconies on each. The windows were of glass, so excellent that it was as clear as water and as bright as day. All manner of furniture adorned the chambers. Pictures hung upon the wall in golden frames—pictures of ships, and men fighting, and of the most beautiful women, and of singular places ; nowhere in the world are there pictures of so bright a colour as those Keawe found hanging in his house. As for the knick-knacks, they were extraordinarily fine : chiming clocks and musical boxes, little men with nodding heads, books filled with pictures, weapons of price from all quarters of the world, and the most elegant puzzles to entertain the leisure of a solitary man. And as no one would care to live in such chambers, only to walk through and view them, the balconies were made so broad that a whole town might have lived upon them in delight ; and Keawe knew not which to prefer, whether the back porch, where you get the land breeze and looked upon the orchards and the flowers, or the front balcony, where you could drink the wind of the sea, and look down the steep wall of the mountain and see the *Hall* going by once a week or so between Hookena and the hills of Pele, or the schooners plying up the coast for wood and ava and bananas.

When they had viewed all, Keawe and Lopaka sat on the porch.

" Well," asked Lopaka, " is it all as you designed ? "

" Words cannot utter it," said Keawe. " It is better than I dreamed, and I am sick with satisfaction."

" There is but one thing to consider," said Lopaka, " all this may be quite natural, and the bottle imp have nothing whatever to say to it. If I were to buy the bottle, and got no schooner after all, I should have put my hand in the fire for nothing. I gave you my word, I know ; but yet I think you would not grudge me one more proof."

" I have sworn I would take no more favours," said Keawe. " I have gone already deep enough."

" This is no favour I am thinking of," replied Lopaka. " It is only to see the imp himself. There is nothing to be gained by that, and so nothing to be ashamed of, and yet, if I once saw him, I should be sure of the whole matter. So indulge me so far, and let me see the imp ; and, after that, here is the money in my hand, and I will buy it."

" There is only one thing I am afraid of," said Keawe. " The imp may be very ugly to view, and if you once set eyes upon him you might be very undesirous of the bottle."

" I am a man of my word," said Lopaka. " And here is the money betwixt us."

" Very well," replied Keawe, " I have a curiosity myself. So come, let us have one look at you, Mr. Imp."

Now as soon as that was said, the imp looked out of the bottle, and in again, swift as a lizard ; and there sat Keawe and Lopaka turned to stone. The night had quite come, before either found a thought to say or voice to say it with ; and then Lopaka pushed the money over and took the bottle.

" I am a man of my word," said he, " and had need to be so, or I would not touch this bottle with my foot. Well, I shall get my schooner and a dollar or two for my pocket ; and then I will be rid of this devil as fast as I can. For to tell you the plain truth, the look of him has cast me down."

" Lopaka," said Keawe, " do not you think any worse of me than you can help ; I know it is night, and the roads bad, and the pass by the tombs an ill place to go by so late, but I declare since I have seen that little face, I cannot eat or sleep or pray till it is gone from me. I will give you a lantern, and a basket to put the bottle in, and any picture or fine thing in all my house that takes your fancy ; and be gone at once, and go sleep at Hookena with Nahinu."

" Keawe," said Lopaka, " many a man would take this ill ; above all, when I am doing you a turn so friendly, as to keep my word and buy the bottle ; and for that matter, the night and the dark, and the way by the tombs, must be all tenfold more dangerous to a man with such a sin upon his conscience and such a bottle under his arm. But for my part, I am so extremely terrified myself, I have not the heart to blame you. Here I go, then ; and I pray God you may be happy in your house, and I fortunate with my schooner, and both get to heaven in the end in spite of the devil and his bottle."

So Lopaka went down the mountain ; and Keawe stood in his front balcony, and listened to the clink of the horse's shoes, and watched the lantern go shining down the path, and along the cliff of caves where the old dead are buried ; and all the time he trembled and clasped his hands, and prayed for his friend, and gave glory to God that he himself was escaped out of that trouble.

But the next day came very brightly, and that new house of his was so delightful to behold that he forgot his terrors. One day followed another, and Keawe dwelt there in perpetual joy. He had his place on the back porch ; it was there he ate and lived, and read the stories in the Honolulu newspapers ; but when any one came by they would go in and view the chambers and the pictures. And the fame of the house went far and wide ; it was called *Ka-Hale Nui* —the Great House—in all Kona ; and sometimes the Bright House, for Keawe kept a Chinaman, who was all day dusting and furbishing ; and the glass, and the gilt, and the fine stuffs, and the pictures, shone as bright as the morning. As for Keawe himself, he could not walk in the chambers without singing, his heart was so enlarged ; and when ships sailed by upon the sea, he would fly his colours on the mast.

So time went by, until one day Keawe went upon a visit as far as Kailua to certain of his friends. There he was well feasted ; and left as soon as he could the next morning, and rode hard, for he was impatient to behold his beautiful house ; and, besides, the night then coming on was the night in which the dead of old days go abroad in the sides of Kona ; and having already meddled with the devil, he was the more chary of meeting with the dead. A little beyond Honaunau, looking far ahead, he was aware of a woman bathing in the edge of the sea ; and she seemed a well-grown girl, but he thought no more of it.   Then he saw her white shift flutter as she put it on, and then her red holoku ; and by the time he came abreast of her she was done with her toilet, and had come up from the sea, and stood by the track-side in her red holoku, and she was all freshened with the bath, and her eyes shone and were kind.   Now Keawe no sooner beheld her than he drew rein.

" I thought I knew every one in this country," said he. " How comes it that I do not know you ? "

" I am Kokua, daughter of Kiano," said the girl, " and I have just returned from Oahu.   Who are you ? "

" I will tell you who I am in a little," said Keawe, dismounting from his horse, " but not now.   For I have a thought in my mind, and if you knew who I was, you might have heard of me, and would not give me a true answer. But tell me, first of all, one thing : are you married ? "

At this Kokua laughed out aloud.   " It is you who ask questions," she said.   " Are you married yourself ? "

" Indeed, Kokua, I am not," replied Keawe, " and never thought to be until this hour.   But here is the plain truth. I have met you here at the road-side, and I saw your eyes, which are like the stars, and my heart went to you as swift as a bird.   And so now, if you want none of me, say so, and I will go on to my own place ; but if you think me no worse than any other young man, say so, too, and I will turn aside to your father's for the night, and to-morrow I will talk with the good man."

Kokua said never a word, but she looked at the sea and laughed.

" Kokua," said Keawe, " if you say nothing, I will take that for the good answer ; so let us be stepping to your father's door."

She went on ahead of him, still without speech ; only sometimes she glanced back and glanced away again, and she kept the strings of her hat in her mouth.

Now, when they had come to the door, Kiano came out on his verandah, and cried out and welcomed Keawe by name.   At that the girl looked over, for the fame of the great house had come to her ears ; and, to be sure, it was a great temptation. All that evening they were very merry together ; and the girl was as bold as brass under the eyes of her parents, and made a mark of Keawe, for she had a quick wit. The next day he had a word with Kiano, and found the girl alone.

" Kokua," said he, " you made a mark of me all the evening ; and it is still time to bid me go. I would not tell you who I was, because I have so fine a house, and I feared you would think too much of that house and too little of the man that loves you. Now you know all, and if you wish to have seen the last of me, say so at once."

" No," said Kokua, but this time she did not laugh, nor did Keawe ask for more.

This was the wooing of Keawe ; things had gone quickly ; but so an arrow goes, and the ball of a rifle swifter still, and yet both may strike the target. Things had gone fast, but they had gone far also, and the thought of Keawe rang in the maiden's head ; she heard his voice in the breach of the surf upon the lava, and for this young man that she had seen but twice she would have left father and mother and her native islands. As for Keawe him-self, his horse flew up the path of the mountain under the cliff of tombs, and the sound of the hoofs, and the sound of Keawe singing to himself for pleasure, echoed in the caverns of the dead. He came to the Bright House, and still he was singing. He sat and ate in the broad balcony, and the Chinaman wondered at his master, to hear how he sang between the mouthfuls. The sun went down into the sea, and the night came ; and Keawe walked the balconies by lamplight, high on the mountains, and the voice of his singing startled men on ships.

" Here am I now upon my high place," he said to him-self. " Life may be no better ; this is the mountain top ; and all shelves about me towards the worse. For the first time I will light up the chambers, and bathe in my fine bath with the hot water and the cold, and sleep above in the bed of my bridal chamber."

So the Chinaman had word, and he must rise from sleep

and light the furnaces ; and as he walked below, beside the boilers, he heard his master singing and rejoicing above him in the lighted chambers. When the water began to be hot the Chinaman cried to his master : and Keawe went into the bathroom ; and the Chinaman heard him sing as he filled the marble basin ; and heard him sing, and the singing broken, as he undressed ; until of a sudden, the song ceased. The Chinaman listened, and listened ; he called up the house to Keawe to ask if all were well, and Keawe answered him " Yes," and bade him go to bed ; but there was no more singing in the Bright House ; and all night long the Chinaman heard his master's feet go round and round the balconies without repose.

Now, the truth of it was this : as Keawe undressed for his bath, he spied upon his flesh a patch like a patch of lichen on a rock, and it was then that he stopped singing. For he knew the likeness of that patch, and knew that he was fallen in the Chinese Evil.*

Now, it is a sad thing for any man to fall into this sickness. And it would be a sad thing for any one to leave a house so beautiful and so commodious, and depart from all his friends to the north coast of Molokai, between the mighty cliff and the sea-breakers. But what was that to the case of the man Keawe, he who had met his love but yesterday and won her but that morning, and now saw all his hopes break, in a moment, like a piece of glass ?

A while he sat upon the edge of the bath, then sprang, with a cry, and ran outside ; and to and fro, to and fro, along the balcony, like one despairing.

" Very willingly could I leave Hawaii, the home of my fathers," Keawe was thinking. " Very lightly could I leave my house, the high-placed, the many-windowed, here upon the mountains. Very bravely could I go to Molokai, to Kalaupapa by the cliffs, to live with the smitten and to sleep there, far from my fathers. But what wrong have I done, what sin lies upon my soul, that I should have encountered Kokua coming cool from the sea-water in the evening ? Kokua, the soul ensnarer ! Kokua, the

* Leprosy.

light of my life ! Her may I never wed, her may I look upon no longer, her may I no more handle with my loving hand ; and it is for this, it is for you, O Kokua ! that I pour my lamentations ! "

Now you are to observe what sort of a man Keawe was, for he might have dwelt there in the Bright House for years, and no one been the wiser of his sickness ; but he reckoned nothing of that, if he must lose Kokua. And again he might have wed Kokua even as he was ; and so many would have done, because they have the souls of pigs ; but Keawe loved the maid manfully, and he would do her no hurt and bring her in no danger.

A little beyond the midst of the night, there came in his mind the recollection of that bottle. He went round to the back porch, and called to memory the day when the devil had looked forth ; and at the thought ice ran in his veins.

" A dreadful thing is the bottle," thought Keawe, " and dreadful is the imp, and it is a dreadful thing to risk the flames of hell. But what other hope have I to cure my sickness or to wed Kokua ? What ! " he thought, " would I beard the devil once, only to get me a house, and not face him again to win Kokua ? "

Thereupon he called to mind it was the next day the *Hall* went by on her return to Honolulu. " There must I go first," he thought, " and see Lopaka. For the best hope that I have now is to find that same bottle I was so pleased to be rid of."

Never a wink could he sleep ; the food stuck in his throat ; but he sent a letter to Kiano, and about the time when the steamer would be coming, rode down beside the cliff of the tombs. It rained ; his horse went heavily ; he looked up at the black mouths of the caves, and he envied the dead that slept there and were done with trouble ; and called to mind how he had galloped by the day before, and was astonished. So he came down to Hookena, and there was all the country gathered for the steamer as usual. In the shed before the store they sat and jested and passed the news ; but there was no matter of speech in Keawe's bosom, and he sat in their midst and looked without on the rain falling on the houses, and the surf beating among the rocks, and the sighs arose in his throat.

"Keawe of the Bright House is out of spirits," said one to another. Indeed, and so he was, and little wonder.

Then the *Hall* came, and the whale-boat carried him on board. The after-part of the ship was full of Haoles *— who had been to visit the volcano, as their custom is; and the midst was crowded with Kanakas, and the fore-part with wild bulls from Hilo and horses from Kaü; but Keawe sat apart from all in his sorrow, and watched for the house of Kiano. There it sat low upon the shore in the black rocks, and shaded by the cocoa-palms, and there by the door was a red holoku, no greater than a fly, and going to and fro with a fly's busyness. "Ah, queen of my heart," he cried, "I'll venture my dear soul to win you!"

Soon after darkness fell and the cabins were lit up, and the Haoles sat and played at the cards and drank whiskey as their custom is; but Keawe walked the deck all night; and all the next day, as they steamed under the lea of Maui or of Molokai, he was still pacing to and fro like a wild animal in a menagerie.

Towards evening they passed Diamond Head, and came to the pier of Honolulu. Keawe stepped out among the crowd and began to ask for Lopaka. It seemed he had become the owner of a schooner—none better in the islands —and was gone upon an adventure as far as Pola-Pola or Kahiki; so there was no help to be looked for from Lopaka. Keawe called to mind a friend of his, a lawyer in the town (I must not tell his name), and inquired of him. They said he was grown suddenly rich, and had a fine new house upon Waikiki shore; and this put a thought in Keawe's head, and he called a hack and drove to the lawyer's house.

The house was all brand new, and the trees in the garden no greater than walking-sticks, and the lawyer, when he came, had the air of a man well pleased.

"What can I do to serve you?" said the lawyer.

* Whites.

"You are a friend of Lopaka's," replied Keawe, "and Lopaka purchased from me a certain piece of goods that I thought you might enable me to trace."

The lawyer's face became very dark. "I do not profess to misunderstand you, Mr. Keawe," said he, "though this is an ugly business to be stirring in. You may be sure I know nothing, but yet I have a guess, and if you would apply in a certain quarter I think you might have news."

And he named the name of a man, which, again, I had better not repeat. So it was for days, and Keawe went from one to another, finding everywhere new clothes and carriages, and fine new houses and men everywhere in great contentment, although, to be sure, when he hinted at his business their faces would cloud over.

"No doubt I am upon the track," thought Keawe. "These new clothes and carriages are all the gifts of the little imp, and these glad faces are the faces of men who have taken their profit and got rid of the accursed thing in safety. When I see pale cheeks and hear sighing, I shall know that I am near the bottle."

So it befell at last he was recommended to a Haole in Beritania Street. When he came to the door, about the hour of the evening meal, there were the usual marks of the new house, and the young garden, and the electric light shining in the windows; but when the owner came, a shock of hope and fear ran through Keawe; for here was a young man, white as a corpse, and black about the eyes, the hair shedding from his head, and such a look in his countenance as a man may have when he is waiting for the gallows.

"Here it is, to be sure," thought Keawe, and so with this man he noways veiled his errand. "I am come to buy the bottle," said he.

At the word, the young Haole of Beritania Street reeled against the wall.

"The bottle!" he gasped. "To buy the bottle!" Then he seemed to choke, and seizing Keawe by the arm, carried him into a room and poured out wine in two glasses.

"Here is my respects," said Keawe, who had been much about with Haoles in his time. "Yes," he added, "I am come to buy the bottle. What is the price by now?"

At that word the young man let his glass slip through his fingers, and looked upon Keawe like a ghost.

"The price," says he; "the price! You do not know the price?"

"It is for that I am asking you," returned Keawe. "But why are you so much concerned? Is there anything wrong about the price?"

"It has dropped a great deal in value since your time, Mr. Keawe," said the young man, stammering.

"Well, well, I shall have the less to pay for it," says Keawe. "How much did it cost you?"

The young man was as white as a sheet. "Two cents," said he.

"What?" cried Keawe, "two cents? Why, then, you can only sell it for one. And he who buys it——" The words died upon Keawe's tongue; he who bought it could never sell it again, the bottle and the bottle imp must abide with him until he died, and when he died must carry him to the red end of hell.

The young man of Beritania Street fell upon his knees. "For God's sake, buy it!" he cried. "You can have all my fortune in the bargain. I was mad when I bought it at that price. I had embezzled money at my store; I was lost else; I must have gone to jail."

"Poor creature," said Keawe, "you would risk your soul upon so desperate an adventure, and to avoid the proper punishment of your own disgrace; and you think I could hesitate with love in front of me. Give me the bottle, and the change which I make sure you have all ready. Here is a five-cent piece."

It was as Keawe supposed; the young man had the change ready in a drawer; the bottle changed hands, and Keawe's fingers were no sooner clasped upon the stalk than he had breathed his wish to be a clean man. And, sure enough, when he got home to his room, and stripped himself before a glass, his flesh was whole like an infant's.

And here was the strange thing : he had no sooner seen this miracle than his mind was changed within him, and he cared naught for the Chinese Evil, and little enough for Kokua ; and had but the one thought, that here he was bound to the bottle imp for time and for eternity, and had no better hope but to be a cinder for ever in the flames of hell. Away ahead of him he saw them blaze with his mind's eye, and his soul shrank, and darkness fell upon the light.

When Keawe came to himself a little, he was aware it was the night when the band played at the hotel. Thither he went, because he feared to be alone ; and there, among happy faces, walked to and fro, and heard the tunes go up and down, and saw Berger beat the measure, and all the while he heard the flames crackle and saw the red fire burning in the bottomless pit. Of a sudden the band played *Hiki-ao-ao ;* that was a song that he had sung with Kokua, and at the strain courage returned to him.

" It is done now," he thought, " and once more let me take the good along with the evil."

So it befell that he returned to Hawaii by the first steamer, and as soon as it could be managed he was wedded to Kokua, and carried her up the mountain side to the Bright House.

Now it was so with these two, that when they were together Keawe's heart was stilled ; but as soon as he was alone he fell into a brooding horror, and heard the flames crackle, and saw the red fire burn in the bottomless pit. The girl, indeed, had come to him wholly ; her heart leaped in her side at sight of him, her hand clung to his ; and she was so fashioned, from the hair upon her head to the nails upon her toes, that none could see her without joy. She was pleasant in her nature. She had the good word always. Full of song she was, and went to and fro in the Bright House, the brightest thing in its three stories, carolling like the birds. And Keawe beheld and heard her with delight, and then must shrink upon one side, and weep and groan to think upon the price that he had paid for her ; and then he must dry his eyes, and wash his face, and go and

H

sit with her on the broad balconies, joining in her songs, and, with a sick spirit, answering her smiles.

There came a day when her feet began to be heavy and her songs more rare ; and now it was not Keawe only that would weep apart, but each would sunder from the other and sit in opposite balconies with the whole width of the Bright House betwixt. Keawe was so sunk in his despair, he scarce observed the change, and was only glad he had more hours to sit alone and brood upon his destiny, and was not so frequently condemned to pull a smiling face on a sick heart. But one day, coming softly through the house, he heard the sound of a child sobbing, and there was Kokua rolling her face upon the balcony floor, and weeping like the lost.

"You do well to weep in this house, Kokua," he said. "And yet I would give the head off my body that you (at least) might have been happy."

"Happy ! " she cried. "Keawe, when you lived alone in your Bright House you were the word of the island for a happy man ; laughter and song were in your mouth, and your face was as bright as the sunrise. Then you wedded poor Kokua ; and the good God knows what is amiss in her—but from that day you have not smiled. Oh ! " she cried, "what ails me ? I thought I was pretty, and I knew I loved him. What ails me, that I throw this cloud upon my husband ? "

"Poor Kokua," said Keawe. He sat down by her side, and sought to take her hand ; but that she plucked away. "Poor Kokua," he said again. "My poor child—my pretty. And I had thought all this while to spare you ! Well, you shall know all. Then, at least, you will pity poor Keawe ; then you will understand how much he loved you in the past—that he dared hell for your possession—and how much he loves you still (the poor condemned one), that he can yet call up a smile when he beholds you."

With that he told her all, even from the beginning.

"You have done this for me ? " she cried. "Ah, well, then what do I care ! " and she clasped and wept upon him.

"Ah, child!" said Keawe, "and yet, when I consider of the fire of hell, I care a good deal!"

"Never tell me," said she, "no man can be lost because he loved Kokua, and no other fault. I tell you, Keawe, I shall save you with these hands, or perish in your company. What! you loved me and gave your soul, and you think I will not die to save you in return?"

"Ah, my dear, you might die a hundred times, and what difference would that make?" he cried, "except to leave me lonely till the time comes for my damnation?"

"You know nothing," said she. "I was educated in a school in Honolulu; I am no common girl. And I tell you I shall save my lover. What is this you say about a cent? But all the world is not American. In England they have a piece they call a farthing, which is about half a cent. Ah! sorrow!" she cried, "that makes it scarcely better, for the buyer must be lost, and we shall find none so brave as my Keawe! But, then, there is France; they have a small coin there which they call a centime, and these go five to the cent, or thereabout. We could not do better. Come, Keawe, let us go to the French islands; let us go to Tahiti, as fast as ships can bear us. There we have four centimes, three centimes, two centimes, one centime; four possible sales to come and go on; and two of us to push the bargain. Come, my Keawe! kiss me, and banish care. Kokua will defend you."

"Gift of God!" he cried. "I cannot think that God will punish me for desiring aught so good. Be it as you will, then, take me where you please: I put my life and my salvation in your hands."

Early the next day Kokua went about her preparations. She took Keawe's chest that he went with sailoring; and first she put the bottle in a corner, and then packed it with the richest of their clothes and the bravest of the knick-knacks in the house. "For," said she, "we must seem to be rich folks, or who would believe in the bottle?" All the time of her preparation she was as gay as a bird; only when she looked upon Keawe the tears would spring in her eye, and she must run and kiss him. As for Keawe, a weight was off his soul; now that he had his secret shared, and some hope in front of him, he seemed like a new man, his feet went lightly on the earth, and his breath was good to him again. Yet was terror still at his elbow; and ever and again, as the wind blows out a taper, hope died in him, and he saw the flames toss and the red fire burn in hell.

It was given out in the country they were gone pleasuring to the States, which was thought a strange thing, and yet not so strange as the truth, if any could have guessed it. So they went to Honolulu in the *Hall*, and thence in the *Umatilla* to San Francisco with a crowd of Haoles, and at San Francisco took their passage by the mail brigantine, the *Tropic Bird*, for Papeete, the chief place of the French in the south islands. Thither they came, after a pleasant voyage, on a fair day of the Trade Wind, and saw the reef with the surf breaking and Motuiti with its palms, and the schooner riding withinside, and the white houses of the town low down along the shore among green trees, and overhead the mountains and the clouds of Tahiti, the wise island.

It was judged the most wise to hire a house, which they did accordingly, opposite the British Consul's, to make a great parade of money, and themselves conspicuous with carriages and horses. This it was very easy to do, so long as they had the bottle in their possession; for Kokua was more bold than Keawe, and, whenever she had a mind, called on the imp for twenty or a hundred dollars. At this rate they soon grew to be remarked in the town; and the strangers from Hawaii, their riding and their driving, the fine holokus, and the rich lace of Kokua, became the matter of much talk.

They got on well after the first with the Tahitia language, which is indeed like to the Hawaiian, with a change of certain letters; and as soon as they had any freedom of speech, began to push the bottle. You are to consider it was not an easy subject to introduce; it was not easy to persuade people you are in earnest, when you offer to sell them for four centimes the spring of health and riches inexhaustible. It was necessary besides to explain the dangers of the bottle; and either people disbelieved the whole thing and laughed, or they thought the more of the darker part, became overcast with gravity, and drew away from Keawe and Kokua, as from persons who had dealings with the devil. So far from gaining ground, these two began to find they were avoided in the town; the children ran away from them screaming, a thing intolerable to Kokua; Catholics crossed themselves as they went by; and all persons began with one accord to disengage themselves from their advances.

Depression fell upon their spirits. They would sit at night in their new house, after a day's weariness, and not exchange one word, or the silence would be broken by Kokua bursting suddenly into sobs. Sometimes they would pray together; sometimes they would have the bottle out upon the floor, and sit all evening watching how the shadow hovered in the midst. At such times they would be afraid to go to rest. It was long ere slumber came to them, and, if either dozed off, it would be to wake and find the other silently weeping in the dark, or, perhaps, to wake alone, the other having fled from the house and the neighbourhood of that bottle, to pace under the bananas in the little garden, or to wander on the beach by moonlight.

One night it was so when Kokua awoke. Keawe was gone. She felt in the bed and his place was cold. Then fear fell upon her, and she sat up in bed. A little moonshine filtered through the shutters. The room was bright, and she could spy the bottle on the floor. Outside it blew high, the great trees of the avenue cried aloud, and the fallen leaves rattled in the verandah. In the midst of this Kokua was aware of another sound; whether of a beast or of a man she could scarce tell, but it was as sad as death, and cut her to the soul. Softly she arose, set the door ajar, and looked forth into the moonlit yard. There, under the bananas, lay Keawe, his mouth in the dust, and as he lay he moaned.

It was Kokua's first thought to run forward and console him; her second potently withheld her. Keawe had borne himself before his wife like a brave man ; it became her little in the hour of weakness to intrude upon his shame. With the thought she drew back into the house.

"Heaven," she thought, "how careless have I been—how weak ! It is he, not I, that stands in this eternal peril ; it was he, not I, that took the curse upon his soul. It is for my sake, and for the love of a creature of so little worth and such poor help, that he now beholds so close to him the flames of hell—ay, and smells the smoke of it, lying without there in the wind and moonlight. Am I so dull of spirit that never till now I have surmised my duty, or have I seen it before and turned aside ? But now, at least, I take up my soul in both the hands of my affection ; now I say farewell to the white steps of heaven and the waiting faces of my friends. A love for a love, and let mine be equalled with Keawe's ! A soul for a soul, and be it mine to perish ! "

She was a deft woman with her hands, and was soon apparelled. She took in her hands the change—the precious centimes they kept ever at their side ; for this coin is little used, and they had made provision at a government office. When she was forth in the avenue clouds came on the wind, and the moon was blackened. The town slept, and she knew not whither to turn till she heard one coughing in the shadow of the trees.

"Old man," said Kokua, "what do you here abroad in the cold night ? "

The old man could scarce express himself for coughing, but she made out that he was old and poor, and a stranger in the island.

"Will you do me a service ? " said Kokua. "As one stranger to another, and as an old man to a young woman, will you help a daughter of Hawaii ? "

"Ah," said the old man. "So you are the witch from the Eight Islands, and even my old soul you seek to entangle. But I have heard of you, and defy your wickedness."

"Sit down here," said Kokua, "and let me tell you a tale." And she told him the story of Keawe from the beginning to the end.

" And now," said she, " I am his wife, whom he bought with his soul's welfare. And what should I do ? If I went to him myself and offered to buy it, he will refuse. But if you go, he will sell it eagerly ; I will await you here ; you will buy it for four centimes, and I will buy it again for three. And the Lord strengthen a poor girl ! "

" If you meant falsely," said the old man, " I think God would strike you dead."

" He would ! " cried Kokua. " Be sure he would. I could not be so treacherous ; God would not suffer it."

" Give me the four centimes and await me here," said the old man.

Now, when Kokua stood alone in the street, her spirit died. The wind roared in the trees, and it seemed to her the rushing of the flames of hell ; the shadows towered in the light of the street lamp, and they seemed to her the snatching hands of evil ones. If she had had the strength, she must have run away, and if she had had the breath, she must have screamed aloud ; but, in truth, she could do neither, and stood and trembled in the avenue, like an affrighted child.

Then she saw the old man returning, and he had the bottle in his hand.

" I have done your bidding," said he, " I left your husband weeping like a child ; to-night he will sleep easy." And he held the bottle forth.

" Before you give it me," Kokua panted, " take the good with the evil—ask to be delivered from your cough."

" I am an old man," replied the other, " and too near the gate of the grave to take a favour from the devil. But what is this ? Why do you not take the bottle ? Do you hesitate ? "

" Not hesitate ! " cried Kokua. " I am only weak. Give me a moment. It is my hand resists, my flesh shrinks back from the accursed thing. One moment only ! "

The old man looked upon Kokua kindly. " Poor child ! " said he, " you fear : your soul misgives you. Well, let me keep it. I am old, and can never more be happy in this world, and as for the next——"

" Give it me ! " gasped Kokua. " There is your money. Do you think I am so base as that ? Give me the bottle."

" God bless you, child," said the old man.

Kokua concealed the bottle under her holoku, said farewell to the old man, and walked off along the avenue, she cared not whither. For all roads were now the same to her, and led equally to hell. Sometimes she walked, and sometimes ran ; sometimes she screamed out loud in the night, and sometimes lay by the wayside in the dust and wept. All that she had heard of hell came back to her ; she saw the flames blaze, and she smelled the smoke, and her flesh withered on the coals.

Near day she came to her mind again, and returned to the house. It was even as the old man said—Keawe slumbered like a child. Kokua stood and gazed upon his face.

" Now, my husband," said she, " it is your turn to sleep. When you wake it will be your turn to sing and laugh. But for poor Kokua, alas ! that meant no evil—for poor Kokua no more sleep, no more singing, no more delight, whether in earth or heaven."

With that she lay down in the bed by his side, and her misery was so extreme that she fell in a deep slumber instantly.

Late in the morning her husband woke her and gave her the good news. It seemed he was silly with delight, for he paid no heed to her distress, ill though she dissembled it. The words stuck in her mouth, it mattered not ; Keawe did the speaking. She ate not a bite, but who was to observe it ? For Keawe cleared the dish. Kokua saw and heard him, like some strange thing in a dream ; there were times when she forgot or doubted, and put her hands to her brow ; to know herself doomed and hear her husband babble, seemed so monstrous.

All the while Keawe was eating and talking, and planning the time of their return, and thanking her for saving him and fondling her, and calling her the true helper after all. He laughed at the old man that was fool enough to buy that bottle.

"A worthy old man he seemed," Keawe said. "But no one can judge by appearances. For why did the old reprobate require the bottle?"

"My husband," said Kokua, humbly, "his purpose may have been good."

Keawe laughed like an angry man.

"Fiddle-de-dee!" cried Keawe. "An old rogue, I tell you; and an old ass to boot. For the bottle was hard enough to sell at four centimes; and at three it will be quite impossible. The margin is not broad enough, the thing begins to smell of scorching—brrr!" said he, and shuddered. "It is true I bought it myself at a cent, when I knew not there were smaller coins. I was a fool for my pains; there will never be found another, and whoever has that bottle now will carry it to the pit."

"O my husband!" said Kokua. "Is it not a terrible thing to save oneself by the eternal ruin of another? It seems to me I could not laugh. I would be humbled. I would be filled with melancholy. I would pray for the poor holder."

Then Keawe, because he felt the truth of what she said, grew the more angry. "Heighty-teighty!" cried he. "You may be filled with melancholy if you please. It is not the mind of a good wife. If you thought at all of me, you would sit shamed."

Thereupon he went out, and Kokua was alone.

What chance had she to sell that bottle at two centimes? None, she perceived. And if she had any, here was her husband hurrying her away to a country where there was nothing lower than a cent. And here—on the morrow of her sacrifice—was her husband leaving her and blaming her.

She would not even try to profit by what time she had, but sat in the house, and now had the bottle out and viewed it with unutterable fear, and now, with loathing, hid it out of sight.

By and by, Keawe came back, and would have her take a drive.

"My husband, I am ill," she said. "I am out of heart. Excuse me, I can take no pleasure."

Then was Keawe more wroth than ever. With her, because he thought she was brooding over the case of the old man ; and with himself, because he thought she was right and was ashamed to be so happy.

" This is your truth," cried he, " and this your affection ! Your husband is just saved from eternal ruin, which he encountered for the love of you—and you can take no pleasure ! Kokua, you have a disloyal heart."

He went forth again furious, and wandered in the town all day. He met friends, and drank with them ; they hired a carriage and drove into the country, and there drank again. All the time Keawe was ill at ease, because he was taking this pastime while his wife was sad, and because he knew in his heart that she was more right than he ; and the knowledge made him drink the deeper.

Now there was an old brutal Haole drinking with him, one that had been a boatswain of a whaler—a runaway, a digger in gold mines, a convict in prisons. He had a low mind and a foul mouth ; he loved to drink and to see others drunken ; and he pressed the glass upon Keawe. Soon there was no more money in the company.

" Here, you ! " says the boatswain, " you are rich, you have been always saying. You have a bottle or some foolishness."

" Yes," says Keawe, " I am rich ; I will go back and get some money from my wife, who keeps it."

" That's a bad idea, mate," said the boatswain. " Never you trust a petticoat with dollars. They're all as false as water ; you keep an eye on her."

Now this word struck in Keawe's mind ; for he was muddled with what he had been drinking.

" I should not wonder but she was false, indeed," thought he. " Why else should she be so cast down at my release ? But I will show her I am not the man to be fooled. I will catch her in the act."

Accordingly, when they were back in town, Keawe bade the boatswain wait for him at the corner, by the old calaboose, and went forward up the avenue alone to the door of his house. The night had come again ; there was a

light within, but never a sound ; and Keawe crept about
the corner, opened the back door softly, and looked in.

There was Kokua on the floor, the lamp at her side ;
before her was a milk-white bottle, with a round belly and a
long neck ; and as she viewed it, Kokua wrung her hands.

A long time Keawe stood and looked in the doorway.
At first he was struck stupid ; and then fear fell upon him
that the bargain had been made amiss, and the bottle had
come back to him as it came at San Francisco ; and at that
his knees were loosened, and the fumes of the wine departed
from his head like mists off a river in the morning. And
then he had another thought ; and it was a strange one,
that made his cheeks to burn.

" I must make sure of this," thought he.

So he closed the door, and went softly round the corner
again, and then came noisily in, as though he were but now
returned. And, lo ! by the time he opened the front door
no bottle was to be seen ; and Kokua sat in a chair and
started up like one awakened out of sleep.

" I have been drinking all day and making merry," said
Keawe. " I have been with good conpanions, and now I
only came back for money, and return to drink and carouse
with them again."

Both his face and voice were as stern as judgment, but
Kokua was too troubled to observe.

" You do well to use your own, my husband," said she,
and her words trembled.

" Oh, I do well in all things," said Keawe, and he went
straight to the chest and took out money. But he looked
besides in the corner where they kept the bottle, and there
was no bottle there.

At that the chest heaved upon the floor like a sea-billow,
and the house span about him like a wreath of smoke, for
he saw she was lost now, and there was no escape. " It is
what I feared," he thought. " It is she who has bought
it."

And then he came to himself a little and rose up ; but
the sweat streamed on his face as thick as the rain and as
cold as the well-water.

"Kokua," said he, "I said to you to-day what ill became me. Now I return to house with my jolly companions," and at that he laughed a little quietly. "I will take more pleasure in the cup if you forgive me."

She clasped his knees in a moment, she kissed his knees with flowing tears.

"Oh," she cried, "I ask but a kind word!"

"Let us never one think hardly of the other," said Keawe, and was gone out of the house.

Now, the money that Keawe had taken was only some of that store of centime pieces they had laid in at their arrival. It was very sure he had no mind to be drinking. His wife had given her soul for him, now he must give his for hers; no other thought was in the world with him.

At the corner, by the old calaboose, there was the boatswain waiting.

"My wife has the bottle," said Keawe, "and, unless you help me to recover it, there can be no more money and no more liquor to-night."

"You do not mean to say you are serious about that bottle?" cried the boatswain.

"There is the lamp," said Keawe. "Do I look as if I was jesting?"

"That is so," said the boatswain. "You look as serious as a ghost."

"Well, then," said Keawe, "here are two centimes; you just go to my wife in the house, and offer her these for the bottle, which (if I am not much mistaken) she will give you instantly. Bring it to me here, and I will buy it back from you for one; for that is the law with this bottle that it still must be sold for a less sum. But whatever you do, never breathe a word to her that you have come from me."

"Mate, I wonder are you making a fool of me?" asked the boatswain.

"It will do you no harm if I am," returned Keawe.

"That is so, mate," said the boatswain.

"And if you doubt me," added Keawe, "you can try. As soon as you are clear of the house, wish to have your pocket full of money, or a bottle of the best rum, or what you please, and you will see the virtue of the thing."

"Very well, Kanaka," says the boatswain. "I will try; but if you are having your fun out of me, I will take my fun out of you with a belaying-pin."

So the whaler-man went off up the avenue; and Keawe stood and waited. It was near the same spot where Kokua had waited the night before; but Keawe was more resolved, and never faltered in his purpose; only his soul was bitter with despair.

It seemed a long time he had to wait before he heard a voice singing in the darkness of the avenue. He knew the voice to be the boatswain's; but it was strange how drunken it appeared upon a sudden.

Next the man himself came stumbling into the light of the lamp. He had the devil's bottle buttoned in his coat; another bottle was in his hand; and even as he came in view he raised it to his mouth and drank.

"You have it," said Keawe. "I see that."

"Hands off!" cried the boatswain, jumping back. "Take a step near me, and I'll smash your mouth. You thought you could make a catspaw of me, did you?"

"What do you mean?" cried Keawe.

"Mean?" cried the boatswain. "This is a pretty good bottle, this is; that's what I mean. How I got it for two centimes I can't make out; but I am sure you sha'nt have it for one."

"You mean you won't sell?" gasped Keawe.

"No, sir," cried the boatswain. "But I'll give you a drink of the rum, if you like."

"I tell you," said Keawe, "the man who has that bottle goes to hell."

"I reckon I'm going anyway," returned the sailor; "and this bottle's the best thing to go with I've struck yet. No, sir!" he cried again, "this is my bottle now, and you can go and fish for another."

"Can this be true?" Keawe cried. "For your own sake, I beseech you, sell it me!"

"I don't value any of your talk," replied the boatswain.

" You thought I was a flat, now you see I'm not ; and there's an end. If you won't have a swallow of the rum, I'll have one myself. Here's your health, and good-night to you ! "

So off he went down the avenue towards town, and there goes the bottle out of the story.

But Keawe ran to Kokua light as the wind ; and great was their joy that night ; and great, since then, has been the peace of all their days in the Bright House.

THE ISLE OF VOICES

THE ISLE OF VOICES

KEOLA was married with Lehua, daughter of Kalamake, the wise man of Molokai, and he kept his dwelling with the father of his wife. There was no man more cunning than that prophet; he read the stars, he could divine by the bodies of the dead, and by the means of evil creatures: he could go alone into the highest parts of the mountain, into the region of the hobgoblins, and there he would lay snares to entrap the spirits of the ancient.

For this reason no man was more consulted in all the Kingdom of Hawaii. Prudent people bought, and sold, and married, and laid out their lives by his counsels; and the King had him twice to Kona to seek the treasures of Kamehameha. Neither was any man more feared: of his enemies, some had dwindled in sickness by the virtue of his incantations, and some had been spirited away, the life and the clay both, so that folk looked in vain for so much as a bone of their bodies. It was rumoured that he had the art or the gift of the old heroes. Men had seen him at night upon the mountains, stepping from one cliff to the next; they had seen him walking in the high forest, and his head and shoulders were above the trees.

This Kalamake was a strange man to see. He was come of the best blood in Molokai and Maui, of a pure descent; and yet he was more white to look upon than any foreigner; his hair the colour of dry grass, and his eyes red and very blind, so that " Blind as Kalamake that can see across to-morrow," was a byword in the islands.

Of all these doings of his father-in-law, Keola knew a little by the common repute, a little more he suspected, and the rest he ignored. But there was one thing troubled him. Kalamake was a man that spared for nothing, whether to eat or to drink, or to wear ; and for all he paid in bright new dollars. " Bright as Kalamake's dollars," was another saying in the Eight Isles. Yet he neither sold, nor planted, nor took hire—only now and then from his sorceries—and there was no source conceivable for so much silver coin.

It chanced one day Keola's wife was gone upon a visit to Kaunakakai on the lee side of the island, and the men were forth at the sea-fishing. But Keola was an idle dog, and he lay in the verandah and watched the surf beat on the shore and the birds fly about the cliff. It was a chief thought with him always—the thought of the bright dollars. When he lay down to bed he would be wondering why they were so many, and when he woke at morn he would be wondering why they were all new ; and the thing was never absent from his mind. But this day of all days he made sure in his heart of some discovery. For it seems he had observed the place where Kalamake kept his treasure, which was a lock-fast desk against the parlour wall, under the print of Kamehameha the fifth, and a photograph of Queen Victoria with her crown ; and it seems again that, no later than the night before, he found occasion to look in, and behold ! the bag lay there empty. And this was the day of the steamer ; he could see her smoke off Kalaupapa ; and she must soon arrive with a month's goods, tinned salmon and gin, and all manner of rare luxuries for Kalamake.

" Now if he can pay for his goods to-day," Keola thought, " I shall know for certain that the man is a warlock, and the dollars come out of the devil's pocket."

While he was so thinking, there was his father-in-law behind him, looking vexed.

" Is that the steamer ? " he asked.

" Yes," said Keola. " She has but to call at Pelekunu, and then she will be here."

" There is no help for it then," returned Kalamake, " and I must take you in my confidence, Keola, for the lack of anyone better. Come here within the house."

So they stepped together into the parlour, which was a

very fine room, papered and hung with prints, and furnished with a rocking-chair, and a table and a sofa in the European style. There was a shelf of books besides, and a family Bible in the midst of the table, and the lock-fast writing-desk against the wall ; so that any one could see it was the house of a man of substance.

Kalamake made Keola close the shutters of the windows, while he himself locked all the doors and set open the lid of the desk. From this he brought forth a pair of neck-laces hung with charms and shells, a bundle of dried herbs, and the dried leaves of trees, and a green branch of palm.

" What I am about," said he, " is a thing beyond wonder. The men of old were wise ; they wrought marvels, and this among the rest ; but that was at night, in the dark, under the fit stars and in the desert. The same will I do here in my own house, and under the plain eye of day." So saying, he put the Bible under the cushion of the sofa so that it was all covered, brought out from the same place a mat of a wonderfully fine texture, and heaped the herbs and leaves on sand in a tin pan. And then he and Keola put on the necklaces, and took their stand upon the opposite corners of the mat.

" The time comes," said the warlock, " be not afraid."

With that he set flame to the herbs, and began to mutter and wave the branch of palm. At first the light was dim because of the closed shutters ; but the herbs caught strongly afire, and the flames beat upon Keola, and the room glowed with the burning ; and next the smoke rose and made his head swim and his eyes darken, and the sound of Kalamake muttering ran in his ears. And suddenly, to the mat on which they were standing came a snatch or twitch, that seemed to be more swift than lightning. In the same wink the room was gone, and the house, the breath all beaten from Keola's body. Volumes of sun rolled upon his eyes and head, and he found himself transported to a beach of the sea, under a strong sun, with a great surf roaring : he and the warlock standing there on the same mat, speechless, gasping and grasping at one another, and passing their hands before their eyes.

"What was this?" cried Keola, who came to himself the first, because he was the younger. "The pang of it was like death."

"It matters not," panted Kalamake. "It is now done."

"And, in the name of God, where are we?" cried Keola.

"That is not the question," replied the sorcerer. "Being here, we have matter in our hands, and that we must attend to. Go, while I recover my breath, into the borders of the wood, and bring me the leaves of such and such an herb, and such and such a tree, which you will find to grow there plentifully—three handfuls of each. And be speedy. We must be home again before the steamer comes; it would seem strange if we had disappeared." And he sat on the sand and panted.

Keola went up the beach, which was of shining sand and coral, strewn with singular shells; and he thought in his heart:

"How do I not know this beach? I will come here again and gather shells."

In front of him was a line of palms against the sky; not like the palms of the Eight Islands, but tall and fresh and beautiful and hanging out withered fans like gold among the green, and he thought in his heart:

"It is strange I should not have found this grove. I will come here again, when it is warm, to sleep." And he thought, "How warm it has grown suddenly!" For it was winter in Hawaii, and the day had been chill. And he thought also, "Where are the grey mountains? And where is the high cliff with the hanging forest and the wheeling birds?" And the more he considered, the less he might conceive in what quarter of the islands he was fallen.

In the border of the grove, where it met the beach, the herb was growing, but the tree farther back. Now, as Keola went towards the tree, he was aware of a young woman who had nothing on her body but a belt of leaves.

"Well!" thought Keola, "they are not very particular about their dress in this part of the country." And he paused, supposing she would observe him and escape; and seeing that she still looked before her, stood and hummed aloud. Up she leaped at the sound. Her face was ashen; she looked this way and that, and her mouth gaped with the terror of her soul. But it was a strange thing that her eyes did not rest upon Keola.

" Good-day," said he. " You need not be so frightened, I will not eat you." And he had scarce opened his mouth before the young woman fled into the bush.

" These are strange manners," thought Keola, and, not thinking what he did, ran after her.

As she ran, the girl kept crying in some speech that was not practised in Hawaii, yet some of the words were the same, and he knew she kept calling and warning others. And presently he saw more people running—men, women, and children, one with another, all running and crying like people at a fire. And with that he began to grow afraid himself, and returned to Kalamake bringing the leaves. Him he told what he had seen.

" You must pay no heed," said Kalamake. " All this is like a dream and shadows. All will disappear and be forgotten."

" It seemed none saw me," said Keola.

" And none did," replied the sorcerer. " We walk here in the broad sun invisible by reason of these charms. Yet they hear us; and therefore it is well to speak softly, as I do."

With that he made a circle round the mat with stones, and in the midst he set the leaves.

" It will be your part," said he, " to keep the leaves alight, and feed the fire slowly. While they blaze (which is but for a little moment) I must do my errand; and before the ashes blacken, the same power that brought us carries us away. Be ready now with the match; and do you call me in good time lest the flames burn out and I be left."

As soon as the leaves caught, the sorcerer leaped like a deer out of the circle, and began to race along the beach like a hound that has been bathing. As he ran, he kept stooping to snatch shells; and it seemed to Keola that they glittered as he took them. The leaves blazed with a clear flame that consumed them swiftly ; and presently Keola had but a handful left, and ᴜne sorcerer was far off, running and stopping.

"Back ! " cried Keola. "Back ! The leaves are near done."

At that Kalamake turned, and if he had run before, now he flew. But fast as he ran, the leaves burned faster. The flame was ready to expire when, with a great leap, he bounded on the mat. The wind of his leaping blew it out ; and with that the beach was gone, and the sun and the sea ; and they stood once more in the dimness of the shuttered parlour, and were once more shaken and blinded ; and on the mat betwixt them lay a pile of shining dollars. Keola ran to the shutters ; and there was the steamer tossing in the swell close in.

The same night Kalamake took his son-in-law apart, and gave him five dollars in his hand.

"Keola," said he ; "if you are a wise man (which I am doubtful of) you will think you slept this afternoon on the verandah, and dreamed as you were sleeping. I am a man of few words, and I have for my helpers people of short memories."

Never a word more said Kalamake, nor referred again to that affair. But it ran all the while in Keola's head—if he were lazy before, he would now do nothing.

"Why should I work," thought he, "when I have a father-in-law who makes dollars of sea-shells ? "

Presently his share was spent. He spent it all upon fine clothes. And then he was sorry :

"For," thought he, "I had done better to have bought a concertina, with which I might have entertained myself all day long." And then he began to grow vexed with Kalamake

"This man has the soul of a dog," thought he. "He can gather dollars when he pleases on the beach, and he leaves me to pine for a concertina ! Let him beware : I am no child, I am as cunning as he, and hold his secret." With that he spoke to his wife Lehua, and complained of her father's manners.

" I would let my father be," said Lehua. " He is a dangerous man to cross."

" I care that for him ! " cried Keola ; and snapped his fingers. " I have him by the nose. I can make him do what I please." And he told Lehua the story.

But she shook her head.

" You may do what you like," said she ; " but as sure as you thwart my father, you will be no more heard of. Think of this person, and that person ; think of Hua, who was a noble of the House of Representatives, and went to Honolulu every year ; and not a bone or a hair of him was found. Remember Kamau, and how he wasted to a thread, so that his wife lifted him with one hand. Keola, you are a baby in my father's hands ; he will take you with his thumb and finger and eat you like a shrimp."

Now Keola was truly afraid of Kalamake, but he was vain too ; and these words of his wife's incensed him.

" Very well," said he, " if that is what you think of me, I will show how much you are deceived." And he went straight to where his father-in-law was sitting in the parlour.

" Kalamake," said he, " I want a concertina."

" Do you, indeed ? " said Kalamake.

" Yes," said he, " and I may as well tell you plainly, I mean to have it. A man who picks up dollars on the beach can certainly afford a concertina."

" I had no idea you had so much spirit," replied the sorcerer. " I thought you were a timid, useless lad, and I cannot describe how much pleased I am to find I was mistaken. Now I begin to think I may have found an assistant and successor in my difficult business. A concertina ? You shall have the best in Honolulu. And to-night, as soon as it is dark, you and I will go and find the money."

" Shall we return to the beach ? " asked Keola.

" No, no ! " replied Kalamake ; " you must begin to learn more of my secrets. Last time I taught you to pick shells ; this time I shall teach you to catch fish. Are you strong enough to launch Pili's boat ? "

" I think I am," returned Keola. " But why should we not take your own, which is afloat already ? "

" I have a reason which you will understand thoroughly before to-morrow," said Kalamake. " Pili's boat is the better suited for my purpose. So, if you please, let us meet there as soon as it is dark ; and in the meanwhile, let us keep our own counsel, for there is no cause to let the family into our business."

Honey is not more sweet than was the voice of Kalamake, and Keola could scarce contain his satisfaction.

" I might have had my concertina weeks ago," thought he, " and there is nothing needed in this world but a little courage."

Presently after he spied Lehua weeping, and was half in a mind to tell her all was well.

" But no," thinks he ; " I shall wait till I can show her the concertina ; we shall see what the chit will do then. Perhaps she will understand in the future that her husband is a man of some intelligence."

As soon as it was dark father and son-in-law launched Pili's boat and set the sail. There was a great sea, and it blew strong from the leeward ; but the boat was swift and light and dry, and skimmed the waves. The wizard had a lantern, which he lit and held with his finger through the ring; and the two sat in the stern and smoked cigars, of which Kalamake had always a provision, and spoke like friends of magic and the great sums of money which they could make by its exercise, and what they should buy first, and what second ; and Kalamake talked like a father.

Presently he looked all about, and above him at the stars, and back at the island, which was already three parts sunk under the sea, and he seemed to consider ripely his position.

" Look ! " says he, " there is Molokai already far behind us, and Maui like a cloud ; and by the bearing of these three stars I know I am come to where I desire. This part of the sea is called the Sea of the Dead. It is in this place extraordinarily deep, and the floor is all covered with the bones of men, and in the holes of this part gods and goblins keep their habitation. The flow of the sea is to the north, stronger than a shark can swim, and any man who shall here be thrown out of a ship it bears away like a wild horse into the uttermost ocean. Presently he is spent and goes down, and his bones are scattered with the rest, and the gods devour his spirit."

Fear came on Keola at the words, and he looked, and by the light of the stars and the lantern, the warlock seemed to change.

" What ails you ? " cried Keola, quick and sharp.

" It is not I who am ailing," said the wizard ; " but there is one here very sick."

With that he changed his grasp upon the lantern, and, behold—as he drew his finger from the ring, the finger stuck and the ring was burst, and his hand was grown to be the bigness of three.

At that sight Keola screamed and covered his face.

But Kalamake held up the lantern. " Look rather at my face ! " said he—and his head was huge as a barrel ; and still he grew and grew as a cloud grows on a mountain, and Keola sat before him screaming, and the boat raced on the great seas.

" And now," said the wizard, " what do you think about that concertina ? and are you sure you would not rather have a flute ? No ? " says he ; " that is well, for I do not like my family to be changeable of purpose. But I begin to think I had better get out of this paltry boat, for my bulk swells to a very unusual degree, and if we are not the more careful, she will presently be swamped."

With that he threw his legs over the side. Even as he did so, the greatness of the man grew thirty-fold and forty-fold as swift as sight or thinking, so that he stood in the deep seas to the armpits, and his head and shoulders rose like a high isle, and the swell beat and burst upon his bosom, as it beats and breaks against a cliff. The boat ran still to the north, but he reached out his hand, and took the gun-wale by the finger and thumb, and broke the side like a biscuit, and Keola was spilled into the sea. And the pieces of the boat the sorcerer crushed in the hollow of his hand and flung miles away into the night.

"Excuse me taking the lantern," said he; "for I have a long wade before me, and the land is far, and the bottom of the sea uneven, and I feel the bones under my toes."

And he turned and went off walking with great strides; and as often as Keola sank in the trough he could see him no longer; but as often as he was heaved upon the crest, there he was striding and dwindling, and he held the lamp high over his head, and the waves broke white about him as he went.

Since first the islands were fished out of the sea, there was never a man so terrified as this Keola. He swam indeed, but he swam as puppies swim when they are cast in to drown, and knew not wherefore. He could but think of the hugeness of the swelling of the warlock, of that face which was great as a mountain, of those shoulders that were broad as an isle, and of the seas that beat on them in vain. He thought, too, of the concertina, and shame took hold upon him; and of the dead men's bones, and fear shook him.

Of a sudden he was aware of something dark against the stars that tossed, and a light below, and a brightness of the cloven sea; and he heard speech of men. He cried out aloud and a voice answered; and in a twinkling the bows of a ship hung above him on a wave like a thing balanced, and swooped down. He caught with his two hands in the chains of her, and the next moment was buried in the rushing seas, and the next hauled on board by seamen.

They gave him gin and biscuit and dry clothes, and asked him how he came where they found him, and whether the light which they had seen was the lighthouse, Lae o Ka Laau. But Keola knew white men are like children and only believe their own stories; so about himself he told them what he pleased, and as for the light (which was Kalamake's lantern) he vowed he had seen none.

This ship was a schooner bound for Honolulu, and then to trade in the low islands; and by a very good chance for Keola she had lost a man off the bowsprit in a squall. It was no use talking. Keola durst not stay in the Eight Islands. Word goes so quickly, and all men are so fond to talk and carry news, that if he hid in the north end of Kauai or in the south end of Kaü, the wizard would have wind of it before a month, and he must perish. So he did what seemed the most prudent, and shipped sailor in the place of the man who had been drowned.

In some ways the ship was a good place. The food was extraordinarily rich and plenty, with biscuits and salt beef every day, and pea-soup and puddings made of flour and suet twice a week, so that Keola grew fat. The captain also was a good man, and the crew no worse than other whites. The trouble was the mate, who was the most difficult man to please Keola had ever met with, and beat and cursed him daily, both for what he did and what he did not. The blows that he dealt were very sure, for he was strong ; and the words he used were very unpalatable, for Keola was come of a good family and accustomed to respect. And what was the worst of all, whenever Keola found a chance to sleep, there was the mate awake and stirring him up with a rope's end. Keola saw it would never do ; and he made up his mind to run away.

They were about a month out from Honolulu when they made the land. It was a fine starry night, the sea was smooth as well as the sky fair ; it blew a steady trade ; and there was the island on their weather bow, a ribbon of palm-trees lying flat along the sea. The captain and the mate looked at it with the night glass, and named the name of it, and talked of it, beside the wheel where Keola was steering. It seemed it was an isle where no traders came. By the captain's way, it was an isle besides where no man dwelt ; but the mate thought otherwise.

"I don't give a cent for the directory," said he. "I've been past here one night in the schooner *Eugenie* : it was just such a night as this ; they were fishing with torches, and the beach was thick with lights like a town."

"Well, well," says the captain, "it's steep-to, that's the great point ; and there ain't any outlying dangers by the chart, so we'll just hug the lee side of it. Keep her ramping full, don't I tell you ! " he cried to Keola, who was listening so hard that he forgot to steer.

And the mate cursed him, and swore that Kanaka was for no use in the world, and if he got started after him with a belaying-pin, it would be a cold day for Keola.

And so the captain and mate lay down on the house together, and Keola was left to himself.

"This island will do very well for me," he thought ; "if no traders deal there, the mate will never come. And as for Kalamake, it is not possible he can ever get as far as this."

With that he kept edging the schooner nearer in. He had to do this quietly, for it was the trouble with these white men, and above all with the mate, that you could never be sure of them ; they would all be sleeping sound, or else pretending, and if a sail shook, they would jump to their feet and fall on you with a rope's end. So Keola edged her up little by little, and kept all drawing. And presently the land was close on board, and the sound of the sea on the sides of it grew loud.

With that, the mate sat up suddenly upon the house.

"What are you doing ? " he roars. "You'll have the ship ashore ! "

And he made one bound for Keola, and Keola made another clean over the rail and plump into the starry sea. When he came up again, the schooner had payed off on her true course, and the mate stood by the wheel himself, and Keola heard him cursing. The sea was smooth under the lee of the island ; it was warm besides, and Keola had his sailor's knife, so he had no fear of sharks. A little way before him the trees stopped ; there was a break in the line of the land like the mouth of a harbour ; and the tide, which was then flowing, took him up and carried him through. One minute he was without, and the next within, had floated there in a wide shallow water, bright with ten thousand stars, and all about him was the ring of the land with its string of palm-trees. And he was amazed, because this was a kind of island he had never heard of.

The time of Keola in that place was in two periods—the period when he was alone, and the period when he was there with the tribe. At first he sought everywhere and found no man ; only some houses standing in a hamlet, and the marks of fires. But the ashes of the fires were cold and the rains had washed them away ; and the winds had blown, and some of the huts were overthrown. It was here he took his dwelling ; and he made a fire drill, and a shell hook, and fished and cooked his fish, and climbed after green cocoa-nuts, the juice of which he drank, for in all the isle there was no water. The days were long to him, and the nights terrifying. He made a lamp of cocoa-shell, and drew the oil off the ripe nuts, and made a wick of fibre ; and when evening came he closed up his hut, and lit his lamp, and lay and trembled till morning. Many a time he thought in his heart he would have been better in the bottom of the sea, his bones rolling there with the others.

All this while he kept by the inside of the island, for the huts were on the shore of the lagoon, and it was there the palms grew best, and the lagoon itself abounded with good fish. And to the outer side he went once only, and he looked but once at the beach of the ocean, and came away shaking. For the look of it, with its bright sand, and strewn shells, and strong sun and surf, went sore against his inclination.

"It cannot be," he thought, "and yet it is very like. And how do I know ? These white men, although they pretend to know where they are sailing, must take their chance like other people. So that after all we may have sailed in a circle, and I may be quite near to Molokai, and this may be the very beach where my father-in-law gathers his dollars."

So after that he was prudent, and kept to the land side.

It was perhaps a month later, when the people of the place arrived—the fill of six great boats. They were a fine race of men, and spoke a tongue that sounded very different from the tongue of Hawaii, but so many of the words were the same that it was not difficult to understand. The men besides were very courteous, and the women very towardly ; and they made Keola welcome, and built him a house, and gave him a wife ; and what surprised him the most, he was never sent to work with the young men.

And now Keola had three periods. First he had a period of being very sad, and then he had a period when he was pretty merry. Last of all, came the third, when he was the most terrified man in the four oceans.

The cause of the first period was the girl he had to wife. He was in doubt about the island, and he might have been in doubt about the speech, of which he had heard so little when he came there with the wizard on the mat. But about his wife there was no mistake conceivable, for she was the same girl that ran from him crying in the wood. So he had sailed all this way, and might as well have stayed in Molokai ; and had left home and wife and all his friends for no other cause but to escape his enemy, and the place he had come to was that wizard's hunting ground, and the place where he walked invisible. It was at this period when he kept the most close to the lagoon side, and as far as he dared, abode in the cover of his hut.

The cause of the second period was talk he had heard from his wife and the chief islanders. Keola himself said little. He was never so sure of his new friends, for he judged they were too civil to be wholesome, and since he had grown better acquainted with his father-in-law the man had grown more cautious. So he told them nothing of himself, but only his name and descent, and that he came from the Eight Islands, and what fine islands they were ; and about the king's palace in Honolulu, and how he was a chief friend of the king and the missionaries. But he put many questions and learned much. The island where he was was called the Isle of Voices ; it belonged to the tribe, but they made their home upon another, three hours' sail to the southward. There they lived and had their permanent houses, and it was a rich island, where were eggs and chickens and pigs, and ships came trading with rum and tobacco. It was there the schooner had gone after Keola deserted ; there, too, the mate had died, like the fool of a white man as he was. It seems, when the ship came, it was the beginning of the sickly season in that isle, when the fish of the lagoon are poisonous, and all who eat of them swell up and die. The mate was told of it ; he saw the boats preparing, because

in that season the people leave that island and sail to the
Isle of Voices ; but he was a fool of a white man, who would
believe no stories but his own, and he caught one of these
fish, cooked it and ate it, and swelled up and died, which
was good news to Keola. As for the Isle of Voices, it lay
solitary the most part of the year, only now and then a
boat's crew came for copra, and in the bad season, when
the fish at the main isle were poisonous, the tribe dwelt there
in a body. It had its name from a marvel, for it seemed the
sea-side of it was all beset with invisible devils ; day and
night you heard them talking with one another in strange
tongues ; day and night little fires blazed up and were
extinguished on the beach ; and what was the cause of
these doings no man might conceive. Keola asked them
if it were the same in their own island where they stayed,
and they told him no, not there ; nor yet in any other of
some hundred isles that lay all about them in that sea ;
but it was a thing peculiar to the Isle of Voices. They
told him also that these fires and voices were ever on the
sea-side and in the seaward fringes of the wood, and a
man might dwell by the lagoon two thousand years (if he
could live so long) and never be any way troubled ; and
even on the sea-side the devils did no harm if let alone.
Only once a chief had cast a spear at one of the voices,
and the same night he fell out of a cocoa-nut palm and was
killed.

Keola thought a good bit with himself. He saw he
would be all right when the tribe returned to the main
island, and right enough where he was, if he kept by the
lagoon, yet he had a mind to make things righter if he could.
So he told the high chief he had once been in an isle
that was pestered the same way, and the folk had found a
means to cure that trouble.

" There was a tree growing in the bush there," says he,
" and it seems these devils came to get the leaves of it.
So the people of the isle cut down the tree wherever it
was found, and the devils came no more."

They asked what kind of a tree this was, and he showed
them the tree of which Kalamake burned the leaves.

They found it hard to believe, yet the idea tickled them. Night after night the old men debated it in their councils, but the high chief (though he was a brave man) was afraid of the matter, and reminded them daily of the chief who cast a spear against the voices and was killed, and the thought of that brought all to a stand again.

Though he could not yet bring about the destruction of the trees, Keola was well enough pleased, and began to look about him and take pleasure in his days ; and, among other things, he was the kinder to his wife, so that the girl began to love him greatly. One day he came to the hut, and she lay on the ground lamenting.

"Why," said Keola, "what is wrong with you now ? "

She declared it was nothing.

The same night she woke him. The lamp burned very low, but he saw by her face she was in sorrow.

"Keola," she said, "put your ear to my mouth that I may whisper, for no one must hear us. Two days before the boats begin to be got ready, go you to the sea-side of the isle and lie in a thicket. We shall choose that place beforehand, you and I ; and hide food ; and every night I shall come near by there singing. So when a night comes and you do not hear me, you shall know we are clean gone out of the island, and you may come forth again in safety."

The soul of Keola died within him.

"What is this ? " he cried. "I cannot live among devils. I will not be left behind upon this isle. I am dying to leave it."

"You will never leave it alive, my poor Keola," said the girl ; "for to tell you the truth, my people are eaters of men ; but this they keep secret. And the reason they will kill you before we leave is because in our island ships come, and Donat-Kimaran comes and talks for the French, and there is a white trader there in a house with a verandah, and a catechist. Oh, that is a fine place indeed ! The trader has barrels filled with flour ; and a French warship once came in the lagoon and gave everybody wine and biscuit. Ah, my poor Keola, I wish I could take you there,

for great is my love to you, and it is the finest place in the
seas except Papeete."

So now Keola was the most terrified man in the four
oceans. He had heard tell of eaters of men in the south
islands, and the thing had always been a fear to him;
and here it was knocking at his door. He had heard
besides, by travellers, of their practices, and how when
they are in a mind to eat a man, they cherish and fondle
him like a mother with a favourite baby. And he saw
this must be his own case; and that was why he had been
housed, and fed, and wived, and liberated from all work;
and why the old men and the chiefs discoursed with him
like a person of weight. So he lay on his bed and railed
upon his destiny; and the flesh curdled on his bones.

The next day the people of the tribe were very civil, as
their way was. They were elegant speakers, and they
made beautiful poetry, and jested at meals, so that a missionary must have died laughing. It was little enough
Keola cared for their fine ways; all he saw was the white
teeth shining in their mouths, and his gorge rose at the
sight; and when they were done eating, he went and lay
in the bush like a dead man.

The next day it was the same, and then his wife followed
him.

" Keola," she said, " if you do not eat, I tell you plainly
you will be killed and cooked to-morrow. Some of the
old chiefs are murmuring already. They think you are
fallen sick and must lose flesh."

With that Keola got to his feet, and anger burned in
him.

" It is little I care one way or the other," said he. " I
am between the devil and the deep sea. Since die I must,
let me die the quickest way; and since I must be eaten
at the best of it, let me rather be eaten by hobgoblins than
by men. Farewell," said he, and he left her standing, and
walked to the sea-side of that island.

It was all bare in the strong sun; there was no sign of
man, only the beach was trodden, and all about him as he
went, the voices talked and whispered, and the little fires

K

sprang up and burned down. All tongues of the earth were spoken there : the French, the Dutch, the Russian, the Tamil, the Chinese. Whatever land knew sorcery, there were some of its people whispering in Keola's ear. That beach was thick as a cried fair, yet no man seen ; and as he walked he saw the shells vanish before him, and no man to pick them up. I think the devil would have been afraid to be alone in such a company ; but Keola was past fear and courted death. When the fires sprang up, he charged for them like a bull. Bodiless voices called to and fro ; unseen hands poured sand upon the flames ; and they were gone from the beach before he reached them.

" It is plain Kalamake is not here," he thought, " as I must have been killed long since."

With that he sat him down in the margin of the wood, for he was tired, and put his chin upon his hands. The business before his eyes continued ; the beach babbled with voices, and the fires sprang up and sank, and the shells vanished and were renewed again even while he looked.

" It was a by-day when I was here before," he thought, " for it was nothing to this."

And his head was dizzy with the thought of these millions and millions of dollars, and all these hundreds and hundreds of persons culling them upon the beach, and flying in the air higher and swifter than eagles.

" And to think how they have fooled me with their talk of mints," says he, " and that money was made there, when it is clear that all the new coin in all the world is gathered on these sands ! But I will know better the next time ! " said he.

And at last, he knew not very well how or when, sleep fell on Keola, and he forgot the island and all his sorrows.

Early the next day, before the sun was yet up, a bustle woke him. He awoke in fear, for he thought the tribe had caught him napping ; but it was no such matter. Only, on the beach in front of him, the bodiless voices called and shouted one upon another, and it seemed they all passed and swept beside him up the coast of the island.

" What is afoot now ? " thinks Keola. And it was plain to him it was something beyond ordinary, for the fires were not lighted nor the shells taken, but the bodiless voices kept posting up the beach, and hailing and dying away ; and others following, and by the sound of them these wizards should be angry.

" It is not me they are angry at," thought Keola, " for they pass me close."

As when hounds go by, or horses in a race, or city folk coursing to a fire, and all men join and follow after, so it was now with Keola ; and he knew not what he did, nor why he did it, but there, lo and behold ! he was running with the voices.

So he turned one point of the island, and this brought him in view of a second ; and there he remembered the wizard trees to have been growing by the score together in a wood. From this point there went up a hubbub of men crying not to be described ; and by the sound of them, those that he ran with shaped their course for the same quarter. A little nearer, and there began to mingle with the outcry the crash of many axes. And at this a thought came at last into his mind that the high chief had consented ; that the men of the tribe had set to cutting down these trees ; that word had gone about the isle from sorcerer to sorcerer, and these were all now assembling to defend their trees. Desire of strange things swept him on. He posted with the voices, crossed the beach, and came into the borders of the wood, and stood astonished. One tree had fallen, others were part hewed away. There was the tribe clustered. They were back to back, and bodies lay, and blood flowed among their feet. The hue of fear was on all their faces ; their voices went up to heaven shrill as a weasel's cry.

Have you seen a child when he is all alone and has a wooden sword, and fights, leaping and hewing with the empty air ? Even so the man-eaters huddled back to back and heaved up their axes and laid on, and screamed as they laid on, and behold ! no man to contend with them ! only here and there Keola saw an axe swinging over against them without hands ; and time and again a man of the tribe would fall before it, clove in twain or burst asunder, and his soul sped howling.

For a while Keola looked upon this prodigy like one that dreams, and then fear took him by the midst as sharp as death, that he should behold such doings. Even in that same flash the high chief of the clan espied him standing, and pointed and called out his name. Thereat the whole tribe saw him also, and their eyes flashed, and their teeth clashed.

"I am too long here," thought Keola, and ran farther out of the wood and down the beach, not caring whither.

"Keola!" said a voice close by upon the empty sand.

"Lehua! is that you!" he cried, and gasped, and looked in vain for her; but by the eyesight he was stark alone.

"I saw you pass before," the voice answered; "but you would not hear me. Quick! get the leaves and the herbs, and let us flee."

"You are there with the mat?" he asked.

"Here, at your side," said she. And he felt her arms about him. "Quick! the leaves and the herbs, before my father can get back!"

So Keola ran for his life, and fetched the wizard fuel; and Lehua guided him back, and set his feet upon the mat, and made the fire. All the time of its burning, the sound of the battle towered out of the wood; the wizards and the man-eaters hard at fight; the wizards, the viewless ones, roaring out aloud like bulls upon a mountain, and the men of the tribe replying shrill and savage out of the terror of their souls. And all the time of the burning, Keola stood there and listened, and shook, and watched how the unseen hands of Lehua poured the leaves. She poured them fast, and the flame burned high, and scorched Keola's hands; and she speeded and blew the burning with her breath. The last leaf was eaten, the flame fell, and the shock followed, and there were Keola and Lehua in the room at home.

Now, when Keola could see his wife at last he was mighty pleased, and he was mighty pleased to be home again in Molokai and sit down beside a bowl of poi — for they made no poi on board ships, and there was none in the Isle of Voices—and he was out of the body with pleasure to be clean escaped out of the hands of the eaters of men. But there was another matter not so clear, and Lehua and Keola talked of it all night and were troubled. There was Kalamake left upon the isle. If, by the blessing of God, he could but stick there, all were well; but should he escape and return to Molokai, it would be an ill day for his daughter and her husband. They spoke of his gift of swelling and whether he could wade that distance in the seas. But Keola knew by this time where that island was —and that is to say, in the Low or Dangerous Archipelago. So they fetched the atlas and looked upon the distance in the map, and by what they could make of it, it seemed a far way for an old gentleman to walk. Still, it would not do to make too sure of a warlock like Kalamake, and they determined at last to take counsel of a white missionary.

So the first one that came by Keola told him everything. And the missionary was very sharp on him for taking the second wife in the low island; but for all the rest, he vowed he could make neither head nor tail of it.

"However," says he, "if you think this money of your father's ill-gotten, my advice to you would be to give some of it to the lepers and some to the missionary fund. And as for this extraordinary rigmarole, you cannot do better than keep it to yourselves."

But he warned the police at Honolulu that, by all he could make out, Kalamake and Keola had been coining false money, and it would not be amiss to watch them.

Keola and Lehua took his advice, and gave many dollars to the lepers and the fund. And no doubt the advice must have been good, for from that day to this, Kalamake has never more been heard of. But whether he was slain in the battle by the trees, or whether he is still kicking his heels upon the Isle of Voices, who shall say?

THE MISADVENTURES OF
JOHN NICHOLSON

The Misadventures of John Nicholson, A Christmas Story, was originally published in *Yule-Tide*, Cassell's Christmas Annual for 1887.

THE MISADVENTURES OF
JOHN NICHOLSON

CHAPTER I

IN WHICH JOHN SOWS THE WIND

JOHN VAREY NICHOLSON was stupid; yet, stupider men than he are now sprawling in Parliament, and lauding themselves as the authors of their own distinction. He was of a fat habit, even from boyhood, and inclined to a cheerful and cursory reading of the face of life; and possibly this attitude of mind was the original cause of his misfortunes. Beyond this hint philosophy is silent on his career, and superstition steps in with the more ready explanation that he was detested of the gods.

His father—that iron gentleman—had long ago enthroned himself on the heights of the Disruption Principles. What these are (and in spite of their grim name they are quite innocent) no array of terms would render thinkable to the merely English intelligence; but to the Scot they often prove unctuously nourishing, and Mr. Nicholson found in them the milk of lions. About the period when the Churches convene at Edinburgh in their annual assemblies, he was to be seen descending the Mound in the company of divers red-headed clergymen: these voluble, he only contributing oracular nods, brief negatives, and the austere spectacle of his stretched upper lip. The names of Candlish and Begg were frequent in these interviews, and occasionally the talk ran on the Residuary Establishment and the doings of one Lee. A stranger to the tight little theological kingdom of Scotland might have listened and gathered literally nothing. And Mr. Nicholson (who was not a dull man) knew this, and raged at it. He knew there was a vast world outside, to whom Disruption Principles were as the chatter of tree-top apes ; the paper brought him chill whiffs from it ; he had met Englishmen who had asked lightly if he did not belong to the Church of Scotland, and then had failed to be much interested by his elucidation of that nice point ; it was an evil, wild, rebellious world, lying sunk in *dozenedness*, for nothing short of a Scot's word will paint this Scotsman's feelings. And when he entered his own house in Randolph Crescent (south side), and shut the door behind him, his heart swelled with security. Here, at least, was a citadel unassailable by right-hand defections or left-hand extremes. Here was a family where prayers came at the same hour, where the Sabbath literature was unimpeachably selected, where the guest who should have leaned to any false opinion was instantly set down, and over which there reigned all week, and grew denser on Sundays, a silence that was agreeable to his ear, and gloom that he found comfortable.

Mrs. Nicholson had died about thirty, and left him with three children : a daughter two years and a son about eight years younger than John ; and John himself, the unfortunate protagonist of the present history. The daughter, Maria, was a good girl—dutiful, pious, dull, but so easily startled that to speak to her was quite a perilous enterprise. " I don't think I care to talk about that, if you please," she would say, and strike the boldest speechless by her unmistakable pain ; this upon all topics — dress, pleasure, morality, politics, in which the formula was changed to " my papa thinks otherwise," and even religion, unless it was approached with a particular whining tone of voice. Alexander, the younger brother, was sickly, clever, fond of books and drawing, and full of satirical remarks. In the midst of these, imagine that natural, clumsy, unintelligent, and mirthful animal, John ; mighty well-behaved in comparison with other lads, although not up to the mark of the house in Randolph Crescent ; full of a sort of blundering affection, full of caresses which were never very warmly received ; full of sudden and loud laughter which rang out in that still house like curses. Mr. Nicholson himself had a great fund of humour, of the Scots order—intellectual, turning on the observation of men ; his own character, for instance—if he could have seen it in another—would have been a rare feast to him ; but his son's empty guffaws over a broken plate, and empty, almost light-hearted remarks, struck him with pain as the indices of a weak mind.

Outside the family John had early attached himself (much as a dog may follow a marquess) to the steps of Alan Houston, a lad about a year older than himself, idle, a trifle wild, the heir to a good estate which was still in the hands of a rigorous trustee, and so royally content with himself that he took John's devotion as a thing of course. The intimacy was gall to Mr. Nicholson ; it took his son from the house, and he was a jealous parent ; it kept him from the office, and he was a martinet ; lastly, Mr. Nicholson was ambitious for his family (in which, and the Disruption Principles, he entirely lived), that he hated to see a son of his play second fiddle to an idler. After some hesitation, he ordered that the friendship should cease—an unfair command, though seemingly inspired by the spirit of prophecy ; and John, saying nothing, continued to disobey the order under the rose.

John was nearly nineteen when he was one day dismissed rather earlier than usual from his father's office, where he was studying the practice of the law. It was Saturday ; and except that he had a matter of four hundred pounds in his pocket which it was his duty to hand over to the British Linen Company's Bank, he had the whole after-noon at his disposal. He went by Princes Street, enjoying the mild sunshine, and the little thrill of easterly wind that tossed the flags along that terrace of palaces, and tumbled the green trees in the garden. The band was playing down in the valley under the castle ; and when it came to the turn of the pipers, he heard their wild sounds with a stirring of the blood. Something distantly martial awoke in him ; and he thought of Miss Mackenzie, whom he was to meet that day at dinner in his father's house.

Now, it is undeniable that he should have gone directly to the bank, but right in the way stood the billiard-room of the hotel where Alan was almost certain to be found ; and the temptation proved too strong. He entered the billiard-room, and was instantly greeted by his friend, cue in hand.

"Nicholson," said he, "I want you to lend me a pound or two till Monday."

"You've come to the right shop, haven't you ? " returned John. "I have twopence."

"Nonsense," said Alan. "You can get some. Go and borrow at your tailor's ; they all do it. Or I'll tell you what : pop your watch."

"Oh, yes, I daresay," said John. "And how about my father ? "

"How is he to know ? He doesn't wind it up for you at night, does he ? " inquired Alan, at which John guffawed. "No, seriously ; I am in a fix," continued the tempter. "I have lost some money to a man here. I'll give it you to-night, and you can get the heirloom out again on Monday. Come ; it's a small service, after all. I would do a good deal more for you."

Whereupon John went forth, and pawned his gold watch under the assumed name of John Froggs, 85 Pleasance. But the nervousness that assailed him at the door of that inglorious haunt—a pawnshop—and the effort necessary to invent the pseudonym (which somehow seemed to him a necessary part of the procedure), had taken more time than he imagined ; and when he returned to the billiard-room with the spoils, the bank had already closed its doors.

This was a shrewd knock. "A piece of business had been neglected." He heard these words in his father's trenchant voice, and trembled, and then dodged the thought. After all, who was to know ? He must carry four hundred pounds about with him till Monday, when the neglect could be surreptitiously repaired ; and meanwhile, he was free to pass the afternoon on the encircling divan of the billiard-room, smoking his pipe, sipping a pint of ale, and enjoying to the mast-head the modest pleasures of admiration.

None can admire like a young man. Of all youth's passions and pleasures, this is the most common and least alloyed ; and every flash of Alan's black eyes ; every aspect of his curly head ; every graceful reach, and easy, stand-off attitude of waiting, everything about him down even to his shirt-sleeves and wrist-links, were seen by John through a luxurious glory. He valued himself by the possession of that royal friend, hugged himself upon the thought, and swam in warm azure ; his own defects, like vanquished difficulties, becoming things on which to plume himself. Only when he thought of Miss Mackenzie there fell upon his mind a shadow of regret ; that young lady was worthy of better things than plain John Nicholson, still known among schoolmates by the derisive name of " Fatty " ; and he felt that if he could chalk a cue or stand at ease, with such a careless grace as Alan, he could approach the object of his sentiments with a less crushing sense of inferiority.

Before they parted, Alan made a proposal that was startling in the extreme. He would be at Collette's that night about twelve, he said. Why should not John come there and get the money ? To go to Collette's was to see life, indeed ; it was wrong ; it was against the laws ; it partook, in a very dingy manner, of adventure. Were it known, it was the sort of exploit that disconsidered a young man for good with the more serious classes, but gave him a standing with the riotous. And yet Collette's was not a hell ; it could not come, without vaulting hyperbole, under the rubric of a gilded saloon ; and, if it was a sin to go there, the sin was merely local and municipal. Collette's (whose name I do not know how to spell, for I was never in epistolary communication with that hospitable outlaw) was simply an unlicensed publican, who gave suppers after eleven at night, the Edinburgh hour of closing. If you belonged to a club, you could get a much better supper at the same hour, and lose not a jot in public esteem.

But if you lacked that qualification, and were an-hungered, or inclined towards conviviality at unlawful hours, Collette's was your only port. You were very ill-supplied. The company was not recruited from the Senate or the Church, though the Bar was very well represented on the only occasion on which I flew in the face of my country's laws, and, taking my reputation in my hand, penetrated into that grim supper-house. And Collette's frequenters, thrillingly conscious of wrong-doing and " that two-handed engine (the policeman) at the door," were perhaps inclined to somewhat feverish excess. But the place was in no sense a very bad one ; and it is somewhat strange to me, at this distance of time, how it had acquired its dangerous repute.

In precisely the same spirit as a man may debate a project to ascend the Matterhorn or to cross Africa, John considered Alan's proposal, and, greatly daring, accepted it. As he walked home, the thoughts of this excursion out of the safe places of life into the wild and arduous, stirred and struggled in his imagination with the image of Flora Mackenzie— incongruous and yet kindred thoughts, for did not each imply unusual tightening of the pegs of resolution ? did not each woo him forth and warn him back again into himself ?

Between these two considerations, at least, he was more than usually moved ; and when he got to Randolph Crescent, he quite forgot the four hundred pounds in the inner pocket of his greatcoat, hung up the coat, with its rich freight, upon his particular pin of the hat-stand ; and in the very action sealed his doom.

CHAPTER II

IN WHICH JOHN REAPS THE WHIRLWIND

ABOUT half-past ten it was John's brave good fortune to offer his arm to Miss Mackenzie, and escort her home. The night was chill and starry; all the way eastward the trees of the different gardens rustled and looked black. Up the stone gully of Leith Walk, when they came to cross it, the breeze made a rush and set the flames of the street-lamps quavering; and when at last they had mounted to the Royal Terrace, where Captain Mackenzie lived, a great salt freshness came in their faces from the sea. These phases of the walk remained written on John's memory, each emphasised by the touch of that light hand on his arm; and behind all these aspects of the nocturnal city he saw, in his mind's eye, a picture of the lighted drawing-room at home where he had sat talking with Flora; and his father, from the other end, had looked on with a kind and ironical smile. John had read the significance of that smile, which might have escaped a stranger. Mr. Nicholson had remarked his son's entanglement with satisfaction, tinged by humour; and his smile, if it still was a thought contemptuous, had implied consent.

At the captain's door the girl held out her hand, with a certain emphasis; and John took it and kept it a little longer, and said, "Good-night, Flora, dear," and was instantly thrown into much fear by his presumption. But she only laughed, ran up the steps, and rang the bell; and while she was waiting for the door to open, kept close in the porch, and talked to him from that point as out of a fortification. She had a knitted shawl over her head; her blue Highland eyes took the light from the neighbouring

street-lamp and sparkled ; and when the door opened and
closed upon her, John felt cruelly alone.

He proceeded slowly back along the terrace in a tender
glow ; and when he came to Greenside Church, he halted
in a doubtful mind. Over the crown of the Calton Hill,
to his left, lay the way to Collette's, where Alan would soon
be looking for his arrival, and where he would now have
no more consented to go than he would have wilfully
wallowed in a bog ; the touch of the girl's hand on his
sleeve, and the kindly light in his father's eyes, both loudly
forbidding. But right before him was the way home,
which pointed only to bed, a place of little ease for one
whose fancy was strung to the lyrical pitch, and whose not
very ardent heart was just then tumultuously moved.
The hill-top, the cool air of the night, the company of the
great monuments, the sight of the city under his feet,
with its hills and valleys and crossing files of lamps,
drew him by all he had of the poetic, and he turned that way ;
and by that quite innocent deflection, ripened the crop of
his venial errors for the sickle of destiny.

On a seat on the hill above Greenside he sat for perhaps
half an hour, looking down upon the lamps of Edinburgh,
and up at the lamps of heaven. Wonderful were the resolves
he formed ; beautiful and kindly were the vistas of future
life that sped before him. He uttered to himself the name
of Flora in so many touching and dramatic keys, that he
became at length fairly melted with tenderness, and could
have sung aloud. At that juncture the sound of a certain
creasing in his greatcoat caught his ear. He put his hand
into his pocket, pulled forth the envelope that held the
money, and sat stupefied. The Calton Hill, about this
period, had an ill name of nights ; and to be sitting there
with four hundred pounds that did not belong to him was
hardly wise. He looked up. There was a man in a very
bad hat a little on one side of him, apparently looking at the
scenery ; from a little on the other a second night-walker
was drawing very quietly near. Up jumped John. The
envelope fell from his hands ; he stooped to get it, and at
the same moment both men ran in and closed with him.

A little after, he got to his feet very sore and shaken, the poorer by a purse which contained exactly one penny postage-stamp, by a cambric handkerchief, and by the all-important envelope.

Here was a young man on whom, at the highest point of loverly exaltation, there had fallen a blow too sharp to be supported alone ; and not many hundred yards away his greatest friend was sitting at supper—ay, and even expecting him. Was it not in the nature of man that he should run there ? He went in quest of sympathy—in quest of that droll article that we all suppose ourselves to want when in a strait, and have agreed to call advice ; and he went, besides, with vague but rather splendid expectations of relief. Alan was rich, or would be so when he came of age. By a stroke of the pen he might remedy this misfortune, and avert that dreaded interview with Mr. Nicholson, from which John now shrunk in imagination as the hand draws back from fire.

Close under the Calton Hill there runs a certain narrow avenue, part street, part by-road. The head of it faces the doors of the prison ; its tail descends into the sunless slums of the Low Calton. On one hand it is overhung by the crags of the hill, on the other by an old grave-yard. Between these two the road-way runs in a trench, sparsely lighted at night, sparsely frequented by day, and bordered, when it has cleared the place of tombs, by dingy and ambiguous houses. One of these was the house of Collette ; and at his door our ill-starred John was presently beating for admittance. In an evil hour he satisfied the jealous inquiries of the contraband hotelkeeper ; in an evil hour he penetrated into the somewhat unsavoury interior. Alan, to be sure, was there, seated in a room lighted by noisy gas-jets, beside a dirty table-cloth, engaged on a coarse meal, and in the company of several tipsy members of the junior bar. But Alan was not sober ; he had lost a thousand pounds upon a horse-race, had received the news at dinner-time, and was now, in default of any possible means of extrication, drowning the memory of his predicament. He to

L

help John! The thing was impossible; he couldn't help himself.

"If you have a beast of a father," said he, "I can tell you I have a brute of a trustee."

"I'm not going to hear my father called a beast," said John, with a beating heart, feeling that he risked the last sound rivet of the chain that bound him to life.

But Alan was quite good-natured.

"All right, old fellow," said he. "Mos' respec'able man your father." And he introduced his friend to his companions as "old Nicholson the what-d'ye-call-um's son."

John sat in dumb agony. Collette's foul walls and maculate table-linen, and even down to Collette's villainous casters, seemed like objects in a nightmare. And just then there came a knock and a scurrying; the police, so lamentably absent from the Calton Hill, appeared upon the scene; and the party, taken *flagrante delicto*, with their glasses at their elbow, were seized, marched up to the police office, and all duly summoned to appear as witnesses in the consequent case against that arch-shebeener, Collette.

It was a sorrowful and a mightily sobered company that came forth again. The vague terror of public opinion weighed generally on them all; but there were private and particular horrors on the minds of individuals. Alan stood in dread of his trustee, already sorely tried. One of the group was the son of a country minister, another of a judge; John, the unhappiest of all, had David Nicholson to father, the idea of facing whom on such a scandalous subject was physically sickening. They stood a while consulting under the buttresses of Saint Giles; thence they adjourned to the lodgings of one of the number in North Castle Street, where (for that matter) they might have had quite as good a supper, and far better drink, than in the dangerous paradise from which they had been routed. There, over an almost tearful glass, they debated their position. Each explained he had the world to lose if the affair went on, and he appeared as a witness. It was remarkable what bright prospects were just then in the very act of opening before each of that little company of youths, and what pious consideration for the feelings of their families began now to well from them. Each, moreover, was in an odd state of destitution. Not one could bear his share of the fine ; not one but evinced a wonderful twinkle of hope that each of the others (in succession) was the very man who could step in to make good the deficit. One took a high hand ; he could not pay his share ; if it went to a trial, he should bolt ; he had always felt the English Bar to be his true sphere. Another branched out into touching details about his family, to which no one listened. John, in the midst of this disorderly competition of poverty and mean-ness, sat stunned, contemplating the mountain bulk of his misfortunes.

At last, upon a pledge that each should apply to his family with a common frankness, this convention of unhappy young asses broke up, went down the common stair, and in the grey of the spring morning, with the streets lying dead empty all about them, the lamps burning on into the daylight in diminished lustre, and the birds begin-ning to sound premonitory notes from the groves of the town gardens, went each his own way with bowed head and echoing footfall.

The rooks were awake in Randolph Crescent ; but the windows looked down, discreetly blinded, on the return of the prodigal. John's pass-key was a recent privilege ; this was the first time it had been used ; and, oh ! with what a sickening sense of his unworthiness he now inserted it into the well-oiled lock and entered that citadel of the proprieties ! All slept ; the gas in the hall had been left faintly burning to light his return ; a dreadful stillness reigned, broken by the deep ticking of the eight-day clock. He put the gas out, and sat on a chair in the hall, waiting and counting the minutes, longing for any human counten-ance. But when at last he heard the alarm-clock spring its rattle in the lower story, and the servants begin to be about, he instantly lost heart, and fled to his own room, where he threw himself upon the bed.

CHAPTER III

IN WHICH JOHN ENJOYS THE HARVEST HOME

SHORTLY after breakfast, at which he assisted with a highly tragical countenance, John sought his father where he sat, presumably in religious meditation, on the Sabbath mornings. The old gentleman looked up with that sour, inquisitive expression that came so near to smiling and was so different in effect.

" This is a time when I do not like to be disturbed," he said.

" I know that," returned John ; " but I have—I want—I've made a dreadful mess of it," he broke out, and turned to the window.

Mr. Nicholson sat silent for an appreciable time, while his unhappy son surveyed the poles in the back green, and a certain yellow cat that was perched upon the wall. Despair sat upon John as he gazed ; and he raged to think of the dreadful series of his misdeeds, and the essential innocence that lay behind them.

" Well," said his father, with an obvious effort, but in very quiet tones, " what is it ? "

" Maclean gave me four hundred pounds to put in the bank, sir," began John ; " and I'm sorry to say that I've been robbed of it ! "

" Robbed of it ? " cried Mr. Nicholson, with a strong rising inflection. " Robbed ? Be careful what you say, John ! "

" I can't say anything else, sir ; I was just robbed of it," said John, in desperation, sullenly.

" And where and when did this extraordinary event take place ? " inquired the father.

"On the Calton Hill about twelve last night."

"The Calton Hill?" repeated Mr. Nicholson. "And what were you doing there at such a time of the night?"

"Nothing, sir," says John.

Mr. Nicholson drew in his breath.

"And how came the money in your hands at twelve last night?" he asked, sharply.

"I neglected that piece of business," said John, anticipating comment; and then in his own dialect: "I clean forgot all about it."

"Well," said his father, "it's a most extraordinary story. Have you communicated with the police?"

"I have," answered poor John, the blood leaping to his face. "They think they know the men that did it. I daresay the money will be recovered, if that was all," said he, with a desperate indifference, which his father set down to levity; but which sprang from the consciousness of worse behind.

"Your mother's watch, too?" asked Mr. Nicholson.

"Oh, the watch is all right!" cried John. "At least, I mean I was coming to the watch—the fact is, I am ashamed to say, I—I had pawned the watch before. Here is the ticket; they didn't find that; the watch can be redeemed; they don't sell pledges." The lad panted out these phrases, one after another, like minute-guns; but at the last word, which rang in that stately chamber like an oath, his heart failed him utterly; and the dreaded silence settled on father and son.

It was broken by Mr. Nicholson picking up the pawn-ticket: "John Froggs, 85 Pleasance," he read; and then turning upon John, with a brief flash of passion and disgust, "Who is John Froggs?" he cried.

"Nobody," said John. "It was just a name."

"An *alias*," his father commented.

"Oh! I think scarcely quite that," said the culprit; "it's a form, they all do it, the man seemed to understand, we had a great deal of fun over the name——"

He paused at that, for he saw his father wince at the

picture like a man physically struck ; and again there was
silence.

" I do not think," said Mr. Nicholson, at last, " that I am
an ungenerous father. I have never grudged you money
within reason, for any avowable purpose ; you had just
to come to me and speak. And now I find that you have
forgotten all decency and all natural feeling, and actually
pawned—pawned—your mother's watch. You must have
had some temptation ; I will do you the justice to suppose
it was a strong one. What did you want with this money ? "

" I would rather not tell you, sir," said John. " It
will only make you angry."

" I will not be fenced with," cried his father. " There
must be an end of disingenuous answers. What did you
want with this money ? "

" To lend it to Houston, sir," says John.

" I thought I had forbidden you to speak to that young
man ? " asked his father.

" Yes, sir," said John ; " but I only met him."

" Where ? " came the deadly question.

And " in a billiard-room " was the damning answer.
Thus, had John's single departure from the truth brought
instant punishment. For no other purpose but to see
Alan would he have entered a billiard-room ; but he had
desired to palliate the fact of his disobedience, and now it
appeared that he frequented these disreputable haunts upon
his own account.

Once more Mr. Nicholson digested the vile tidings in
silence ; and when John stole a glance at his father's countenance, he was abashed to see the marks of suffering.

" Well," said the old gentleman, at last, " I cannot
pretend not to be simply bowed down. I rose this morning
what the world calls a happy man—happy, at least, in a son
of whom I thought I could be reasonably proud——"

But it was beyond human nature to endure this longer,
and John interrupted almost with a scream. " Oh,
wheest ! " he cried, " that's not all, that's not the worst of
it—it's nothing ! How could I tell you were proud of me ?
Oh ! I wish, I wish that I had known ; but you always said I

was such a disgrace ! And the dreadful thing is this :
we were all taken up last night, and we have to pay Collette's
fine among the six, or we'll be had up for evidence—she-
beening it is. They made me swear to tell you ; but for
my part," he cried, bursting into tears, " I just wish that I
was dead ! " And he fell on his knees before a chair and
hid his face.

Whether his father spoke, or whether he remained long
in the room or at once departed, are points lost to history.
A horrid turmoil of mind and body ; bursting sobs ;
broken, vanishing thoughts, now of indignation, now of
remorse ; broken elementary whiffs of consciousness, of the
smell of the horse-hair on the chair bottom, of the jang-
ling of church bells that now began to make day horrible
throughout the confines of the city, of the hard floor that
bruised his knees, of the taste of tears that found their way
into his mouth : for a period of time, the duration of which
I cannot guess, while I refuse to dwell longer on its agony,
these were the whole of God's world for John Nicholson.

When at last, as by the touching of a spring, he returned
again to clearness of consciousness and even a measure of
composure, the bells had but just done ringing, and the
Sabbath silence was still marred by the patter of belated
feet. By the clock above the fire, as well as by these more
speaking signs, the service had not long begun ; and the
unhappy sinner, if his father had really gone to church,
might count on near two hours of only comparative unhappi-
ness. With his father, the superlative degree returned
infallibly. He knew it by every shrinking fibre in his body,
he knew it by the sudden dizzy whirling of his brain, at
the mere thought of that calamity. An hour and a half,
perhaps an hour and three quarters, if the doctor was long-
winded, and then would begin again that active agony
from which, even in the dull ache of the present, he shrunk
as from the bite of fire. He saw, in a vision, the family
pew, the somnolent cushions, the Bibles, the Psalm-books,
Maria with her smelling-salts, his father sitting spectacled
and critical ; and at once he was struck with indignation,
not unjustly   It was inhuman to go off to church, and leave

a sinner in suspense, unpunished, unforgiven. And at the
very touch of criticism, the paternal sanctity was lessened ;
yet the paternal terror only grew ; and the two strands of
feeling pushed him in the same direction.

And suddenly there came upon him a mad fear lest his
father should have locked him in. The notion had no
ground in sense ; it was probably no more than a reminiscence of similar calamities in childhood, for his father's
room had always been the chamber of inquisition and the
scene of punishment ; but it stuck so rigorously in his
mind that he must instantly approach the door and prove
its untruth. As he went, he struck upon a drawer left
open in the business table. It was the money-drawer, a
measure of his father's disarray : the money-drawer—
perhaps a pointing providence ! Who is to decide, when
even divines differ between a providence and a temptation ?
or who, sitting calmly under his own vine, is to pass a
judgment on the doings of a poor, hunted dog, slavishly
afraid, slavishly rebellious, like John Nicholson on that
particular Sunday ? His hand was in the drawer, almost
before his mind had conceived the hope ; and rising to his
new situation, he wrote, sitting in his father's chair and
using his father's blotting-pad, his pitiful apology and farewell :

"MY DEAR FATHER,—I have taken the money, but I will pay
it back as soon as I am able. You will never hear of me again.
I did not mean any harm by anything, so I hope you will try
and forgive me. I wish you would say good-bye to Alexander
and Maria, but not if you don't want to. I could not wait to
see you, really. Please try to forgive me. Your affectionate son.
                                        "JOHN NICHOLSON."

The coins abstracted and the missive written, he could
not be gone too soon from the scene of these transgressions ;
and remembering how his father had once returned from
church, on some slight illness, in the middle of the second
psalm, he durst not even make a packet of a change of
clothes. Attired as he was, he slipped from the paternal
doors, and found himself in the cool spring air, the thin

spring sunshine, and the great Sabbath quiet of the city, which was now only pointed by the cawing of the rooks. There was not a soul in Randolph Crescent, nor a soul in Queensferry Street ; in this out-door privacy and the sense of escape, John took heart again ; and with a pathetic sense of leave-taking, he even ventured up the lane and stood a while, a strange peri at the gates of a quaint paradise, by the west end of St. George's Church. They were singing within ; and by a strange chance, the tune was "St. George's, Edinburgh," which bears the name, and was first sung in the choir of that church. "Who is this King of Glory ? " went the voices from within ; and to John this was like the end of all Christian observances, for he was now to be a wild man like Ishmael, and his life was to be cast in homeless places and with godless people.

It was thus, with no rising sense of the adventurous, but in mere desolation and despair, that he turned his back on his native city, and set out on foot for California, with a more immediate eye to Glasgow.

CHAPTER IV

THE SECOND SOWING

IT is no part of mine to narrate the adventures of John Nicholson, which were many, but simply his more momentous misadventures, which were more than he desired, and, by human standards, more than he deserved; how he reached California, how he was rooked, and robbed, and beaten, and starved; how he was at last taken up by charitable folk, restored to some degree of self-complacency, and installed as a clerk in a bank in San Francisco, it would take too long to tell; nor in these episodes were there any marks of the peculiar Nicholsonic destiny, for they were just such matters as befell some thousands of other young adventurers in the same days and places. But once posted in the bank, he fell for a time into a high degree of good fortune, which, as it was only a longer way about to fresh disaster, it behoves me to explain.

It was his luck to meet a young man in what is technically called a " dive," and thanks to his monthly wages, to extricate this new acquaintance from a position of present disgrace and possible danger in the future. This young man was the nephew of one of the Nob Hill magnates, who run the San Francisco Stock Exchange, much as more humble adventurers, in the corner of some public park at home, may be seen to perform the simple artifice of pea and thimble: for their own profit, that is to say, and the discouragement of public gambling. It was thus in his power—and, as he was of grateful temper, it was among the things that he desired—to put John in the way of growing rich; and thus, without thought or industry, or so much as even understanding the game at which he played, but by simply buying and selling what he was told to buy and sell, that plaything of fortune was presently at the head of between eleven and twelve thousand pounds, or, as he reckoned it, of upward of sixty thousand dollars.

How he had come to deserve this wealth, any more than how he had formerly earned disgrace at home, was a problem beyond the reach of his philosophy. It was true that he had been industrious at the bank, but no more so than the cashier, who had seven small children and was visibly sinking in decline. Nor was the step which had determined his advance—a visit to a dive with a month's wages in his pocket—an act of such transcendent virtue, or even wisdom, as to seem to merit the favour of the gods. From some sense of this, and of the dizzy see-saw—heaven-high, hell-deep—on which men sit clutching; or perhaps fearing that the sources of his fortune might be insidiously traced to some root in the field of petty cash; he stuck to his work, said not a word of his new circumstances, and kept his account with a bank in a different quarter of the town. The concealment, innocent as it seems, was the first step in the second tragi-comedy of John's existence.

Meanwhile, he had never written home. Whether from diffidence or shame, or a touch of anger, or mere procrastination, or because (as we have seen) he had no skill in literary arts, or because (as I am sometimes tempted to suppose) there is a law in human nature that prevents young men —not otherwise beasts—from the performance of this simple act of piety—months and years had gone by, and John had never written. The habit of not writing, indeed, was already fixed before he had begun to come into his fortune; and it was only the difficulty of breaking this long silence that withheld him from an instant restitution of the money he had stolen or (as he preferred to call it) borrowed. In vain he sat before paper, attending on inspiration; that heavenly nymph, beyond suggesting the words, "my dear father," remained obstinately silent; and presently John would crumple up the sheet and decide, as soon as he had "a good chance," to carry the money home in person. And this delay, which is indefensible, was his second step into the snares of fortune.

Ten years had passed, and John was drawing near to thirty. He had kept the promise of his boyhood, and was now of a lusty frame, verging toward corpulence ; good features, good eyes, a genial manner, a ready laugh, a long pair of sandy whiskers, a dash of an American accent, a close familiarity with the great American joke, and a certain likeness to a R-y-l P-rs-n-ge, who shall remain nameless for me, made up the man's externals as he could be viewed in society. Inwardly, in spite of his gross body and highly masculine whiskers, he was more like a maiden lady than a man of twenty-nine.

It chanced one day, as he was strolling down Market Street on the eve of his fortnight's holiday, that his eye was caught by certain railway bills, and in very idleness of mind he calculated that he might be home for Christmas if he started on the morrow. The fancy thrilled him with desire, and in one moment he decided he would go.

There was much to be done : his portmanteau to be packed, a credit to be got from the bank where he was a wealthy customer, and certain offices to be transacted for that other bank in which he was an humble clerk ; and it chanced, in conformity with human nature, that out of all this business it was the last that came to be neglected. Night found him, not only equipped with money of his own, but once more (as on that former occasion) saddled with a considerable sum of other people's.

Now it chanced there lived in the same boarding-house a fellow-clerk of his, an honest fellow, with what is called a weakness for drink—though it might, in this case, have been called a strength, for the victim had been drunk for weeks together without the briefest intermission. To this unfortunate John intrusted a letter with an inclosure of bonds, addressed to the bank manager. Even as he did so he thought he perceived a certain haziness of eye and speech in his trustee ; but he was too hopeful to be stayed, silenced the voice of warning in his bosom, and with one and the same gesture committed the money to the clerk, and himself into the hands of destiny.

I dwell, even at the risk of tedium, on John's minutest errors, his case being so perplexing to the moralist; but we have done with them now, the roll is closed, the reader has the worst of our poor hero, and I leave him to judge for himself whether he or John has been the less deserving. Henceforth we have to follow the spectacle of a man who was a mere whip-top for calamity; on whose unmerited misadventures not even the humourist can look without pity, and not even the philosopher without alarm.

That same night the clerk entered upon a bout of drunkenness so consistent as to surprise even his intimate acquaintance. He was speedily ejected from the boarding-house; deposited his portmanteau with a perfect stranger, who did not even catch his name; wandered he knew not where, and was at last hove-to, all standing, in a hospital at Sacramento. There, under the impenetrable *alias* of the number of his bed, the crapulous being lay for some more days unconscious of all things, and of one thing in particular: that the police were after him. Two months had come and gone before the convalescent in the Sacramento hospital was identified with Kirkman, the absconding San Francisco clerk; even then, there must elapse nearly a fortnight more till the perfect stranger could be hunted up, the portmanteau recovered, and John's letter carried at length to its destination, the seal still unbroken, the enclosure still intact.

Meanwhile, John had gone upon his holidays without a word, which was irregular; and there had disappeared with him a certain sum of money, which was out of all bounds of palliation. But he was known to be careless, and believed to be honest; the manager besides had a regard for him; and little was said, although something was no doubt thought, until the fortnight was finally at an end, and the time had come for John to reappear. Then, indeed, the affair began to look black; and when inquiries were made, and the penniless clerk was found to have amassed thousands of dollars, and kept them secretly in a rival establishment, the stoutest of his friends abandoned him, the books were overhauled for traces of ancient and artful fraud, and though none were found, there still prevailed a general impression of loss. The telegraph was set in motion; and the correspondent of the bank in Edinburgh, for which place it was understood that John had armed himself with extensive credits, was warned to communicate with the police.

Now this correspondent was a friend of Mr. Nicholson's; he was well acquainted with the tale of John's calamitous disappearance from Edinburgh; and putting one thing with another, hasted with the first word of this scandal, not to the police, but to his friend. The old gentleman had long regarded his son as one dead; John's place had been taken, the memory of his faults had already fallen to be one of those old aches, which awaken again indeed upon occasion, but which we can always vanquish by an effort of the will; and to have the long lost resuscitated in a fresh disgrace was doubly bitter.

"MacEwen," said the old man, "this must be hushed up, if possible. If I give you a check for this sum, about which they are certain, could you take it on yourself to let the matter rest?"

"I will," said MacEwen. "I will take the risk of it."

"You understand," resumed Mr. Nicholson, speaking precisely, but with ashen lips, "I do this for my family, not for that unhappy young man. If it should turn out that these suspicions are correct, and he has embezzled large sums, he must lie on his bed as he has made it." And then looking up at MacEwen with a nod, and one of his strange smiles: "Good-bye," said he; and MacEwen, perceiving the case to be too grave for consolation, took himself off and blessed God on his way home that he was childless.

CHAPTER V

THE PRODIGAL'S RETURN

BY a little after noon on the eve of Christmas, John had left his portmanteau in the cloak-room, and stepped forth into Princes Street with a wonderful expansion of the soul, such as men enjoy in the completion of long-nourished schemes. He was at home again, incognito and rich ; presently he could enter his father's house by means of the pass-key, which he had piously preserved through all his wanderings ; he would throw down the borrowed money ; there would be a reconciliation, the details of which he frequently arranged ; and he saw himself, during the next month, made welcome in many stately houses at many frigid dinner-parties, taking his share in the conversation with the freedom of the man and the traveller, and laying down the law upon finance with the authority of the successful investor. But this programme was not to be begun before evening—not till just before dinner, indeed, at which meal the reassembled family were to sit roseate, and the best wine (the modern fatted calf) should flow for the prodigal's return.

Meanwhile he walked familiar streets, merry reminiscences crowding round him, sad ones also, both with the same surprising pathos. The keen frosty air ; the low, rosy, wintery sun ; the castle, hailing him like an old acquaintance ; the names of friends on door-plates ; the sight of friends whom he seemed to recognise, and whom he eagerly avoided, in the streets ; the pleasant chant of the north country accent ; the dome of St. George's reminding him of his last penitential moments in the lane, and of that King of Glory whose name had echoed ever since in the

saddest corner of his memory; and the gutters where he
had learned to slide, and the shop where he had bought his
skates, and the stones on which he had trod, and the railings
in which he had rattled his clachan as he went to school;
and all those thousand and one nameless particulars, which
the eye sees without noting, which the memory keeps indeed
yet without knowing, and which, taken one with another,
build up for us the aspect of the place that we call home:
and all these besieged him, as he went, with both delight
and sadness.

His first visit was for Houston, who had a house on
Regent's Terrace, kept for him in old days by an aunt.
The door was opened (to his surprise) upon the chain, and
a voice asked him from within what he wanted.

"I want Mr. Houston—Mr. Alan Houston," said he.

"And who are ye?" said the voice.

"This is most extraordinary," thought John; and then
aloud he told his name.

"No, young Mr. John?" cried the voice, with a sudden
increase of Scottish accent, testifying to a friendlier feeling.

"The very same," said John.

And the old butler removed his defences, remarking
only, "I thocht ye were that man." But his master was
not there; he was staying, it appeared, at the house in
Murrayfield; and though the butler would have been glad
enough to have taken his place and given all the news of
the family, John, struck with a little chill, was eager to be
gone. Only, the door was scarce closed again, before he
regretted that he had not asked about "that man."

He was to pay no more visits till he had seen his father
and made all well at home; Alan had been the only possible
exception, and John had not time to go as far as Murrayfield. But here he was on Regent's Terrace; there was
nothing to prevent him going round the end of the hill,
and looking from without on the Mackenzies' house. As
he went, he reflected that Flora must now be a woman of
near his own age, and it was within the bounds of possi-
bility that she was married; but this dishonourable doubt
he damned down.

There was the house, sure enough ; but the door was of another colour, and what was this—two door-plates ? He drew nearer ; the top one bore, with dignified simplicity the words, " Mr. Proudfoot " ; the lower one was more explicit, and informed the passer-by that here was likewise the abode of " Mr. J. A. Dunlop Proudfoot, Advocate." The Proudfoots must be rich, for no advocate could look to have much business in so remote a quarter ; and John hated them for their wealth and for their name, and for the sake of the house they desecrated with their presence. He remembered a Proudfoot he had seen at school, not known : a little, whey-faced urchin, the despicable member of some lower class. Could it be this abortion that had climbed to be an advocate, and now lived in the birthplace of Flora and the home of John's tenderest memories ? The chill that had first seized upon him when he heard of Houston's absence deepened and struck inward. For a moment, as he stood under the doors of that estranged house, and looked east and west along the solitary pavement of the Royal Terrace, where not a cat was stirring, the sense of solitude and desolation took him by the throat, and he wished himself in San Francisco.

And then the figure he made, with his decent portliness, his whiskers, the money in his purse, the excellent cigar that he now lighted, recurred to his mind in consolatory comparison with that of a certain maddened lad who, on a certain spring Sunday ten years before, and in the hour of church-time silence, had stolen from that city by the Glasgow road. In the face of these changes, it were impious to doubt fortune's kindness. All would be well yet ; the Mackenzies would be found, Flora, younger and lovelier and kinder than before ; Alan would be found, and would have so nicely discriminated his behaviour as to have grown, on the one hand, into a valued friend of Mr. Nicholson's, and to have remained, upon the other, of that exact shade of joviality which John desired in his companions. And so, once more, John fell to work discounting the delightful future ; his first appearance in the family pew ; his first visit to his uncle Greig, who thought himself so great a

M

financier, and on whose purblind Edinburgh eyes John was
to let in the dazzling daylight of the West; and the details
in general of that unrivalled transformation scene, in which
he was to display to all Edinburgh a portly and successful
gentleman in the shoes of the derided fugitive.

The time began to draw near when his father would have
returned from the office, and it would be the prodigal's cue
to enter. He strolled westward by Albany Street, facing
the sunset embers, pleased, he knew not why, to move in
that cold air and indigo twilight, starred with street-lamps.
But there was one more disenchantment waiting him by the
way.

At the corner of Pitt Street he paused to light a fresh
cigar; the vesta threw, as he did so, a strong light upon his
features, and a man of about his own age stopped at sight
of it.

"I think your name must be Nicholson," said the
stranger.

It was too late to avoid recognition; and besides, as
John was now actually on the way home, it hardly mattered,
and he gave way to the impulse of his nature.

"Great Scott!" he cried, "Beatson!" and shook hands
with warmth. It scarce seemed he was repaid in kind.

"So you're home again?" said Beatson. "Where
have you been all this long time?"

"In the States," said John—"California. I've made my
pile though; and it suddenly struck me it would be a
noble scheme to come home for Christmas."

"I see," said Beatson. "Well, I hope we'll see something of you now you're here."

"Oh, I guess so," said John, a little frozen.

"Well, ta-ta," concluded Beatson, and he shook hands
again and went.

This was a cruel first experience. It was idle to blink
facts: here was John home again, and Beatson—Old
Beatson—did not care a rush. He recalled Old Beatson in
the past—that merry and affectionate lad—and their joint
adventures and mishaps, the window they had broken with
a catapult in India Place, the escalade of the Castle rock,

and many another inestimable bond of friendship ; and his hurt surprise grew deeper. Well, after all, it was only on a man's own family that he could count ; blood was thicker than water, he remembered ; and the net result of this encounter was to bring him to the doorstep of his father's house, with tenderer and softer feelings.

The night had come ; the fanlight over the door shone bright ; the two windows of the dining-room where the cloth was being laid, and the three windows of the drawing-room where Maria would be waiting dinner, glowed softlier through yellow blinds. It was like a vision of the past. All this time of his absence, life had gone forward with an equal foot, and the fires and the gas had been lighted, and the meals spread, at the accustomed hours. At the accustomed hour, too, the bell had sounded thrice to call the family to worship. And at the thought a pang of regret for his demerit seized him ; he remembered the things that were good and that he had neglected and the things that were evil and that he had loved ; and it was with a prayer upon his lips that he mounted the steps and thrust the key into the key-hole.

He stepped into the lighted hall, shut the door softly behind him, and stood there fixed in wonder. No surprise of strangeness could equal the surprise of that complete familiarity. There was the bust of Chalmers near the stair railings, there was the clothes-brush in the accustomed place ; and there, on the hat-stand, hung hats and coats that must surely be the same as he remembered. Ten years dropped from his life, as a pin may slip between the fingers ; and the ocean and the mountains, and the mines, and crowded marts and mingled races of San Francisco, and his own fortune and his own disgrace, became, for that one moment, the figures of a dream that was over.

He took off his hat, and moved mechanically towards the stand ; and there he found a small change that was a great one to him. The pin that had been his from boyhood, where he had flung his balmoral hat when he loitered home from the academy, and his first hat when he came briskly back from college or the office—his pin was occupied.

" They might have at least respected my pin ! " he thought, and he was moved as by a slight, and began at once to recollect that he was here an interloper, in a strange house, which he had entered almost by a burglary, and where at any moment he might be scandalously challenged.

He moved at once, his hat still in his hand, to the door of his father's room, opened it, and entered. Mr. Nicholson sat in the same place and posture as on that last Sunday morning ; only he was older, and greyer, and sterner ; and as he now glanced up and caught the eye of his son, a strange commotion and a dark flush sprang into his face.

" Father," said John, steadily, and even cheerfully, for this was a moment against which he was long ago prepared, " father, here I am, and here is the money that I took from you. I have come back to ask your forgiveness, and to stay Christmas with you and the children."

" Keep your money," said the father, " and go ! "

" Father ! " cried John ; " For God's sake don't receive me this way. I've come for——"

" Understand me," interrupted Mr. Nicholson ; " you are no son of mine ; and in the sight of God, I wash my hands of you. One last thing I will tell you ; one warning I will give you ; all is discovered, and you are being hunted for your crimes ; if you are still at large it is thanks to me ; but I have done all that I mean to do ; and from this time forth I would not raise one finger—not one finger—to save you from the gallows ! And now," with a low voice of absolute authority, and a single weighty gesture of the finger, " and now—go ! "

CHAPTER VI

THE HOUSE AT MURRAYFIELD

HOW John passed the evening, in what windy confusion of mind, in what squalls of anger and lulls of sick collapse, in what pacing of streets and plunging into public-houses, it would profit little to relate. His misery, if it were not progressive, yet tended in no way to diminish; for in proportion as grief and indignation abated, fear began to take their place. At first, his father's menacing words lay by in some safe drawer of memory, biding their hour. At first, John was all thwarted affection and blighted hope; next bludgeoned vanity raised its head again, with twenty mortal gashes: and the father was disowned even as he had disowned the son. What was this regular course of life, that John should have admired it? what were these clockwork virtues, from which love was absent? Kindness was the test, kindness the aim and soul; and judged by such a standard, the discarded prodigal—now rapidly drowning his sorrows and his reason in successive drams—was a creature of a lovelier morality than his self-righteous father. Yes, he was the better man; he felt it, glowed with the consciousness, and entering a public-house at the corner of Howard Place (whither he had somehow wandered) he pledged his own virtues in a glass—perhaps the fourth since his dismissal. Of that he knew nothing, keeping no account of what he did or where he went; and in the general crashing hurry of his nerves, unconscious of the approach of intoxication. Indeed, it is a question whether he were really growing intoxicated, or whether at first the spirits did not even sober him. For it was even as he drained this last glass that his father's ambiguous and menacing words — popping from their hiding-place in memory—startled him like a hand laid upon his shoulder. " Crimes, hunted, the gallows." They were ugly words ; in the ears of an innocent man, perhapsall the uglier ; for if some judicial error were in act against him, who should set a limit to its grossness or to how far it might be pushed ? Not John, indeed ; he was no believer in the powers of innocence, his cursed experience pointing in quite other ways ; and his fears, once wakened, grew with every hour and hunted him about the city streets.

It was perhaps nearly nine at night ; he had eaten nothing since lunch, he had drunk a good deal, and he was exhausted by emotion, when the thought of Houston came into his head. He turned, not merely to the man as a friend, but to his house as a place of refuge. The danger that threatened him was still so vague that he knew neither what to fear nor where he might expect it ; but this much at least seemed undeniable, that a private house was safer than a public inn. Moved by these counsels, he turned at once to the Caledonian Station, passed (not without alarm) into the bright lights of the approach, redeemed his portmanteau from the cloak-room, and was soon whirling in a cab along the Glasgow road. The change of movement and position, the sight of the lamps twinkling to the rear, and the smell of damp and mould and rotten straw which clung about the vehicle, wrought in him strange alternations of lucidity and mortal giddiness.

" I have been drinking," he discovered ; " I must go straight to bed, and sleep." And he thanked Heaven for the drowsiness that came upon his mind in waves.

From one of these spells he was wakened by the stoppage of the cab ; and, getting down, found himself in quite a country road, the last lamp of the suburb shining some way below, and the high walls of a garden rising before him in the dark. The Lodge (as the place was named), stood, indeed, very solitary. To the south it adjoined another house, but standing in so large a garden as to be well out of cry ; on all other sides, open fields stretched upward to the woods of Corstorphine Hill, or backward to the dells of Ravelston, or downward toward the valley of the Leith. The effect of seclusion was aided by the great height of the garden walls, which were, indeed, conventual, and, as John had tested in former days, defied the climbing schoolboy. The lamp of the cab threw a gleam upon the door and the not brilliant handle of the bell.

" Shall I ring for ye ? " said the cabman, who had descended from his perch and was slapping his chest, for the night was bitter.

" I wish you would," said John, putting his hand to his brow in one of his accesses of giddiness.

The man pulled at the handle, and the clanking of the bell replied from farther in the garden ; twice and thrice he did it, with sufficient intervals ; in the great, frosty silence of the night, the sounds fell sharp and small.

" Does he expect ye ? " asked the driver, with that manner of familiar interest that well became his port-wine face ; and when John had told him no, " Well, then," said the cabman, " if ye'll tak' my advice of it, we'll just gang back. And that's disinterested, mind ye, for my stables are in the Glesgie road."

" The servants must hear," said John.

" Hout ! " said the driver. " He keeps no servants here, man. They're a' in the town house ; I drive him often ; it's just a kind of hermitage, this."

" Give me the bell," said John ; and he plucked at it like a man desperate.

The clamour had not yet subsided before they heard steps upon the gravel, and a voice of singular nervous irritability cried to them through the door, " Who are you, and what do you want ? "

" Alan," said John, " it's me—it's Fatty—John, you know. I'm just come home, and I've come to stay with you."

There was no reply for a moment, and then the door was opened.

" Get the portmanteau down," said John to the driver.

" Do nothing of the kind," said Alan ; and then to John, " Come in here a moment. I want to speak to you."

John entered the garden, and the door was closed behind him. A candle stood on the gravel walk, winking a little in the draughts; it threw inconstant sparkles on the clumped holly, struck the light and darkness to and fro like a veil on Alan's features, and set his shadow hovering behind him. All beyond was inscrutable; and John's dizzy brain rocked with the shadow. Yet even so, it struck him that Alan was pale, and his voice, when he spoke, unnatural.

"What brings you here to-night?" he began. "I don't want, God knows, to seem unfriendly; but I cannot take you in, Nicholson; I cannot do it."

"Alan," said John, "you've just got to! You don't know the mess I'm in; the governor's turned me out, and I daren't show my face in an inn, because they're down on me for murder or something!"

"For what?" cried Alan, starting.

'Murder, I believe," says John.

"Murder!" repeated Alan, and passed his hand over his eyes. "What was that you were saying?" he asked again.

"That they were down on me," said John. "I'm accused of murder, by what I can make out; and I've really had a dreadful day of it, Alan, and I can't sleep on the road-side on a night like this—at least, not with a portmanteau," he pleaded.

"Hush!" said Alan, with his head on one side; and then, "did you hear nothing?" he asked.

"No," said John, thrilling, he knew not why, with communicated terror. "No, I heard nothing; why?" And then, as there was no answer, he reverted to his pleading: "But I say, Alan, you've just got to take me in. I'll go right away to bed if you have anything to do. I seem to have been drinking; I was that knocked over. I wouldn't turn you away, Alan, if you were down on your luck."

"No?" returned Alan. "Neither will I you, then. Come and let's get your portmanteau."

The cabman was paid, and drove off down the long, lamp-lit hill, and the two friends stood on the side-walk

beside the portmanteau till the last rumble of the wheels
had died in silence. It seemed to John as though Alan
attached importance to this departure of the cab ; and
John, who was in no state to criticise, shared profoundly
in the feeling.

When the stillness was once more perfect, Alan shouldered the portmanteau, carried it in, and shut and locked
the garden door ; and then, once more, abstraction seemed
to fall upon him, and he stood with his hand on the key,
until the cold began to nibble at John's fingers.

" Why are we standing here ? " asked John.

" Eh ? " said Alan, blankly.

" Why, man, you don't seem yourself," said the other.

" No, I'm not myself," said Alan ; and he sat down on
the portmanteau and put his face in his hands.

John stood beside him swaying a little, and looking about
him at the swaying shadows, the flitting sparkles, and the
steady stars overhead, until the windless cold began to
touch him through his clothes on the bare skin. Even in
his bemused intelligence, wonder began to awake.

" I say, let's come on to the house," he said at last.

" Yes, let's come on to the house," repeated Alan.

And he rose at once, re-shouldered the portmanteau,
and taking the candle in his other hand, moved forward
to the Lodge. This was a long, low building, smothered in creepers ; and now, except for some chinks of
light between the dining-room shutters, it was plunged in
darkness and silence.

In the hall Alan lighted another candle, gave it to John,
and opened the door of a bedroom.

" Here," said he ; " go to bed. Don't mind me, John.
You'll be sorry for me when you know."

" Wait a bit," returned John ; " I've got so cold with
all that standing about. Let's go into the dining-room a
minute. Just one glass to warm me, Alan."

On the table in the hall stood a glass, and a bottle with
a whisky label on a tray. It was plain that the bottle had
just been opened, for the cork and corkscrew lay beside
it.

" Take that," said Alan, passing John the whisky, and then with a certain roughness pushed his friend into the bedroom, and closed the door behind him.

John stood amazed ; then he shook the bottle, and, to his further wonder, found it partly empty. Three or four glasses were gone. Alan must have uncorked a bottle of whisky and drank three or four glasses one after the other, without sitting down, for there was no chair, and that in his own cold lobby on this freezing night ! It fully explained his eccentricities, John reflected sagely, as he mixed himself a grog. Poor Alan ! He was drunk ; and what a dreadful thing was drink, and what a slave to it poor Alan was, to drink in this unsociable, uncomfortable fashion ! The man who would drink alone, except for health's sake—as John was now doing—was a man utterly lost. He took the grog out, and felt hazier, but warmer. It was hard work opening the portmanteau and finding his night things ; and before he was undressed, the cold had struck home to him once more. " Well," said he ; " just a drop more. There's no sense in getting ill with all this other trouble." And presently dreamless slumber buried him.

When John awoke it was day. The low winter sun was already in the heavens, but his watch had stopped, and it was impossible to tell the hour exactly. Ten, he guessed it, and made haste to dress, dismal reflections crowding on his mind. But it was less from terror than from regret that he now suffered ; and with his regret there were mingled cutting pangs of penitence. There had fallen upon him a blow, cruel, indeed, but yet only the punishment of old misdoing ; and he had rebelled and plunged into fresh sin. The rod had been used to chasten, and he had bit the chastening fingers. His father was right ; John had justified him ; John was no guest for decent people's houses, and no fit associate for decent people's children. And had a broader hint been needed, there was the case of his old friend. John was no drunkard, though he could at times exceed ; and the picture of Houston drinking neat spirits at his hall-table struck him with something like disgust. He hung from meeting his old friend. He could have wished he had not come to him ; and yet, even now, where else was he to turn ?

These musings occupied him while he dressed and accompanied him into the lobby of the house. The door stood open on the garden ; doubtless, Alan had stepped forth ; and John did as he supposed his friend had done. The ground was hard as iron, the frost still rigorous as he brushed among the hollies, icicles jingled and glittered in their fall ; and wherever he went, a volley of eager sparrows followed him. Here were Christmas weather and Christmas morning duly met, to the delight of children. This was the day of reunited families, the day to which he had so long looked forward, thinking to awake in his own bed in Randolph Crescent, reconciled with all men and repeating the foot-prints of his youth ; and here he was alone, pacing the alleys of a wintery garden and filled with penitential thoughts.

And that reminded him : why was he alone ? and where was Alan ? The thought of the festal morning and the due salutations reawakened his desire for his friend, and he began to call for him by name. As the sound of his voice died away, he was aware of the greatness of the silence that environed him. But for the twittering of the sparrows and the crunching of his own feet upon the frozen snow, the whole windless world of air hung over him entranced, and the stillness weighed upon his mind with a horror of solitude.

Still calling at intervals, but now with a moderated voice, he made the hasty circuit of the garden, and finding neither man nor trace of man in all its evergreen coverts, turned at last to the house. About the house the silence seemed to deepen strangely. The door, indeed, stood open as before ; but the windows were still shuttered, the chimneys breathed no stain into the bright air, there sounded abroad none of the low stir (perhaps audible rather to the ear of the spirit than to the ear of the flesh) by which a house announces and betrays its human lodgers. And yet Alan must be there—Alan locked in drunken slumbers, forgetful of the return of day, of the holy season, and of the friend whom he

had so coldly received and was now so churlishly neglecting.
John's disgust redoubled at the thought ; but hunger was
beginning to grow stronger than repulsion, and as a step
to breakfast, if nothing else, he must find and arouse the
sleeper.

He made the circuit of the bedroom quarters. All,
until he came to Alan's chamber, were locked from without,
and bore the marks of a prolonged disuse. But Alan's
was a room in commission, filled with clothes, knick-
knacks, letters, books, and the conveniences of a solitary
man. The fire had been lighted ; but it had long ago
burned out, and the ashes were stone cold. The bed
had been made, but it had not been slept in.

Worse and worse, then ; Alan must have fallen where
he sat, and now sprawled brutishly, no doubt, upon the
dining-room floor.

The dining-room was a very long apartment, and was
reached through a passage ; so that John, upon his entrance,
brought but little light with him, and must move toward
the windows with spread arms, groping and knocking on
the furniture. Suddenly he tripped and fell his length
over a prostrate body. It was what he had looked for,
yet it shocked him ; and he marvelled that so rough an
impact should not have kicked a groan out of the drunkard.
Men had killed themselves ere now in such excesses, a
dreary and degraded end had made John shudder. What if
Alan were dead ? There would be a Christmas Day !

By this, John had his hand upon the shutters, and flinging
them back, beheld once again the blessed face of the day.
Even by that light the room had a discomfortable air. The
chairs were scattered, and one had been overthrown ; the
table-cloth, laid as if for dinner, was twitched upon one
side, and some of the dishes had fallen to the floor.
Behind the table lay the drunkard, still unaroused, only one
foot visible to John.

But now that light was in the room, the worst seemed
over ; it was a disgusting business, but not more than
disgusting ; and it was with no great apprehension that
John proceeded to make the circuit of the table : his last

comparatively tranquil moment for that day. No sooner had he turned the corner, no sooner had his eye alighted on the body, than he gave a smothered, breathless cry, and fled out of the room and out of the house.

It was not Alan who lay there, but a man well up in years, of stern countenance and iron-grey locks ; and it was no drunkard, for the body lay in a black pool of blood, and the open eyes stared upon the ceiling.

To and fro walked John before the door. The extreme sharpness of the air acted on his nerves like an astringent, and braced them swiftly. Presently, he not relaxing in his disordered walk, the images began to come clearer and stay longer in his fancy ; and next the power of thought came back to him, and the horror and danger of his situation rooted him to the ground.

He grasped his forehead, and staring on one spot of gravel, pieced together what he knew and what he suspected. Alan had murdered some one : possibly " that man " against whom the butler chained the door in Regent's Terrace ; possibly another ; some one at least : a human soul, whom it was death to slay and whose blood lay spilled upon the floor. This was the reason of the whisky drinking in the passage, of his unwillingness to welcome John, of his strange behaviour and bewildered words ; this was why he had started at and harped upon the name of murder ; this was why he had stood and hearkened, or sat and covered his eyes, in the black night. And now he was gone, now he had basely fled ; and to all his perplexities and dangers John stood heir.

" Let me think—let me think," he said, aloud, impatiently, even pleadingly, as if to some merciless interrupter. In the turmoil of his wits, a thousand hints and hopes and threats and terrors dinning continuously in his ears, he was like one plunged in the hubbub of a crowd. How was he to remember—he, who had not a thought to spare—that he was himself the author, as well as the theatre, of so much confusion ? But in hours of trial the junto of man's nature is dissolved, and anarchy succeeds.

It was plain he must stay no longer where he was, for

here was a new Judicial Error in the very making. It was
not so plain where he must go, for the old Judicial Error,
vague as a cloud, appeared to fill the habitable world ;
whatever it might be, it watched for him, full-grown, in
Edinburgh ; it must have had its birth in San Francisco ;
it stood guard no doubt, like a dragon, at the bank where he
should cash his credit ; and though there were doubtless
many other places, who should say in which of them it
was not ambushed ? No, he could not tell where he was
to go ; he must not lose time on these insolubilities.
Let him go back to the beginning. It was plain he must
stay no longer where he was. It was plain, too, that he
must not flee as he was, for he could not carry his portmanteau, and to flee and leave it, was to plunge deeper in
the mire. He must go, leave the house unguarded, find a
cab, and return—return after an absence ? Had he
courage for that ?

And just then he spied a stain about a hand's breadth
on his trouser-leg, and reached his finger down to touch
it. The finger was stained red ; it was blood ; he stared
upon it with disgust, and awe, and terror, and in the sharpness of the new sensation, fell instantly to act.

He cleansed his finger in the snow, returned into the
house, drew near with hushed footsteps to the dining-room
door, and shut and locked it. Then he breathed a little
freer, for here at least was an oaken barrier between himself and what he feared. Next, he hastened to his room,
tore off the spotted trousers which seemed in his eyes a
link to bind him to the gallows, flung them in a corner,
donned another pair, breathlessly crammed his night
things into his portmanteau, locked it, swung it with an
effort from the ground, and with a rush of relief, came forth
again under the open heavens.

The portmanteau, being of Occidental build, was no
feather-weight ; it had distressed the powerful Alan ; and
as for John, he was crushed under its bulk, and the sweat
broke upon him thickly. Twice he must set it down to
rest before he reached the gate ; and when he had come
so far, he must do as Alan did, and take his seat upon one

corner. Here, then, he sat a while and panted ; but now his thoughts were sensibly lightened ; now, with the trunk standing just inside the door, some part of his dissociation from the house of crime had been effected, and the cabman need not pass the garden wall. It was wonderful how that relieved him ; for the house, in his eyes, was a place to strike the most cursory beholder with suspicion, as though the very windows had cried murder.

But there was to be no remission of the strokes of fate. As he thus sat, taking breath in the shadow of the wall and hopped about by sparrows, it chanced that his eye roved to the fastening of the door ; and what he saw plucked him to his feet. The thing locked with a spring ; once the door was closed, the bolt shut of itself ; and without a key, there was no means of entering from without.

He saw himself obliged to one of two distasteful and perilous alternatives ; either to shut the door altogether and set his portmanteau out upon the way-side, a wonder to all beholders ; or to leave the door ajar, so that any thievish tramp or holiday school-boy might stray in and stumble on the grisly secret. To the last, as the least desperate, his mind inclined ; but he must first insure himself that he was unobserved. He peered out, and down the long road : it lay dead empty. He went to the corner of the by-road that comes by way of Dean ; there also not a passenger was stirring. Plainly it was, now or never, the high tide of his affairs ; and he drew the door as close as he durst, slipped a pebble in the chink, and made off down hill to find a cab.

Half-way down a gate opened, and a troop of Christmas children sallied forth in the most cheerful humour, followed more soberly by a smiling mother.

" And this is Christmas Day ! " thought John ; and could have laughed aloud in tragic bitterness of heart.

CHAPTER VII

A TRAGI-COMEDY IN A CAB

IN front of Donaldson's Hospital, John counted it good
fortune to perceive a cab a great way off, and by much
shouting and waving of his arm to catch the notice of the
driver. He counted it good fortune, for the time was long
to him till he should have done for ever with the Lodge;
and the farther he must go to find a cab, the greater the
chance that the inevitable discovery had taken place, and
that he should return to find the garden full of angry
neighbours. Yet when the vehicle drew up he was sensibly
chagrined to recognise the port-wine cabman of the night
before. " Here," he could not but reflect, " here is another
link in the Judicial Error."

The driver, on the other hand, was pleased to drop again
upon so liberal a fare; and as he was a man—the reader
must already have perceived—of easy, not to say familiar
manners, he dropped at once into a vein of friendly talk,
commenting on the weather, on the sacred season, which
struck him chiefly in the light of a day of liberal gratuities,
on the chance which had reunited him to a pleasing customer,
and on the fact that John had been (as he was pleased to
call it) visibly " on the ran-dan " the night before.

" And ye look dreidful bad the-day, sir, I must say that,"
he continued. " There's nothing like a dram for ye—if
ye'll take my advice of it; and bein' as it's Christmas,
I'm no' saying," he added, with a fatherly smile, " but
what I would join ye mysel'."

John had listened with a sick heart.

" I'll give you a dram when we've got through," said he,
affecting a sprightliness which sat on him most unhand-

somely, " and not a drop till then. Business first, and pleasure afterward."

With this promise the jarvey was prevailed upon to clamber to his place and drive, with hideous deliberation, to the door of the Lodge. There were no signs as yet of any public emotion ; only, two men stood not far off in talk, and their presence, seen from afar, set John's pulses buzzing. He might have spared himself his fright, for the pair were lost in some dispute of a theological complexion, and with lengthened upper lip and enumerating fingers, pursued the matter of their difference, and paid no heed to John.

But the cabman proved a thorn in the flesh. Nothing would keep him on his perch ; he must clamber down, comment upon the pebble in the door (which he regarded as an ingenious but unsafe device), help John with the portmanteau, and enliven matters with a flow of speech, especially of questions, which I thus condense :—

" He'll no' be here himsel', will he ? No ? Well, he's an eccentric man—a fair oddity—if ye ken the expression. Great trouble with his tenants, they tell me. I've driven the fam'ly for years. I drove a cab at his father's waddin'. What'll your name be ?—I should ken your face. Baigrey, ye say ? There were Baigreys about Gilmerton ; ye'll be one of that lot ? Then this'll be a friend's portmantie, like ? Why ? Because the name upon it's Nucholson ! Oh, if ye're in a hurry, that's another job. Waverley Brig' ? Are ye for away ? "

So the friendly toper prated and questioned and kept John's heart in a flutter. But to this also, as to other evils under the sun, there came a period ; and the victim of circumstances began at last to rumble towards the railway terminus at Waverley Bridge. During the transit, he sat with raised glasses in the frosty chill and mouldy fetor of his chariot, and glanced out sidelong on the holiday face of things, the shuttered shops, and the crowds along the pavement, much as the rider in the Tyburn cart may have observed the concourse gathering to his execution.

At the station his spirits rose again ; another stage of

N

his escape was fortunately ended—he began to spy blue water. He called a railway porter, and bade him carry the portmanteau to the cloak-room : not that he had any notion of delay ; flight, instant flight was his design, no matter whither ; but he had determined to dismiss the cabman ere he named, or even chose his destination, thus possibly balking the Judicial Error of another link. This was his cunning aim, and now with one foot on the road-way, and one still on the coach-step, he made haste to put the thing in practice, and plunged his hand into his trousers pocket.

There was nothing there !

Oh, yes ; this time he was to blame. He should have remembered, and when he deserted his blood-stained pantaloons, he should not have deserted along with them his purse. Make the most of his error, and then compare it with the punishment ! Conceive his new position, for I lack words to picture it ; conceive him condemned to return to that house, from the very thought of which his soul revolted, and once more to expose himself to capture on the very scene of the misdeed : conceive him linked to the mouldy cab and the familiar cabman. John cursed the cabman silently, and then it occurred to him that he must stop the incarceration of his portmanteau ; that, at least, he must keep close at hand, and he turned to recall the porter. But his reflections, brief as they had appeared, must have occupied him longer than he supposed, and there was the man already returning with the receipt.

Well, that was settled ; he had lost his portmanteau also ; for the sixpence with which he had paid the Murrayfield Toll was one that had strayed alone into his waistcoat pocket, and unless he once more successfully achieved the adventure of the house of crime, his portmanteau lay in the cloak-room in eternal pawn, for lack of a penny fee. And then he remembered the porter, who stood suggestively attentive, words of gratitude hanging on his lips.

John hunted right and left ; he found a coin—prayed God that it was a sovereign—drew it out, beheld a half-penny, and offered it to the porter.

The man's jaw dropped.

" It's only a halfpenny ! " he said, startled out of railway decency.

" I know that," said John, piteously.

And here the porter recovered the dignity of man.

" Thank you, sir," said he, and would have returned the base gratuity. But John, too, would none of it ; and as they struggled, who must join in but the cabman ?

" Hoots, Mr. Baigrey," said he, " you surely forget what day it is ! "

" I tell you I have no change ! " cried John.

" Well," said the driver, " and what then ? I would rather give a man a shillin' on a day like this than put him off with a derision like a baw-bee. I'm surprised at the like of you, Mr. Baigrey ! "

" My name is not Baigrey ! " broke out John, in mere childish temper and distress.

" Ye told me it was yoursel'," said the cabman.

" I know I did ; and what the devil right had you to ask ? " cried the unhappy one.

" Oh, very well," said the driver. " I know my place, if you know yours—if you know yours ! " he repeated, as one who should imply grave doubt ; and muttered inarticulate thunders, in which the grand old name of gentleman was taken seemingly in vain.

Oh, to have been able to discharge this monster, whom John now perceived, with tardy clear-sightedness, to have begun betimes the festivities of Christmas ! But far from any such ray of consolation visiting the lost, he stood bare of help and helpers, his portmanteau sequestered in one place, his money deserted in another and guarded by a corpse ; himself, so sedulous of privacy, the cynosure of all men's eyes about the station ; and, as if these were not enough mischances, he was now fallen in ill-blood with the beast to whom his poverty had linked him ! In ill-blood, as he reflected dismally, with the witness who perhaps might hang or save him. There was no time to be lost ; he durst not linger any longer in that public spot ; and whether he had recourse to dignity or concilia-

tion, the remedy must be applied at once. Some happily
surviving element of manhood moved him to the former.

"Let us have no more of this," said he, his foot once
more upon the step. "Go back to where we came from."

He had avoided the name of any destination, for there
was now quite a little band of railway folk about the cab,
and he still kept an eye upon the Court of Justice, and
laboured to avoid concentric evidence. But here again the
fatal jarvey out-manœuvred him.

"Back to the Ludge?" cried he, in shrill tones of
protest.

"Drive on at once!" roared John, and slammed the
door behind him, so that the crazy chariot rocked and
jingled.

Forth trundled the cab into the Christmas streets, the
fare within plunged in the blackness of a despair that
neighboured on unconsciousness, the driver on the box
digesting his rebuke and his customer's duplicity. I would
not be thought to put the pair in competition; John's
case was out of all parallel. But the cabman, too, is worth
the sympathy of the judicious; for he was a fellow of
genuine kindliness and a high sense of personal dignity
incensed by drink; and his advances had been cruelly
and publicly rebuffed. As he drove, therefore, he counted
his wrongs, and thirsted for sympathy and drink. Now,
it chanced he had a friend, a publican, in Queensferry
Street, from whom, in view of the sacredness of the
occasion, he thought he might extract a dram. Queensferry Street lies something off the direct road to Murrayfield. But then there is the hilly cross-road that passes
by the valley of the Leith and the Dean Cemetery; and
Queensferry Street is on the way to that. What was to
hinder the cabman, since his horse was dumb, from choos-
ing the cross-road, and calling on his friend in passing?
So it was decided; and the charioteer, already somewhat
mollified, turned aside his horse to the right.

John, meanwhile, sat collapsed, his chin sunk upon his
chest, his mind in abeyance. The smell of the cab was
still faintly present to his senses, and a certain leaden chill

about his feet ; all else had disappeared in one vast oppression of calamity and physical faintness. It was drawing on to noon—two-and-twenty hours since he had broken bread ; in the interval, he had suffered tortures of sorrow and alarm, and been partly tipsy ; and though it was impossible to say he slept, yet when the cab stopped and the cabman thrust his head into the window, his attention had to be recalled from depths of vacancy.

" If you'll no' *stand* me a dram," said the driver, with a well-merited severity of tone and manner, " I daresay ye'll have no objection to my taking one mysel' ? "

" Yes—no—do what you like," returned John ; and then, as he watched his tormenter mount the stairs and enter the whisky-shop, there floated into his mind a sense as of something long ago familiar. At that he started fully awake, and stared at the shop-fronts. Yes, he knew them ; but when ? and how ? Long since, he thought ; and then, casting his eye through the front glass, which had been recently occluded by the figure of the jarvey, he beheld the tree-tops of the rookery in Randolph Crescent. He was close to home—home, where he had thought, at that hour, to be sitting in the well-remembered drawing-room in friendly converse ; and, instead——!

It was his first impulse to drop into the bottom of the cab ; his next, to cover his face with his hands. So he sat, while the cabman toasted the publican, and the publican toasted the cabman, and both reviewed the affairs of the nation ; so he still sat, when his master condescended to return, and drive off at last down-hill, along the curve of Lynedoch Place ; but even so sitting, as he passed the end of his father's street, he took one glance from between shielding fingers, and beheld a doctor's carriage at the door.

" Well, just so," thought he ; " I'll have killed my father ! And this is Christmas Day ! "

If Mr. Nicholson died, it was down this same road he must journey to the grave ; and down this road, on the same errand, his wife had preceded him years before ; and many other leading citizens, with the proper trappings and attendance of the end. And now, in that frosty, ill-smelling, straw-carpeted, and ragged-cushioned cab, with his breath congealing on the glasses, where else was John himself advancing to ?

The thought stirred his imagination, which began to manufacture many thousand pictures, bright and fleeting, like the shapes in a kaleidoscope ; and now he saw himself, ruddy and comfortered, sliding in the gutter ; and, again, a little woe-begone, bored urchin tricked forth in crape and weepers, descending this same hill at the foot's-pace of mourning coaches, his mother's body just preceding him ; and yet again, his fancy, running far in front, showed him the house at Murrayfield—now standing solitary in the low sunshine, with the sparrows hopping on the threshold and the dead man within staring at the roof—and now, with a sudden change, thronged about with white-faced, hand-uplifting neighbours, and doctor bursting through their midst and fixing his stethoscope as he went, the policeman shaking a sagacious head beside the body. It was to this he feared that he was driving ; in the midst of this he saw himself arrive, heard himself stammer faint explanations, and felt the hand of the constable upon his shoulder. Heavens ! how he wished he had played the manlier part ; how he despised himself that he had fled that fatal neighbourhood when all was quiet, and should now be tamely travelling back when it was thronging with avengers !

Any strong degree of passion lends, even to the dullest, the forces of the imagination. And so now as he dwelt on what was probably awaiting him at the end of this distressful drive—John, who saw things little, remembered them less, and could not have described them at all, beheld in his mind's eye the garden of the Lodge, detailed as in a map ; he went to and fro in it, feeding his terrors ; he saw the hollies, the snowy borders, the paths where he had sought Alan, the high, conventual walls, the shut door—what ! was the door shut ? Ay, truly, he had shut it—shut in his money, his escape, his future life—shut it with these hands, and none could now open it ! He heard the snap of the spring-lock like something bursting in his brain, and sat astonied.

And then he woke again, terror jarring through his vitals. This was no time to be idle ; he must be up and doing, he must think. Once at the end of this ridiculous cruise, once at the Lodge door, there would be nothing for it but to turn the cab and trundle back again. Why, then, go so far ? why add another feature of suspicion to a case already so suggestive ? why not turn at once ? It was easy to say, turn ; but whither ? He had nowhere now to go to ; he could never—he saw it in letters of blood—he could never pay that cab ; he was saddled with that cab for ever. Oh, that cab ! his soul yearned to be rid of it. He forgot all other cares. He must first quit himself and this ill-smelling vehicle and of the human beast that guided it— first do that ; do that at least ; do that at once.

And just then the cab suddenly stopped, and there was his persecutor rapping on the front glass. John let it down, and beheld the port-wine countenance inflamed with intellectual triumph.

" I ken wha ye are ! " cried the husky voice. " I mind ye now. Ye're a Nucholson. I drove ye to Hermiston to a Christmas party, and ye came back on the box, and I let ye drive."

It is a fact. John knew the man ; they had been even friends. His enemy, he now remembered, was a fellow of great good-nature—endless good-nature—with a boy ; why not with a man ? Why not appeal to his better side ? He grasped at the new hope.

" Great Scott ! and so you did," he cried, as if in a transport of delight, his voice sounding false in his own ears. " Well, if that's so, I've something to say to you. I'll just get out, I guess. Where are we, anyway ? "

The driver had fluttered his ticket in the eyes of the branch toll-keeper, and they were now brought to on the highest and most solitary part of the by-road. On the left, a row of fieldside trees beshaded it ; on the right, it was bordered by naked fallows, undulating down-hill to the Queensferry Road ; in front, Corstorphine Hill raised its

snow-bedabbled, darkling woods against the sky. John
looked all about him, drinking the clear air like wine ; then
his eyes returned to the cabman's face as he sat, not unglee-
fully, awaiting John's communication, with the air of one
looking to be tipped.

The features of that face were hard to read, drink had so
swollen them, drink had so painted them, in tints that varied
from brick red to mulberry. The small grey eyes blinked,
the lips moved, with greed ; greed was the ruling passion ;
and though there was some good-nature, some genuine
kindliness, a true human touch, in the old toper, his greed
was now so set afire by hope, that all other traits of character
lay dormant. He sat there a monument of gluttonous
desire.

John's heart slowly fell. He had opened his lips, but
he stood there and uttered naught. He sounded the well
of his courage, and it was dry. He groped in his treasury
of words, and it was vacant. A devil of dumbness had
him by the throat ; the devil of terror babbled in his ears ;
and suddenly, without a word uttered, with no conscious
purpose formed in his will, John whipped about, tumbled
over the road-side wall, and began running for his life
across the fallows.

He had not gone far, he was not past the midst of the
first field, when his whole brain thundered within him,
" Fool ! You have your watch ! " The shock stopped
him, and he faced once more towards the cab. The driver
was leaning over the wall, brandishing his whip, his face
empurpled, roaring like a bull. And John saw (or thought)
that he had lost the chance. No watch would pacify the
man's resentment now ; he would cry for vengeance also.
John would be under the eye of the police ; his tale would
be unfolded, his secret plumbed, his destiny would close
on him at last, and for ever.

He uttered a deep sigh ; and just as the cabman, taking
heart of grace, was beginning at last to scale the wall,
his defaulting customer fell again to running, and disappeared into the farther fields.

CHAPTER VIII

SINGULAR INSTANCE OF THE UTILITY OF PASS-KEYS

WHERE he ran at first, John never very clearly knew ;
nor yet how long a time elapsed ere he found himself in the by-road near the lodge of Ravelston, propped
against the wall, his lungs heaving like bellows, his legs
leaden-heavy, his mind possessed by one sole desire—to
lie down and be unseen. He remembered the thick
coverts round the quarry-hole pond, an untrodden corner
of the world where he might surely find concealment till
the night should fall. Thither he passed down the lane ;
and when he came there, behold ! he had forgotten the
frost, and the pond was alive with young people skating,
and the pond-side coverts were thick with lookers-on.
He looked on a while himself. There was one tall, graceful
maiden, skating hand in hand with a youth, on whom she
bestowed her bright eyes perhaps too patently ; and it was
strange with what anger John beheld her. He could have
broken forth in curses ; he could have stood there, like a
mortified tramp, and shaken his fist and vented his gall
upon her by the hour—or so he thought ; and the next
moment his heart bled for the girl. " Poor creature, it's
little she knows ! " he sighed. " Let her enjoy herself
while she can ! " But was it possible, when Flora used to
smile at him on the Braid ponds, she could have looked so
fulsome to a sick-hearted bystander ?

The thought of one quarry, in his frozen wits, suggested
another ; and he plodded off towards Craig Leith. A wind
had sprung up out of the north-west ; it was cruel keen,
it dried him like a fire, and racked his finger-joints. It
brought clouds, too ; pale, swift, hurrying clouds, that

blotted heaven and shed gloom upon the earth. He
scrambled up among the hazelled rubbish heaps that
surround the caldron of the quarry, and lay flat upon the
stones. The wind searched close along the earth, the
stones were cutting and icy, the bare hazels wailed about
him ; and soon the air of the afternoon began to be vocal
with those strange and dismal harpings that herald snow.
Pain and misery turned in John's limbs to a harrowing
impatience and blind desire of change ; now he would roll
in his harsh lair, and when the flints abraded him, was
almost pleased ; now he would crawl to the edge of the
huge pit and look dizzily down. He saw the spiral of the
descending roadway, the steep crags, the clinging bushes,
the peppering of snow - wreaths, and far down in the
bottom, the diminished crane. Here, no doubt, was a
way to end it. But it somehow did not take his fancy.

And suddenly he was aware that he was hungry ; ay,
even through the tortures of the cold, even through the
frosts of despair, a gross, desperate longing after food,
no matter what, no matter how, began to wake and spur
him. Suppose he pawned his watch ? But no, on Christmas Day—this was Christmas Day !—the pawn-shop would
be closed. Suppose he went to the public-house close
by at Blackhall, and offered the watch, which was worth
ten pounds, in payment for a meal of bread and cheese ?
The incongruity was too remarkable ; the good folks would
either put him to the door, or only let him in to send for
the police. He turned his pockets out one after another ;
some San Francisco tram-car checks, one cigar, no lights,
the pass-key to his father's house, a pocket-handkerchief,
with just a touch of scent : no, money could be raised on
none of these. There was nothing for it but to starve ; and
after all, what mattered it ? That also was a door of exit.

He crept close among the bushes, the wind playing round
him like a lash ; his clothes seemed thin as paper, his
joints burned, his skin curdled on his bones. He had a
vision of a high-lying cattle-drive in California, and the
bed of a dried stream with one muddy pool, by which the
vaqueros had encamped : splendid sun over all, the big

bonfire blazing, the strips of cow browning and smoking
on a skewer of wood ; how warm it was, how savoury the
steam of scorching meat ! And then again he remembered
his manifold calamities, and burrowed and wallowed in
the sense of his disgrace and shame. And next he was
entering Frank's restaurant in Montgomery Street, San
Francisco ; he had ordered a pan-stew and venison chops,
of which he was immoderately fond, and as he sat waiting,
Munroe, the good attendant, brought him a whisky punch ;
he saw the strawberries float on the delectable cup, he
heard the ice chink about the straws. And then he woke
again to his detested fate, and found himself sitting, humped
together in a windy combe of quarry refuse—darkness thick
about him, thin flakes of snow flying here and there like
rags of paper, and the strong shuddering of his body
clashing his teeth like a hiccough.

We have seen John in nothing but the stormiest condi-
tion ; we have seen him reckless, desperate, tried beyond
his moderate powers ; of his daily self, cheerful, regular,
not unthrifty, we have seen nothing ; and it may thus be a
surprise to the reader, to learn that he was studiously careful
of his health. This favourite preoccupation now awoke.
If he were to sit there and die of cold, there would be
mighty little gained ; better the police cell and the chances
of a jury trial, than the miserable certainty of death at a
dike-side before the next winter's dawn, or death a little
later in the gas-lighted wards of an infirmary.

He rose on aching legs, and stumbled here and there
among the rubbish-heaps, still circumvented by the yawn-
ing crater of the quarry ; or perhaps he only thought so,
for the darkness was already dense, the snow was growing
thicker, and he moved like a blind man, and with a blind
man's terrors. At last he climbed a fence, thinking to drop
into the road, and found himself staggering, instead, among
the iron furrows of a ploughland, endless, it seemed, as a
whole county. And next he was in a wood, beating among
young trees ; and then he was aware of a house with many
lighted windows, Christmas carriages waiting at the doors,
and Christmas drivers (for Christmas has a double edge)

becoming swiftly hooded with snow. From this glimpse
of human cheerfulness, he fled like Cain ; wandered in
the night, unpiloted, careless of whither he went ; fell,
and lay, and then rose again and wandered farther ; and
at last, like a transformation scene, behold him in the lighted
jaws of the city, staring at a lamp which had already donned
the tilted night-cap of the snow. It came thickly now, a
" Feeding Storm " ; and while he yet stood blinking at the
lamp, his feet were buried. He remembered something
like it in the past, a street-lamp crowned and caked upon
the windward side with snow, the wind uttering its mourn-
ful hoot, himself looking on, even as now ; but the cold
had struck too sharply on his wits, and memory failed him
as to the date and sequel of the reminiscence.

His next conscious moment was on the Dean Bridge ;
but whether he was John Nicholson of a bank in a California street, or some former John, a clerk in his father's
office, he had now clean forgotten. Another blank, and
he was thrusting his pass-key into the door-lock of his
father's house.

Hours must have passed. Whether crouched on the
cold stones or wandering in the fields among the snow,
was more than he could tell ; but hours had passed. The
finger of the hall clock was close on twelve ; a narrow peep
of gas in the hall-lamp shed shadows ; and the door of the
back room—his father's room—was open and emitted a
warm light. At so late an hour, all this was strange ;
the lights should have been out, the doors locked, the good
folk safe in bed. He marvelled at the irregularity, leaning
on the hall table ; and marvelled to himself there ; and
thawed and grew once more hungry, in the warmer air
of the house.

The clock uttered its premonitory catch ; in five minutes
Christmas Day would be among the days of the past—
Christmas !—what a Christmas ! Well, there was no use
waiting ; he had come into that house, he scarce knew how ;
if they were to thrust him forth again, it had best be done
at once ; and he moved to the door of the back room and
entered.

Oh, well, then he was insane, as he had long believed.

There, in his father's room, at midnight, the fire was roaring and the gas blazing ; the papers, the sacred papers —to lay a hand on which was criminal—had all been taken off and piled along the floor ; a cloth was spread, and a supper laid, upon the business table ; and in his father's chair a woman, habited like a nun, sat eating. As he appeared in the doorway, the nun rose, gave a low cry, and stood staring. She was a large woman, strong, calm, a little masculine, her features marked with courage and good sense ; and as John blinked back at her, a faint resemblance dodged about his memory, as when a tune haunts us, and yet will not be recalled.

" Why, it's John ! " cried the nun.

" I daresay I'm mad," said John, unconsciously following King Lear ; " but, upon my word, I do believe you're Flora."

" Of course I am," replied she.

And yet it is not Flora at all, thought John ; Flora was slender, and timid, and of changing colour, and dewy-eyed ; and had Flora such an Edinburgh accent ? But he said none of these things, which was perhaps as well. What he said was, " Then why are you a nun ? "

" Such nonsense ! " said Flora. " I'm a sick-nurse ; and I am here nursing your sister, with whom, between you and me, there is precious little the matter. But that is not the question. The point is : How do you come here ? and are you not ashamed to show yourself ? "

" Flora," said John, sepulchrally, " I haven't eaten anything for three days. Or, at least, I don't know what day it is ; but I guess I'm starving."

" You unhappy man ! " she cried. " Here, sit down and eat my supper ; and I'll just run upstairs and see my patient, not but what I doubt she's fast asleep ; for Maria is a *malade imaginaire*."

With this specimen of the French, not of Stratford-atte-Bowe, but of a finishing establishment in Moray Place, she left John alone in his father's sanctum. He fell at once upon the food ; and it is to be supposed that Flora had

found her patient wakeful, and been detained with some
details of nursing, for he had time to make a full end of all
there was to eat, and not only to empty the teapot, but to
fill it again from a kettle that was fitfully singing on his
father's fire. Then he sat torpid, and pleased, and bewildered ; his misfortunes were then half forgotten ; his
mind considering, not without regret, this unsentimental
return to his old love.

He was thus engaged, when that bustling woman noise-
lessly re-entered.

"Have you eaten ? " said she. "Then tell me all about it."

It was a long and (as the reader knows) a pitiful story ;
but Flora heard it with compressed lips. She was lost in
none of those questionings of human destiny that have, from
time to time, arrested the flight of my own pen ; for women,
such as she, are no philosophers, and behold the concrete
only. And women, such as she, are very hard on the imperfect man.

"Very well," said she, when he had done ; " then down
upon your knees at once, and beg God's forgiveness."

And the great baby plumped upon his knees, and did as
he was bid ; and none the worse for that ! But while he
was heartily enough requesting forgiveness on general
principles, the rational side of him distinguished, and wondered if, perhaps, the apology were not due upon the other
part. And when he rose again from that becoming exercise, he first eyed the face of his old love doubtfully, and
then, taking heart, uttered his protest.

"I must say, Flora," said he, " in all this business, I
can see very little fault of mine."

"If you had written home," replied the lady, " there
would have been none of it. If you had even gone to
Murrayfield reasonably sober, you would never have slept
there, and the worst would not have happened. Besides,
the whole thing began years ago. You got into trouble,
and when your father, honest man, was disappointed, you
took the pet, or got afraid, and ran away from punishment.
Well, you've had your own way of it, John, and I don't
suppose you like it."

" I sometimes fancy I'm not much better than a fool," sighed John.

" My dear John," said she, " not much ! "

He looked at her, and his eye fell. A certain anger rose within him ; here was a Flora he disowned ; she was hard ; she was of a set colour ; a settled, mature, undecorative manner ; plain of speech, plain of habit— he had come near saying, plain of face. And this change- ling called herself by the same name as the many-coloured, clinging maid of yore ; she of the frequent laughter, and the many sighs, and the kind, stolen glances. And to make all worse, she took the upper hand with him, which (as John knew well) was not the true relation of the sexes. He steeled his heart against this sick-nurse.

" And how do you come to be here ? " he asked.

She told him how she had nursed her father in his long illness, and when he died, and she was left alone, had taken to nurse others, partly from habit, partly to be of some service in the world ; partly, it might be, for amusement. " There's no accounting for taste," said she. And she told him how she went largely to the houses of old friends, as the need arose ; and how she was thus doubly welcome, as an old friend first, and then as an experienced nurse, to whom doctors would confide the gravest cases.

" And, indeed, it's a mere farce my being here for poor Maria," she continued ; " but your father takes her ailments to heart, and I cannot always be refusing him. We are great friends, your father and I ; he was very kind to me long ago—ten years ago."

A strange stir came in John's heart. All this while had he been thinking only of himself ? All this while, why had he not written to Flora ? In penitential tenderness, he took her hand, and, to his awe and trouble, it remained in his, compliant. A voice told him this was Flora, after all —told him so quietly, yet with a thrill of singing.

" And you never married ? " said he.

" No, John, I never married," she replied.

The hall clock striking two recalled them to the sense of time.

" And now," said she, " you have been fed and warmed, and I have heard your story, and now it's high time to call your brother."

" Oh ! " cried John, chap-fallen ; " do you think that absolutely necessary ? "

" *I* can't keep you here ; I am a stranger," said she. " Do you want to run away again ? I thought you had enough of that."

He bowed his head under the reproof. She despised him, he reflected, as he sat once more alone ; a monstrous thing for a woman to despise a man ; and strangest of all, she seemed to like him Would his brother despise him, too ? And would his brother like him ?

And presently the brother appeared, under Flora's escort ; and, standing afar off beside the door-way, eyed the hero of this tale.

" So this is you ? " he said, at length.

" Yes, Alick, it's me—it's John," replied the elder brother, feebly.

" And how did you get in here ? " inquired the younger.

" Oh, I had my pass-key," says John.

" The deuce you had ! " said Alexander. " Ah, you lived in a better world ! There are no pass-keys going now."

" Well, father was always averse to them," sighed John.

And the conversation then broke down, and the brothers looked askance at one another in silence.

" Well, and what the devil are we to do ? " said Alexander. " I suppose if the authorities got wind of you, you would be taken up ? "

" It depends on whether they've found the body or not," returned John. " And then there's that cabman, to be sure ! "

" Oh, bother the body ! " said Alexander. " I mean about the other thing. That's serious."

" Is that what my father spoke about ? " asked John. " I don't even know what it is."

" About your robbing your bank in California, of course," replied Alexander.

It was plain, from Flora's face, that this was the first she had heard of it ; it was plainer still, from John's, that he was innocent.

" I ! " he exclaimed. " I rob my bank ! My God ! Flora, this is too much ; even you must allow that."

" Meaning you didn't ? " asked Alexander.

" I never robbed a soul in all my days," cried John : " except my father, if you call that robbery ; and I brought him back the money in this room, and he wouldn't even take it ! "

" Look here, John," said his brother ; " let us have no misunderstanding upon this. MacEwen saw my father ; he told him a bank you had worked for in San Francisco was wiring over the habitable globe to have you collared—that it was supposed you had nailed thousands ; and it was dead certain you had nailed three hundred. So MacEwen said, and I wish you would be careful how you answer. I may tell you also, that your father paid the three hundred on the spot."

" Three hundred ? " repeated John. " Three hundred pounds, you mean ? That's fifteen hundred dollars. Why, then, it's Kirkman ! " he broke out. " Thank Heaven ! I can explain all that. I gave them to Kirkman to pay for me the night before I left—fifteen hundred dollars, and a letter to the manager. What do they suppose I would steal fifteen hundred dollars for ? I'm rich ; I struck it rich in stocks. It's the silliest stuff I ever heard of. All that's needful is to cable to the manager : Kirkman has the fifteen hundred—find Kirkman. He was a fellow-clerk of mine, and a hard case ; but to do him justice, I didn't think he was as hard as this."

" And what do you say to that, Alick ? " asked Flora.

" I say the cablegram shall go to-night ! " cried Alexander, with energy. " Answer prepaid, too. If this can be cleared away—and upon my word I do believe it can—we shall all be able to hold up our heads again. Here, you John, you stick down the address of your bank manager. You, Flora, you can pack John into my bed, for which I have no further use to-night. As for me, I am off to the post-

o

office, and thence to the High Street about the dead body.
The police ought to know, you see, and they ought to know
through John ; and I can tell them some rigmarole about
my brother being a man of highly nervous organisation,
and the rest of it.   And then, I'll tell you what, John—did
you notice the name upon the cab ? "

John gave the name of the driver, which, as I have not
been able to commend the vehicle, I here suppress.

"Well," resumed Alexander, " I'll call round at their
place before I come back, and pay your shot for you.
In that way, before breakfast-time, you'll be as good as
new."

John murmured inarticulate thanks.   To see his brother
thus energetic in his service moved him beyond expression ;
if he could not utter what he felt, he showed it legibly
in his face ; and Alexander read it there, and liked it the
better in that dumb delivery.

"But there's one thing," said the latter, " cablegrams
are dear ;   and I daresay you remember enough of the
governor to guess the state of my finances."

"The trouble is," said John, " that all my stamps are
in that beastly house."

" All your what ? " asked Alexander.

"Stamps—money," explained John.   " It's an American expression ;   I'm afraid I contracted one or two."

" I have some," said Flora.   " I have a pound-note
upstairs."

"My dear Flora," returned Alexander, " a pound-note
won't see us very far ;   and besides, this is my father's
business, and I shall be very much surprised if it isn't my
father who pays for it."

" I would not apply to him yet ;   I do not think that can
be wise," objected Flora.

"You have a very imperfect idea of my resources, and
none at all of my effrontery," replied Alexander.   " Please
observe."

He put John from his way, chose a stout knife among
the supper things, and with surprising quickness broke
into his father's drawer.

"There's nothing easier when you come to try," he observed, pocketing the money.

"I wish you had not done that," said Flora. "You will never hear the last of it."

"Oh, I don't know," returned the young man; "the governor is human after all. And now, John, let me see your famous pass-key. Get into bed, and don't move for anyone till I come back. They won't mind you not answering when they knock; I generally don't myself."

CHAPTER IX

IN WHICH MR. NICHOLSON CONCEDES THE
PRINCIPLE OF AN ALLOWANCE

IN spite of the horrors of the day and the tea-drinking of the night, John slept the sleep of infancy. He was awakened by the maid, as it might have been ten years ago, tapping at the door. The winter sunrise was painting the east; and as the window was to the back of the house, it shone into the room with many strange colours of re-fracted light. Without, the houses were all cleanly roofed with snow; the garden walls were coped with it a foot in height; the greens lay glittering. Yet strange as snow had grown to John during his years upon the Bay of San Francisco, it was what he saw within that most affected him. For it was to his own room that Alexander had been promoted; there was the old paper with the device of flowers, in which a cunning fancy might yet detect the face of Skinny Jim, of the Academy, John's former dominie; there was the old chest of drawers; there were the chairs—one, two, three—three as before. Only the carpet was new, and the litter of Alexander's clothes and books and drawing materials, and a pencil-drawing on the wall which (in John's eyes) appeared a marvel of proficiency.

He was thus lying, and looking, and dreaming, hanging, as it were, between two epochs of his life, when Alexander came to the door, and made his presence known in a loud whisper. John let him in, and jumped back into the warm bed.

"Well, John," said Alexander, "the cablegram is sent in your name, and twenty words of answer paid. I have been to the cab-office and paid your cab, even saw the old gentleman himself, and properly apologised. He was mighty placable, and indicated his belief you had been drinking. Then I knocked up old MacEwen out of bed, and explained affairs to him as he sat and shivered in a dressing-gown. And before that I had been to the High Street, where they have heard nothing of your dead body, so that I incline to the idea that you dreamed it."

" Catch me ! " said John.

" Well, the police never do know anything," assented Alexander ; " and at any rate, they have dispatched a man to inquire and to recover your trousers and your money, so that really your bill is now fairly clean ; and I see but one lion in your path—the governor."

" I'll be turned out again, you'll see," said John, dismally.

" I don't imagine so," returned the other ; " not if you do what Flora and I have arranged ; and your business now is to dress, and lose no time about it. Is your watch right ? Well, you have a quarter of an hour. By five minutes before the half-hour you must be at table, in your old seat, under Uncle Duthie's picture. Flora will be there to keep you countenance ; and we shall see what we shall see."

" Wouldn't it be wiser for me to stay in bed ? " said John.

" If you mean to manage your own concerns, you can do precisely what you like," replied Alexander ; " but if you are not in your place five minutes before the half-hour I wash my hands of you, for one."

And thereupon he departed. He had spoken warmly, but the truth is, his heart was somewhat troubled. And as he hung over the banisters, watching for his father to appear, he had hard ado to keep himself braced for the encounter that must follow.

" If he takes it well, I shall be lucky," he reflected. " If he takes it ill, why it'll be a herring across John's tracks, and perhaps all for the best. He's a confounded muff, this brother of mine, but he seems a decent soul."

At that stage a door opened below with a certain emphasis, and Mr. Nicholson was seen solemnly to descend the stairs, and pass into his own apartment. Alexander followed, quaking inwardly, but with a steady face. He knocked, was bidden to enter, and found his father standing in front of the forced drawer, to which he pointed as he spoke.

"This is a most extraordinary thing," said he; "I have been robbed!"

"I was afraid you would notice it," observed his son; "it made such a beastly hash of the table."

"You were afraid I would notice it?" repeated Mr. Nicholson. "And, pray, what may that mean?"

"That I was a thief, sir," returned Alexander. "I took all the money in case the servants should get hold of it; and here is the change, and a note of my expenditure. You were gone to bed, you see, and I did not feel at liberty to knock you up; but I think when you have heard the circumstances, you will do me justice. The fact is, I have reason to believe there has been some dreadful error about my brother John; the sooner it can be cleared up the better for all parties; it was a piece of business, sir— and so I took it, and decided, on my own responsibility, to send a telegram to San Francisco. Thanks to my quickness we may hear to-night. There appears to be no doubt, sir, that John has been abominably used."

"When did this take place?" asked the father.

"Last night, sir, after you were asleep," was the reply.

"It's most extraordinary," said Mr. Nicholson. "Do you mean to say you have been out all night?"

"All night, as you say, sir. I have been to the telegraph and the police-office, and Mr. MacEwen's. Oh, I had my hands full," said Alexander.

"Very irregular," said the father. "You think of no one but yourself."

"I do not see that I have much to gain in bringing back my elder brother," returned Alexander, shrewdly.

The answer pleased the old man; he smiled. "Well, well, I will go into this after breakfast," said he.

"I'm sorry about the table," said the son.

"The table is a small matter; I think nothing of that," said the father.

" It's another example," continued the son, " of the awkwardness of a man having no money of his own. If I had a proper allowance, like other fellows of my age, this would have been quite unnecessary."

" A proper allowance ! " repeated his father, in tones of blighting sarcasm, for the expression was not new to him. " I have never grudged you money for any proper purpose."

" No doubt, no doubt," said Alexander, " but then you see you ar'n't always on the spot to have the thing explained to you. Last night for instance——"

" You could have wakened me last night," interrupted his father.

" Was it not some similar affair that first got John into a mess ? " asked the son, skilfully evading the point.

But the father was not less adroit. " And pray, sir, how did you come and go out of the house ? " he asked.

" I forgot to lock the door, it seems," replied Alexander.

" I have had cause to complain of that too often," said Mr. Nicholson. " But still I do not understand. Did you keep the servants up ? "

" I propose to go into all that at length after breakfast," returned Alexander. " There is the half-hour going ; we must not keep Miss Mackenzie waiting."

And greatly daring, he opened the door.

Even Alexander, who it must have been perceived, was on terms of comparative freedom with his parent ; even Alexander had never before dared to cut short an interview in this high-handed fashion. But the truth is the very mass of his son's delinquencies daunted the old gentleman. He was like the man with the cart of apples—this was beyond him ! That Alexander should have spoiled his table, taken his money, stayed out all night, and then coolly acknowledged all, was something undreamed of in the Nicholsonian philosophy, and transcended comment. The return of the change, which the old gentleman still carried in his hand, had been a feature of imposing impudence ; it had dealt him a staggering blow. Then there was the reference to John's original flight—a subject which he always kept resolutely curtained in his own mind ; for he was a man who loved to have made no mistakes, and when he feared he might have made one kept the papers sealed. In view of all these surprises and reminders, and of his son's composed and masterful demeanour, there began to creep on Mr. Nicholson a sickly misgiving. He seemed beyond his depth ; if he did or said anything, he might come to regret it. The young man, besides, as he had pointed out himself, was playing a generous part. And if wrong had been done—and done to one who was, after, and in spite of, all, a Nicholson—it should certainly be righted.

All things considered, monstrous as it was to be cut short in his inquiries, the old gentleman submitted, pocketed the change, and followed his son into the dining-room. During these few steps he once more mentally revolted, and once more, and this time finally, laid down his arms : a still, small voice in his bosom having informed him authentically of a piece of news ; that he was afraid of Alexander. The strange thing was that he was pleased to be afraid of him. He was proud of his son ; he might be proud of him ; the boy had character and grit, and knew what he was doing.

These were his reflections as he turned the corner of the dining-room door. Miss Mackenzie was in the place of honour, conjuring with a teapot and a cozy ; and, behold ! there was another person present, a large, portly, whiskered man of a very comfortable and respectable air, who now rose from his seat and came forward, holding out his hand.

" Good-morning, father," said he.

Of the contention of feeling that ran high in Mr. Nicholson's starched bosom, no outward sign was visible ; nor did he delay long to make a choice of conduct. Yet in that interval he had reviewed a great field of possibilities both past and future ; whether it was possible he had not been perfectly wise in his treatment of John ; whether it was possible that John was innocent ; whether, if he turned John out a second time, as his outraged authority suggested, it was possible to avoid a scandal ; and whether, if he went to that extremity, it was possible that Alexander might rebel.

"Hum!" said Mr. Nicholson, and put his hand, limp and dead, into John's.

And then, in an embarrassed silence, all took their places; and even the paper—from which it was the old gentleman's habit to suck mortification daily, as he marked the decline of our institutions—even the paper lay furled by his side.

But presently Flora came to the rescue. She slid into the silence with a technicality, asking if John still took his old inordinate amount of sugar. Thence it was but a step to the burning question of the day; and in tones a little shaken, she commented on the interval since she had last made tea for the prodigal, and congratulated him on his return. And then addressing Mr. Nicholson, she congratulated him also in a manner that defied his ill-humour; and from that launched into the tale of John's misadventures not without some suitable suppressions.

Gradually Alexander joined; between them, whether he would or no, they forced a word or two from John; and these fell so tremulously, and spoke so eloquently of a mind oppressed with dread, that Mr. Nicholson relented. At length even he contributed a question: and before the meal was at an end all four were talking even freely.

Prayers followed, with the servants gaping at this newcomer whom no one had admitted; and after prayers there came that moment on the clock which was the signal for Mr. Nicholson's departure.

"John," said he, "of course you will stay here. Be very careful not to excite Maria, if Miss Mackenzie thinks it desirable that you should see her.—Alexander, I wish to speak with you alone." And then, when they were both in the back-room: "You need not come to the office to-day," said he; "you can stay and amuse your brother, and I think it would be respectful to call on Uncle Greig. And by-the-by" (this spoken with a certain—dare we say?—bashfulness), "I agree to concede the principle of an allowance; and I will consult with Dr. Durie, who is quite a man of the world and has sons of his own, as to the amount. And, my fine fellow, you may consider yourself in luck ! " he added, with a smile.

" Thank you," said Alexander.

Before noon a detective had restored to John his money, and brought news, sad enough in truth, but perhaps the least sad possible. Alan had been found in his own house in Regent's Terrace, under care of the terrified butler. He was quite mad, and instead of going to prison, had gone to Morningside Asylum. The murdered man, it appeared, was an evicted tenant who had for nearly a year pursued his late landlord with threats and insults ; and beyond this, the cause and details of the tragedy were lost.

When Mr. Nicholson returned for dinner they were able to put a dispatch into his hands : " John V. Nicholson, Randolph Crescent, Edinburgh.—Kirkman has disappeared ; police looking for him. All understood. Keep mind quite easy. — Austin." Having had this explained to him, the old gentleman took down the cellar key and departed for two bottles of the 1820 port. Uncle Greig dined there that day, and Cousin Robina, and, by an odd chance, Mr. MacEwen ; and the presence of these strangers relieved what might have been otherwise a somewhat strained relation. Ere they departed, the family was welded once more into a fair semblance of unity.

In the end of April John led Flora—or, let us say, as more descriptive, Flora led John—to the altar, if altar that may be called which was indeed the drawing - room mantel-piece in Mr. Nicholson's house, with the Reverend Dr. Durie posted on the hearth-rug in the guise of Hymen's priest.

The last I saw of them, on a recent visit to the north, was at a dinner-party in the house of my old friend Gellatly Macbride ; and after we had, in classic phrase, " rejoined the ladies," I had an opportunity to overhear Flora conversing with another married woman on the much canvassed matter of a husband's tobacco.

" Oh, yes ! " said she ; " I only allow Mr. Nicholson

four cigars a day.   Three he smokes at fixed times—after a
meal, you know, my dear ; and the fourth he can take
when he likes with any friend."

"Bravo !" thought I to myself ; "this is the wife for
my friend John ! "

THE EDINBURGH PRESS, 9 AND 11 YOUNG STREET, EDINBURGH